Sylvester Young was born in England of Jamaican parents. A keen all-round sportsman, he studied karate at one of Europe's toughest and most successful karate clubs. He was a member of the British karate team at under-21 level and won a silver medal at the European championships and also won several British individual and team titles. He now lives in Ontario, Canada.

MORE THAN A GAME

A Story About Football and Other Stuff

Sylvester Young

Raldon Books

First Published in 2006 by
Raldon Books
Cnoc Abhainn, Old Church Road,
Passage West, County Cork, Eire
www.raldonbooks.com

© Sylvester Young 2006
All rights reserved

The right of Sylvester Young to be identified as the Author of the Work has been asserted by him in accordance with Copyright, Designs and Patents Act 1988.

No part of this publication may be copied, reproduced, or transmitted in any form, or by any means without the prior permission of the publisher, nor be otherwise circulated in any form of binding or cover other than that in which it is first published and without a similar condition being imposed on the subsequent purchaser.

Although this novel contains references to actual people, places and events it is entirely a work of fiction and these references are used only to lend a realistic setting for the novel. All other names, characters, places and incidents are the products of the author's imagination. Any resemblance to actual persons, living or dead, events or locales is entirely incidental.

A CIP catalogue record for this book is available
from the British Library.

ISBN: 0-9552169-0-7
ISBN 13: 978-0-9552169-0-9

Cover design by Eric Dunne-Magner
Typeset by Dominic Carroll, Ardfield, Co. Cork
Printed and bound in the Republic of Ireland by Colourbooks Ltd., Dublin

*To Rosemarie Hudson,
a publisher and unsung heroine*

Prologue

Before I begin to tell you what befell the young men who made up the Sabina Park Rangers football team I feel I should first give you a few ideas about the place and time in which they played.

The place was a town in decline called Wolverhampton. It was mostly known for the factories and foundries that, for the most part, no longer existed and the Wolves team that had won the League Championship three times during the 1950s. Besides footballers such as Billy Wright, Jimmy Mullen, Ron Flowers and, much later, Derek Dougan, one of its most well-known inhabitants was the local MP Enoch Powell. He represented the town for almost a quarter of a century and in an infamous speech he drew a nation's attention to a fading political career when he made it clear that he did not want so many black and brown people in England. Whatever the other consequences, his speech linked the name of Wolverhampton with prejudice and anti-immigrant movements for a very long time to come. No one involved with Sabina Park Rangers, who were all of a Caribbean background, could tell you what Powell had said. But they knew, if only because of the reaction in the media, that there had been no mention of an appreciation of calypso or reggae music – and he certainly wasn't looking to embrace any of his West Indian constituents whilst proclaiming 'One love!'

The time in which this story took place is 1981. As I recall, it was a time of unreliable cars and scratchy vinyl records, of industrial strife and mass unemployment, most of which was blamed on the prime minister Margaret Thatcher, who was doing a fair impression of the Wicked Witch of the North. People who had become surplus to requirements reacted to her government's policies throughout the land with protest, riot and rage.

To me, the early 1980s now seem a strange and backward time: there were no mobile phones, nor home computers; there were only three terrestrial stations and no satellite TV. It was a time of different labels and descriptions: *Starbursts* were called *Opal Fruits* and *Snickers* were *Marathon* bars. It was a time when Michael Jackson was still black and people of a skin tone similar to the one he was born with were called nig-nogs in British TV sit-coms – just for a laugh.

The players of Sabina Park Rangers were not the sort to watch a lot of TV; they were too busy with other things. To varying degrees, it was football that was their passion. Football was so woven into some of their lives that life without it seemed unimaginable. For other members of the team, talented as they were, it was simply something for them to do as most of them had left school without any real chance of getting a job. It was hard for anyone to find work back then but it was even more difficult if you were black. Amongst a few other things, it was the vexation caused by the lack of job opportunities that had led to widespread rioting during the previous year.

During the riots of 1980 in nearby Birmingham some of the people I'm going to tell you about evaded police roadblocks and joined in the mayhem. Some wanted to bounce a few 'rakstones' off the heads of policemen in revenge for the harassment that was part of their daily lives, while others saw the rioting as a rare business opportunity. A fleet of vans and small trucks carried off such an amount of electrical appliances that six months later it was still possible to buy a very cheap, brand new video recorder, washing machine, or fridge-freezer in Wolverhampton, if you knew where to go.

By then the team had been going for over a decade and had changed its name twice but had finally settled with

'Sabina Park Rangers' for over half that period. It was a name that evoked happy memories for the coach, who as a youth had watched the Jamaican national team play in Sabina Park stadium in Kingston. Horace McIntosh had ambitions for the young men who played for him, they were not particularly grand but he wanted them to expand their horizons a little further than the town's smoky boundaries. He believed football would give them a purpose and a sense of achievement that wasn't exactly plentiful – as he saw it – in a lot of their lives. When his team moved from a town to an area league he decided on a new name, one that had a cultural reference but that was not overtly provocative to some of the white teams. In the early 1970s his players had travelled to areas where there were few or no black people and the team members were sometimes greeted as if they had just landed from outer space. Normally such trips passed without trouble but in rougher areas home teams would often bring a gang with them if they saw their next fixture was against a side whose name included words such as 'Afro', 'West Indian', 'Caribbean', 'Punjab' or 'Black'. The thugs were rarely up to much, they'd jeer during the match and throw stones at the minibus as the team was *leaving* but there had been incidents that had escalated into more serious violence. Once, after some guys on the sidelines made monkey noises, a mass brawl broke out. It involved the spectators; all twenty-two players; substitutes; and coaching staff. Two other white teams also got stuck in; they had been playing on an adjoining pitch but got involved when it became obvious that those in Horace's team who had dabbled in boxing and the martial arts were getting the upper hand. There had been talk of setting up a black league after that but it was eventually decided that it would be tantamount to a surrender to racists and so the team changed its name for a final time and joined another, bigger, amateur league.

I first met Horace McIntosh as a boy when my father used to take me to a house just off the Newhampton Road, which stretched from the Molinuex football ground at one end to the plusher Tettenhall area at the other. The road was lined with terraces of old blackened brick houses that had a few small shops and a bookies in amongst them. There was also a large clearing that accommodated a newly built shopping precinct and a car dealer's showroom from which few of the local inhabitants could afford to buy. From the outside, Horace's place looked like just another terraced house but at the top of a narrow green lino-covered stairs was a front bedroom that had been converted into a barbershop. At ground level was a door to the left of the grimy hallway, through which I was never allowed to go. My father would hurry past it and guide me up to Horace and tell him that there was "no rush for the bwoy" before going downstairs again and entering the forbidden room. Years later, when I was old enough to go to the barbers by myself, I opened the door to see groups of black men seated around small tables. All of them sat with cigarettes hanging from the corners of their mouths and one eye closed against the fumes as they studied and then slapped down their dominoes. Around the perimeters of the room sat bored women: they were mostly white and bottle-blonde, usually with a can of beer in one hand and a cigarette in the other. The first time I entered the gambling room one of them looked around and puckered her lips at me and the shock of it had me frozen to the spot. I had never seen women act or dressed like that before and I trotted home wondering what my father would be doing in such company. In the mind of a twelve-year-old it was about as close to a den of iniquity as you could get.

Horace McIntosh had set up business in 1957 after listening to his recently arrived compatriots grumble about their inability to get a decent haircut from an English barber. In the following twenty-four years his trade hadn't altered much: even though the seventies was the decade of the big Afro, for a lot of his younger customers it was still mostly all about a trim and a touch of *Dax*, or a shave and a splash of *Brut*. It was the shop's interior that had undergone the most changes during the time he had cut my hair. Over the years the walls had become covered with posters of black football players. When I first went there in the sixties there were only creased sepia-tinted photos of The Caribbean All Stars and Jamaican sides of the 1950s. The only exception to the football theme was a framed photo of the all-conquering West Indies cricket team. As time went by the walls began to be covered with pictures of mainly South American footballers as it would be years before Jamaica's 'Reggae Boyz', or the Trinidad and Tobago side made their appearances at the World Cup finals. Up until then most of Wolverhampton's West Indian soccer fans supported Brazil – or failing that *any* side that happened to be playing England. As I headed into adolescence black players were still a rarity – some said an exotic curiosity – in English soccer, as there seemed to be a common belief amongst professional managers that black men were not robust enough for the rigours of the British game. That began to change in the mid-seventies when Ron Atkinson of nearby West Bromwich Albion became the first high-profile manager to challenge the notion of racially based fragility and put three black players into his team. Photos of Regis, Batson and Cunningham were promptly added to join the lonely figure of Clyde Best, a Bermudan who once played for West Ham United. Wolves followed suit a few years later and put a couple of black players called Hazell and Berry into the first team and gave the town's black people more than a passing interest about what they were up to. Looking back from a time when nearly one in four of the superstars in the English Premier League are black, the 1980s really do seem a very strange and backward time.

But whatever the achievements of black players at national or international levels, pride of place in Horace's shop was reserved for the Sabina Park Rangers. Next to the large mirror was a collage of yellowed newspaper cuttings detailing his team's exploits. The latest – and therefore brightest – addition was a report of Sabina Park Rangers' greatest victory to date.

I was waiting my turn when Frank Grant stilled his broom. "White people don't want to read about black people's tings, me-a tell unno," he said. The wooden handle tapped the small press cutting. "Look 'pon it, to rasclart, a black team mek it to de final fe de first time an' dat's all dem write. But watch it now, if there's riot like de one in London last week black people is back on de front page, to ras."

"To ras," grunted Venton as his chin dropped to his chest.

Horace's brow furrowed in concentration as he ran his electric razor over the back of Venton's neck. Like Horace McIntosh, Frank Grant was dark-skinned, large, pot-bellied and beginning to grey. They had arrived in Wolverhampton from Jamaica at the same time but that's where the similarities ended. Horace had a much more positive outlook on life: he had been happily married for over a quarter of a century and both his son and daughter had gone to university and got themselves good jobs. To Frank the world was a disappointing, cruel, place full of racist white people, conniving black women (all of whom had left him) and 'bad pickney' (the ungrateful fruit of his loins). To sum them up, Horace was always willing to light a candle but Frank was just as ready to cuss the darkness. And, man, did he cuss.

Horace put away the razor and flicked a soft brush over Venton's nape before he said, "When we win de final, dem can't ignore it, to ras."

"To rasclart," muttered Venton excitedly, "yeah if dem win dem can't *h*ignore it!"

"Not if," replied Horace, "*when* dem win."

Frank resumed his sweeping. "When dem win?" he snorted. "Mi ras," he added scornfully, "watch it now, if it a white team dem-a play de referee will teef dem."

Before I carry on with this story I feel I should explain something about Jamaican cussing – most of which I picked up from Frank – and manner of speech for those who are not conversant with it. 'Rasclart' in its most literal term means 'bottom wipe'. This is not to be confused with the moist and scented disposable sort that is used on the posteriors of young babies. Also, in Jamaican patois the same word can have several different meanings depending on how it is pronounced. 'Rasclart' is a popular word because of its two constituent parts: 'ras' and 'clart'. 'Ras' as in "Mi ras!" is often used as an expression of astonishment or derision – the meaning dependent on the tenor of delivery, whereas "to ras" comes at the end of a sentence to underline a point or can act as an acknowledgement of a truth uttered by another. For example: "The bwoy wukless" – that is to say "the young man is not very good" is strengthened by the addition of "to ras"; which in turn is uttered should one agree with the point raised. However, Jamaican men would never utter, "You can kiss my ras!" Rather, they would say: "Kiss mi neck-back!" as this is a part of the anatomy that is far away enough from an area that otherwise might give the impression one is inviting another to take part in some "batty-bwoy ting" – that is to say an act of homosexuality. 'Clart' too has several meanings from "pass me clart so me can wipe de table", to "shut your clart", to the extreme "Me will kill your clart!" The adding and subtracting of aitches is a little harder to explain as it usually occurs without any consistency or conscious thought. For some older Jamaicans adding aitches to words that have never possessed them is associated with speaking correctly, though this is only in the mind of the speaker and is a sort of compensation for all those aitches that are dropped in more common speech. But for a younger, somewhat cruder, generation, the adding of an aitch serves to reinforce a point. For example: "The ting ugly" might be used to describe a young lady or an object that was not to a young man's liking but: "The ting *h*ugly!" tends to convey that whom or what being described has profound problems – at least in the eye of the beholder. Now with that out of the way I will continue.

As Horace put a red plastic cape over my shoulders I read the headline '*Sabina reaches final with wonder goal*'. The date of the game was 20 April 1981; the venue was a pitch on Fowler's Park, Wolverhampton. Three and a half weeks before Ricardo Villa left the Manchester City defence mesmerised by a magical dribble and won the FA Cup final replay for Tottenham Hotspur, another, some say better, goal was scored by Mark Beckford for Sabina Park Rangers. It happened in the semifinal of the Watney's Red Barrel Challenge Cup and excluding the players and match officials, probably no more than a dozen people witnessed it. There were the coaches, a netball team who were cheering for SPR and a man in an overcoat and flat cap who stood on his own – he turned out to be a scout for Aston Villa.

With the score standing at one-all, there was less than a minute of normal time left to play. Sabina Park Rangers were down to ten men after Nestor Riley had reacted badly to a tackle and threatened to "juk" (that is to stab) the offender's "bloodclart"(an imaginary piece of sanitary wear). Once he had left the pitch the free kick was taken and the Rangers' goalkeeper, Carl Hooper, heaved his massive frame into the air to catch the ball with one hand in the way Pat Jennings of Tottenham Hotspur, Arsenal and Northern Ireland used to do. Members of the JA City netball team, who acted as unofficial cheerleaders during the home matches, screamed their approval and drowned out Horace's command to kick the ball deep into the other half of the pitch. As he would recount on many subsequent occasions, he had turned away in disgust as Carl rolled the ball to his right-back Donovan Brown. As the tired opposing team plodded back into their defensive positions, Donovan played a short ball inside to Courtney Wright who in turn passed it left to Vince 'Buckshot' Pinnock. Horace had turned around again at this point and repeated his order for the ball to be booted up the field but it was already on its way to Ian Beckford. Ian, the youngest SPR player, was slender and nimble. He laid it back to Buckshot as a defender clattered against his heels but he stayed on his feet and in an instant he had spun around and started his run up the wing. The ball from Buckshot was perfectly weighted and dropped onto Ian's left foot. Without a pause in his stride, he then dropped his right shoulder but moved to his left and had an opposing player kicking at fresh air as he darted towards the penalty box. Another defender fell on his backside after buying a dummy before Ian made a pass to Audley Robinson. Audley, on the edge of the box with his back towards goal, shielded the ball with his sinewy frame as he took the pass and in one fluid movement he had flicked it up and put it overhead before getting a defender's size ten in his gut for his trouble. No foul was called as Cecil Grant, the aggressive and muscular striker, jumped highest and headed the ball back towards Ian Beckford's brother Mark who had sprinted at least sixty yards to join the attack. He was still running and outside the area as he struck the ball. It was the perfect strike, onlookers could tell by the sound, as few of them could keep track of the ball because of its speed once it had left his boot. For one long awe-struck moment Mark Beckford was the only one to have registered that the ball was in the net. His hands aloft, his team-mates roared and the netball girls whooped, while Horace McIntosh hugged the person closest to him – a perplexed linesman. The final whistle blew within seconds of the restart and signalled the beginning of celebrations that went long into the night.

As Horace cut my hair he was still basking in that moment of victory. The truth of the story I'm about to tell would only fully emerge years later; it is a tale of a series of events that took place in the weeks before the final of the 1981 Watney's Red Barrel Challenge Cup. It is the story of work and dedication and of struggles against almost overwhelming odds. It's a story of ambition, of love and loathing, of greed and generosity, of loyalty and treachery, of small triumphs and catastrophic failure. What I'm about to recount for the first time is the whole, never-told-before truth about what happened to the players of Sabina Park Rangers.

1

On Tuesday evenings Sabina Park Rangers' training sessions took place at the YMCA in Whitmore Reans. It wasn't really that suitable a venue as there was no football pitch but there were showers in the changing rooms and once the netball players were done, their court was used for five-a-side sessions. Horace McIntosh continued using the YMCA facilities partly out of sentimentality, as it was the place where he'd brought his first team together over a decade before in 1970. But also it was out of practicality as his house was less than a quarter of a mile away, a mere petrol bomb's throw (as they used to say in those days) from the nearby Dunstall Road police station. There was also another reason for him persevering with the YMCA: the shapely figures of the JA City netball players who always ensured a good attendance at training. The young women were acutely aware of the admiring glances they drew and were always immaculately turned out. Without exception, their legs were smooth and oiled; and their pleated short skirts ensured every male who watched them play became admirers of the large rounded batty long before Jennifer Lopez brought hers to the attention of the world. They were the scented roses for Horace's team of bees who were only too ready to pollinate if they were given the chance.

As usual, the first player to arrive was Ian Beckford. He did not even bother to go home and change out of his school uniform. Such was his stamina, he would usually play a game of football with his friends in West Park before trotting a half a mile to the YMCA to train and play for another hour and a half. Norman Longmore, the team captain, nearly always turned up next. He had played for Horace McIntosh's teams for nine years and at thirty-one was the oldest player. He was a few years past his best and as he put on weight the rest of the team used to joke that he was the only one who wore a padded shirt. Despite his thickening waist, he remained a good passer of the ball and an all-round sportsman who was already looking forward to knocking a cricket ball around the place during the summer months. Yet in some ways Norman embodied why Sabina Park Rangers languished near the bottom of the league. He could still amble about the pitch and be effective in a Sunday or a town league but against fitter, more dedicated players of an area league he was at least a yard too slow in pace. Not that he was the only player who found it difficult to compete at a higher level but Horace McIntosh put their lethargy in the league down to losing the first six games of the season. The cup run had shown what the team was capable of if properly motivated and Horace was already thinking about how he would break it to his captain and most loyal player that the cup final would be his last game for the team.

Norman Longmore had arrived in Wolverhampton at the age of nineteen, found himself a college place and eventually became a primary school teacher, which, back then, was an even rarer sight than a black footballer. His Jamaican education had left him a puritanical streak, and throughout his training course he was reminded that corporal punishment was not permitted, even if he used his own belt. Once Norman had qualified he had returned to Jamaica and, as promised, married his childhood sweetheart Euphemia – which had led to a two-year long battle with the immigration authorities to allow her to join him in England.

Norman had rubbed horse liniment into his thick legs and put on the strip that, because of the similarity in their names, had been chosen to resemble that of Queens Park Rangers, when the massive goalkeeper Carl Hooper arrived next in the changing room. Carl did not talk to Norman; then again, he did little more than grunt to anyone else. Carl was suspicious of authority and in his view that Norman was a teacher made him part of an establishment that had never done him any favours. All the players thought Norman talked to them as if he were still in the classroom and his big trouble was he thought he had to know all the answers, even if no one was asking the questions. Carl had arrived in England six years before, at the age of thirteen, from the island of Grenada. While at school there Carl had been thought of as backward until it was discovered in England that in fact he was hard of hearing. But by then he had lost all trust in adults except for his maternal grandmother whose death had made his journey to join his mother in Wolverhampton a necessary one.

"A'right, mi spar?" Norman said to him on his way outside. Carl had had an operation to rectify his hearing and now he was 'selectively' slightly deaf – particularly when talking to someone from Social Security. When there was no reply Norman convinced himself that Carl had not heard him.

As the whistle blew to signal the end of the netball game more than twenty guys had turned up for training, although quite a few were not officially registered as SPR players, success as well as short skirts had proved alluring. A man with a camera clasped to his chest looked nervously over his shoulder as Cecil Grant inspected the photographer's gleaming Ford Escort RS 2000 as the players made two lines. "Nice car, man," Cecil said as he jogged past to join his team-mates. The newspaperman mumbled something back in acknowledgement. He should have been more grateful: Cecil rarely talked to white people and when he did they were often the other side of a counter and he was yelling for them to stay away from any alarm and to hand over all their money. The JA City netball players hovered before changing and called out to the man to take their photo. They were never lost for a pose but when they turned around and bent over to show those lovely round batties they produced a fearsome roar from the assembled SPR players for the photographer to quickly turn around. What little colour he had drained from his face as he tried to make sense of what they were screaming at him but by the time his frightened mind understood the girls were heading for the changing rooms playfully shaking their heads. Try as he might, the man from *The Wolverhampton Ad News* could not get the men in front of him to lift the scowls from their faces and the only one who smiled for the photo was Horace. "A idyatt like that nah deserve a nice car," growled Cecil. "I would-a even paid him for that photo, to ras."

"To ras!" spat several others in unison.

Norman Longmore led the players through the warm-up exercises as Horace chatted to the photographer and gave him the names of the players he had photographed. "Which one's Mark Beckford, Mr McIntosh?"

"Well, now you mention it, I can't see Mark." Horace turned and called out, "Hey, Ian, where ya brodda?" Ian Beckford looked up and responded with a shrug of his shoulders. "Arks Marcia when she's finished changin," he called out. "She sees more of him than I do." Marcia Yuell was the captain of the netball team and it was an open secret amongst the team that she and Mark had been seeing each other for a while.

"Pity," said the photographer, "our sports reporter Alf Turley wanted me to take a photo of him on his own. He reckons that goal he scored has Aston Villa very interested."

Horace tried to act as if he already knew. "Yeah, but Mark's not the only player that has interested professional teams, you know. Over the years we've had a few go fe trials an' ting."

"But it must be a thrill to have the champions interested in one of your players."

The lines on Horace's face deepened. On one level he would have been proud that the newly-crowned First

Division champions even knew of one of his players but at the same time he was also concerned that he might be about to be deprived of his best player for the cup final. "Yeah," he said, "but I wouldn't call it a t'rill. There's a lotta hurdles for a young player to climb before him mek the big-time. There's a couple more if him black."

The photographer, neither interested in nor prepared to believe Horace's stories of racism in football, glanced anxiously back to his car again. "Alf will probably give you a call in the week and have a chat about that," he said before he scurried back to his prized possession.

The five-a-side games were more competitive than usual. Those who had not played in the semifinal were now doing their best to stake a claim for a place in the cup final, the exception being Nestor Riley. Because he had been sent off during that famous victory he would be automatically banned from taking any further part in the cup. Jealousy as well as personal ambition put a little extra bite into the tackles and had Horace bringing the session to a premature halt. "Right," he said, "nice to see so many at trainin 'ere dis evenin. We got circuit trainin at Aldersley Stadium on Thursday an' me want to see all-a unno there. Friday night we 'ave been invited to de Star an' Moon nightclub because we reach de final, yours truly has been *h*invited to be a judge fe de beauty pageant an' you all will get a free ticket from me . . ." Horace waited for the whoops and whistles to subside before he added, ". . . after trainin on Thursday." His players groaned as he went on, "De weekend after dat we 'ave a tournament in Nottingham. It a long-standin commitment an' because it's not long before de final we gonna 'ave plenty-a substitutions. As usual, as guests of de Beeston Caribs Football Club, we will go on to de dinner an' dance. Now we 'ave reached de Watney's final all me arks *h*everyone is to realise wha' a great *h*achievement it would be fe a black team to win dis cup. Dis is more than football, more than jus a game, it is about wha' it represents fe all-a black people in dis town. So stay fit an'outta trouble. An', please, please, dis year stay away from de Nottingham gal dem. Please!"

Norman Longmore nodded his head vigorously and was happy to shoulder the burden of representing the cause of black people throughout the town but the young men around him just laughed. It wasn't as though they hadn't a sense of representing their community; it was that they were more sceptical about how winning a cup might change anything. And they laughed because of Horace's pleas to stay away from the fair maidens of Nottingham: several of them had already made their plans for the dance that took place after the tournament and nothing their coach could say would change that.

2

It had taken sixty-three years for Mervyn Palmer to get himself banged up. He woke in the early hours of the morning to the muffled screams from the cell next door and tried to figure out where he was. There were angry shouts from the corridor outside and the jangling of a large set of keys before the screaming stopped. Mervyn kept his ear close to the wall and tried to hear what was going on. The opening of a metal flap in the door straightened him and a set of hard blue eyes peered through the slot.

"'Ello," said Mervyn, "where am I?"

"Red Lion Street police station, Mr Palmer. Sobered up, have we?"

"Wha'? You mean you was drunk too?"

"Watch your lip, sambo."

"Oi, there's nah need fe the *h*abuse, superintendent. When can I go 'ome?"

"I'll give it half an hour and see if your attitude has improved, all right?"

Mervyn was about to give an assurance of his sobriety but the flap slammed shut. After a moment or two of wondering about his now silent neighbour he sat down again on the slatted bench and tried to recall what had happened since Saturday afternoon. He'd gone out feeling king of the world in his platform shoes of green and red patented leather and the pair of purple flares he saved for special occasions. But instead of his local in Whitmore Reans, Mervyn went to the Little Swan pub on the edge of the town centre. He thought he might have gone home that night but couldn't be sure and ended up being arrested while walking through town the following evening, or was it the evening after that? The tip of his tongue found the caked remains of vomit at the corners of his mouth and it was only then that he realised that his false teeth were missing. A vague memory shifted his eyes to the corner of the cell where there was a foul-smelling toilet with all sorts of stuff streaked down its sides. He hoped that it was his 'stuff' and tottered over and looked into the bowl. "Rasclart, mi teet dem," he whined as he saw his upper plate in amongst what looked liked vegetable matter. There was no sign of his bottom teeth.

He put his top set back in. They tasted no worse than the inside of his mouth. Mervyn needed his teeth in to think properly: had he said anything, had he let the reason for his celebration (like his teeth) slip out? He thought not. When he was younger he could always handle his alcohol and there wasn't enough liquor in the town to dull his sharp brain. He lifted out his teeth and wiped them on his best purple flares and by the time they were back in his mouth he was convinced that his secret was safe.

There were two pieces of bad news waiting for him as he collected his belongings from the custody sergeant. Firstly, he had been bailed to appear at the magistrate's court in a fortnight on a charge of being drunk and disorderly and, secondly, this was not Monday morning, it wasn't even Tuesday, it was Wednesday-rahteed-morning. Mervyn hurried outside; all certainty had vanished. If he had not realised his celebrations had lasted for nigh on three days how could he be sure that he hadn't blurted out something during that length of time? The answer lay with his friends at the barbershop. Mervyn called into Horace and Frank almost every day and knew there wasn't much that happened around the town without them hearing about it. If there were rumours, they would have heard them by now.

After going home and finding his spare set of dentures, Mervyn washed and changed before driving his Austin Cambridge to the Newhampton Road. Up until very recently he had been happy with his car despite it being fifteen years old and having the aerodynamics of a brick on four wheels. Now he was thinking of something a bit more stylish, something like a sleek Austin Princess – he'd often fantasised about one day owning the 2000cc HL model with metallic bronze paintwork and black vinyl roof covering. He parked outside the barbershop and decided against taking a diversion through the door on the left and went straight upstairs. As soon as he opened the door he could tell by the look on their faces that they had found out. Mervyn tried to return their smiles. "So wha' happen?" he asked them, hoping he was wrong.

"Whoy," laughed Frank Grant, "t'irty-five t'ousand pounds, to blues beat, t'irty-five t'ousand pounds!"

It crossed Mervyn's mind to deny it, or at least make out that the amount had been exaggerated. "An' who de 'ell tell you dat?" he said scornfully.

Frank was still shaking Mervyn's reluctant hand as

Horace McIntosh walked over and showed him the front page of Monday's *Express and Star*. Under the headline 'Local man wins pools' was a photograph of Mervyn holding up what the article called his 'winning coupon'. He studied the photo. His bottom teeth were missing and his eyes were glazed as he smiled idiotically for the camera. Mervyn blasphemed; he thought he had only dreamt of walking into the newspaper's Queen Street offices and demanding that he see a reporter. A list of gravelitious, that is to say money-grabbing, relatives and 'lady friends' ran through his mind. They had probably been trying to track him down since Monday evening. He pulled his hand from Frank's and turned on his heels and made for the stairs.

"Oi," called Frank, "where you-a go?"

"De *h*Austin dealer in Chapel Ash before de vultures dem come try an' tek all mi money."

"There goes a worried man," Horace said to Frank.

"Him'd be even more worried if you'd told him wha' it seh in de paper 'bout him givin money to im five pickney in Jamaica," Frank said. "An' him got four pickney 'ere an' me know dat dem all will want dem share. It don't leave a lot fe sponsorship. You still goin to arks him fe money?"

"I'll arks him once he gets im new car, Mervyn will be in a better mood by then."

Frank Grant laughed quietly to himself. Both he and Horace knew that Mervyn Palmer was rarely in a 'better mood'. He had called to the shop for the best part of twenty years and shared his unremittingly gloomy view of the world. For Horace, one compensation was that once a week Mervyn would come with a blackened dutch-pot full of 'cow-cock' soup. But that would normally only happen Saturdays and during weekdays Mervyn would arrive about ten and sit in a corner and spend a few hours sipping a cup of tea sweetened with condensed milk, while sharing his opinions about the various articles in his *Daily Mail* he thought interesting. Frank agreed with most of his points of view and saw Mervyn as a kindred spirit, or a "breddren" as he called him. Like Mervyn, Frank had had his share of 'thankless' children and thought the black youth in 'Hinglan' needed more beating than understanding: what was a matter with them all? They had free education and then welfare payments when they left school, they had it soft and yet they were still bleating about unfairness. Unfairness to Mervyn was working six days a week, twelve hours a day, chopping sugar cane under an unrelenting sun for a pittance. "True, true," Frank had often murmured on hearing such pearls of wisdom, "de pickney too *h*ungrateful, to ras."

"To ras."

Mervyn's special abuse was saved for Rastafarians (who featured with surprising regularity within the pages of his daily newspaper) or any black person who had ideas above their station. "The Rastaman," he would say, "him like a beast on hind legs, a dutty beast. In Jamaica we used to 'unt dem down. Wha' dis 'bout *h*Africa? We nah *h*Africans, to blues beat, we's West *h*Indians. A *h*Indian *h*is a different ting from a *h*African! . . . You hear 'bout dat woman who set up a Caribbean takeaway in Worcester Street? Rasclart, 'er 'usband should control her. Who de 'ell is goin to buy stuff dem can cook in dem own kitchen?"

"White people," Horace had suggested.

The notion of people actually buying rice and peas that someone else had cooked seemed ridiculous to both Mervyn and Frank but the thought that those people might be white was a cause for side-splitting hilarity.

Once Mervyn had finished thundering down the stairs, Frank said to Horace, "Quiet today. Look, man, me-a go to the bookies. You fancy anyting?"

Horace shook his head and remained seated as he gazed out of the window and watched Mervyn's Austin Cambridge pull away. On quiet days Horace usually cleaned his razor, polished his mirror and dusted the photographs on his walls before going down to the gambling room for a game of dominoes – while listening out for anyone climbing the stairs looking for a haircut. But today he was too preoccupied for dominoes. His mind was full of tactical possibilities for the cup final and he was already thinking about Thursday night's training session and hoping everyone would turn up. With exception of Ian Beckford and Norman Longmore, punctuality and reliability were not the strongest points of the Sabina Park Rangers' squad. In particular he hoped Ian's brother Mark would be there: his appearance would tell him that he had not lost his best player to the First Division champions before the final.

While driving to the car dealers, Mervyn Palmer came across an example of the low-key policing for which the West Midlands' force was well known. Low-key policing in Whitmore Reans took the shape of four large white vans patrolling the quiet streets at ten miles per hour with grills on the outside of the windows and a dozen frazzled cops inside each of them. Wolverhampton cops had a reputation for making evenings out for black men a disagreeable experience, whether they were in a car or on foot. Back then black guys had no need for stuff like sky-diving, or bungee-jumping to get an adrenalin kick – all a black man had to do for adventure was to try and make it to a club for the night. When outnumbered and confronted by aggressive cops the best means of defence was usually a sub-ten-second hundred metres sprint. Hence, it was argued, there were so many black sprinters representing Britain: it wasn't to do with twitch fibres or anything genetic, it was down to practise. But the police in the vans patrolling Whitmore Reans weren't even local cops; they were on secondment from Birmingham and were really intent on getting themselves involved with some action with members of the local community. The police van in front of Mervyn's car came to a halt as Courtney Wright ambled along the pavement dressed in jeans and a tight yellow tee-shirt. Maybe it was the bright colours he wore, perhaps it was the bulging masculine figure beneath his shirt – but just the way he carried himself was enough to provoke the cops. Like love, hate comes in many forms and this particular form was racism – and man-to-man racism can be often violent and testosterone-fuelled; and not too dissimilar to the stuff that has bull elephants charging at each other and cracking heads. The cause and origin of prejudice has provoked many debates and arguments but as the police van drew to a halt both they and Courtney knew what this was all about: deep down it was to do with territory – and deep, deep down it was about pussy.

"Hey," a bored and irritable cop called to him from the front seat of the van, "when are you black bastards going to have a go, eh? Fancy yourself do you, you black bastard." Uncomfortable and sweaty balls can do that to a man. Courtney pulled a puzzled face as he pawed at his short dreads his Trinidadian father detested (as a minority within a minority, Lancelot Wright thought his son's hair and speech had been too influenced by Jamaicans.) Smirking to himself, Courtney flexed one of his large biceps at the cops and walked on. Like a lot of the guys he knew, Courtney was at a stage in his life in which he definitely didn't talk to cops unless he had to – and especially if he was outnumbered and they were ready for a ruck. He knew only too well what it was like for one person to take on a dozen men. It wasn't like the kung fu films he enjoyed at the Colosseum cinema on Friday nights in which the gang of thugs had the good grace to attack the hero one at the time. In real life the bastards piled in from all directions and Courtney's own experience of this cowardly tactic came three years before when he was set upon on his way to the Molinuex and beaten by a gang of Wolves supporters. They came at him from behind and he was left badly injured and then, to cap it all, *he* was the only one arrested for affray (although the charges were later dropped.) Courtney never went to another Wolves game. In his time watching matches, he'd had to tell people around him to quit the 'nigger' chants every time a black player got a touch of the ball. He had also, on occasions, gone down to the areas from where bananas were thrown onto the pitch. He was prepared to put up with all that aggravation – but that he had been set upon by people who were supporting the same team made him think about spending his time playing, rather than watching, football. The injuries took a time to heal and when he lost his job as a labourer he supported Lynette and their two kids by hustling and selling a little ganja. That was the other reason for him not reacting to the cops: the herbal matter hidden in the soles of his shoes. The cops jeered as Courtney coolly saluted old Mervyn Palmer as he went by.

Courtney was late for his meeting with his fellow defenders Desmond Palmer (who was Mervyn's youngest son) and Nestor Riley at the gambling room below Horace's barbershop but he knew they would not be on time either. They had "a ting 'bout a ting" to discuss with him. They said it was a legit money-making opportunity but their smiles told him something different. There were those who played for Sabina Park Rangers who walked the virtuous road; there were a few, like Courtney, who travelled on its margins; and while there were a number of serious criminals within the squad, there were two in particular who were even more scornful of the righteous route. They had made their own path – and trampled everything in their way as they did so. Everyone in the team knew what Desmond and Nestor were all about: they were both just eighteen but for at least a third of their relatively short lives had pulled – or tried to pull – every skank imaginable. Their antics got so bad that

Mervyn had put Desmond out of his house at the age of sixteen. The final straw was a neighbour – a very angry Mr Singh – who had turned up on Mervyn's doorstep shouting he wanted the return of the money he had given for what was supposed to be a brand new VCR. It turned out that Desmond had sold him a shell of a video recorder that only had a pair of house bricks inside to give it weight. As Mervyn looked on, Mr Singh got back his money but on his way to the council's Housing Department to look for a place to live, Desmond sold the same piece of useless machinery to a cousin of Mr Singh who lived a little further down the road.

Both he and Nestor were charming in their own peculiar ways, but beneath their easy smiles lurked a pair of nature's most voracious predators who had no scruples about how they made their money, none at all. They referred to each other as 'spars', 'breddren' or 'friends' but words like that had as little meaning for them as 'love' or 'respect'. In reality theirs was a relationship of convenience because they both knew they each needed at least one person to cover their double-crossing backs. Normally Courtney would have told them he wasn't interested but Lynette was giving him grief about his dealing in weed and asking what would become of her and their kids if he were banged up. She asked him were the risks he was taking worth fifty pounds a week. Truth was it was nearer one hundred pounds after giving Lynette a share – but no, what he was left with still wasn't worth prison. So he thought he'd talk to Desmond and Nestor and see what they were offering. After all, there was no harm in just talking.

3

Courtney Wright was only one of the many who were living on the margins of the 'straight and narrow' in and around Wolverhampton. Many factories in the midlands area known as the Black Country had closed and thousands of people had been put out of work in the two previous years. With the loss of money coming into so many households came changes in attitudes: the stuff that used to frighten people into staying law-abiding were sometimes ignored or forgotten about. It was hardly an outbreak of serious crime but cars weren't taxed, TVs were not licensed and the odd piece of cheese or meat was slipped into a bag and not paid for. Few people set out to be that way and they did not consider themselves as criminals, they were just struggling to make ends meet. Courtney was more active than most in finding alternative ways to earn money and sold a little weed. He justified his actions with the thought that he could have sold a lot more serious shit than ganja. Back then there had been no studies of the long-term effects of ganja and Courtney had convinced himself that in some ways he was doing the Government a favour. In lives full of unhappiness a spliff was one of the few ways to mellow out before the despair turned into something worse. He'd often say that unlike the man who had swallowed a good share of alcohol, there was rarely a sight more peaceable than a man who'd had a draw.

Others made their money by the selling and buying of all sorts of stuff that was not always legit. For Courtney's youngest brother Patrick the nicking of car radios progressed to the stealing of tellies and videos by the means of ram-raiding, which was a very common line of business in the early eighties. For those who are unaware of the methodology of such an operation, it involved a car (usually, though not always, stolen); a pair of ramps; and then the manoeuvring of the vehicle up the ramps at high speed and through the protective screen and plate glass window of an electrical store. The occupants then jumped out and loaded as much gear as they could into the boot before making their getaway. More professional gangs used a van and put up 'road closed' signs at the ends of the street so they had more time to break into the stockroom rather than just gather up the goods on show.

Now these guys wouldn't have been robbing if no one were buying; black, white or brown, they were never short of customers. This sort of robbery was viewed as a social service, there were no threats, no weapons, and no one was physically hurt unless they cut themselves on a piece of broken glass as they took the gear out of the shop. But the danger of making a living in this way was that a line had been crossed, risks and been taken and the cops had been revealed as piss-poor thief-takers. It was now easier to be tempted to take another step into areas of a more serious criminal nature. And if you knew someone who had got away with that kind of stuff, it was a step that could cross a mind more than once or twice if you were short of readies. Desmond Palmer and Nestor Riley were already considered to be two serious criminals and just by the way they carried on (and mostly got away with it) provided a temptation for some guys to follow in their footsteps. Even if you were unlucky enough to get caught, like Nestor did once when he was fifteen, you could still learn a lot to make you a much better criminal while banged up.

Courtney wasn't surprised when Desmond and Nestor failed to show, as they were never the most reliable sort. But that Courtney had turned up was a sign that he was starting to consider taking a step into a place that was a lot more serious than selling weed. Not much of a domino player, he went upstairs to Horace. "Me jus saw the millionaire," he said, referring to Mervyn Palmer.

"Him jus gone down to Charles Clarke's to buy imself a brand new *h*Austin Princess."

"Mi rahteed," snorted Courtney, "him wastin im money already on a pile-a shit? Him never hear of BMW?"

"Him say him buyin it before de vultures come for im winnins. You trainin tomorra?"

"Yeah, man, you know I never miss circuits."

"Have you seen Mark aroun?"

"Not since Saturday."

"De guy from de newspaper said dat de Villa could be interested in him."

"Cha, there's interest an' interest, if you unnerstan me. Them tell you turn up an' if you're lucky you might see twenty minutes of a game," he said referring to his own disappointing experience of the trials process at professional clubs. It was often a more haphazard than a scientific method of finding out new talent back then. In his first trial he only got three kicks of the ball, mostly because the other players wouldn't make a pass to him, and was told he hadn't imposed himself enough. Courtney 'imposed' himself at his next trial and was told that he needed to be less aggressive. He got the feeling they were just making excuses.

"So wha' happen to Mark?" asked Horace. "How come he ain't been in contact since Saturday?"

Courtney laughed quietly. "A complicated love life, as far as I know. If the worst come to the worst you can always play Nestor an' call him Mark."

Impersonation was not a tactic Horace was willing to consider but before he could rebuke Courtney for having such an idea, even if he were only joking, what sounded like the dull thud of a shotgun blast took them to the window. A young black guy with a scarf around his face was running from the post office with a sawn-off in one hand and a bag in the other. They watched the scrawny youth jump into a car that screeched its way down the Newhampton Road. People had streamed out of the shops, including the bookies, to line the pavements and hurl abuse at the car as it sped by with one of its doors flapping wildly. Horace shook his head and put the scene down to a quirk of Jamaican culture, as most other people would look for cover rather than run outside – and possibly into the line of fire – just to see what was happening.

"Where's the police now?" sneered Courtney. "Them patrol aroun the place lookin for trouble so how come they ain't out there now?"

Horace didn't reply as he thought Courtney's question was really more of a statement and he was just relieved that – by his build – the masked robber did not resemble any of his players. Now a trophy was a mere ninety minutes away, he could not shake the strange feeling of foreboding that Fate was about to snatch away his moment of glory.

It turned out that the young robber was a kid called Joe Stuart. He was a reckless seventeen-year-old and an avid admirer of Cecil Grant (who had committed his first armed robbery at sixteen). But in striving to emulate his hero, Joe had made the mistake of attempting to stick up the bookies only minutes before running from the post office. The hysterics which accompanied a photo-finish had just subsided as he entered the shop shouting for everybody to lie down when he was confronted by the six-feet-four frame of Carl Hooper. Not one for talking much, Carl let his stare communicate just how he felt. He had a winning docket in his hand and no scrawny youth was going to stop him from collecting his money. He had barred the robber's route to the counter and when no shot came, an emboldened Frank Grant positioned himself next to, if slightly to the rear, of Carl.

"Wha' you tink you-a do?" Frank asked the hesitant

youth. "Go tek yuhself down to de post office an' go steal de government money. G'wan, tek yuhself down deh now an' don't come lookin fe money dat belong to we. G'wan, man. You 'ave ten minutes before it closes fe lunch. G'wan, man, move yuhself."

By now the rest of the customers were gesticulating wildly and calling out for young Joe to remove himself. The bookies was filled with raucous laughter and questions about what was going wrong with the modern youth as he ran the short distance up the road to the post office that was situated on the edge of the Avion shopping precinct.

Frank later repeated the question of what was going wrong with the youth as he finished giving Horace and a customer his slightly exaggerated account of what had happened in the bookies. In his version of the story Carl Hooper's actions did not get much of a mention. "Me tell de yout where he should-a go but everyone knows dat you nah rob de post office if it nah pension day, to ras."

"To ras," Horace and the customer sighed.

No one could say what was going wrong in the lives of the youth but for Joe Stuart life had already taken a turn for the worst. After a not very successful career in crime, six days before his nineteenth birthday, he began a fourteen years sentence for a robbery in which he'd shot and wounded a fifty-three year old security man. Seven months into the sentence he was found hanging in a prison cell.

The reason Desmond Palmer and Nestor Riley never got to meet up with Courtney was because of the message Nestor's mother had passed onto him. She had woken Nestor just before midday and told him Steve Patel had been on the phone and that he had a job for him and Des. He wanted to roll over and go back to sleep not only because had he been kept awake by the baby who had cried most of the night but also because his leg was still causing a lot of pain. It still bore the stud marks left by the late tackle that had led to his sending off. He winced as he got out of bed and thought if he could find that guy who had fouled him he would have juked his bloodclart for sure. His mom had left his black suit and white shirt on the landing, together with the black tie and socks she had pressed and his black shoes that she had polished. She wasn't exactly happy about his new line of work but he'd stuck at it for five months now, which was roughly four-and-a-half months longer than any job he'd had before. She'd once asked him about where his money had come from when he didn't have a job and Nestor had mumbled something about gambling and that was enough for her not to ask again. Claudette and Rupert Riley had four sons; the youngest of them was Nestor, the only one of them to be born in England. Rupert reckoned it was his youngest boy's place of birth that had made him so bad and wukless.

Rupert Riley had never got on with his English-born pickney, and their relationship had got increasingly violent as Nestor grew older. For Rupert, Nestor embodied everything that had proved such a disappointment about England. He had tried his hand at many things and eventually bought a small grocery that failed when a supermarket opened less than a mile away. Eventually, he was forced to sell up and shortly after that he returned to Jamaica without asking if any of his family wanted to go with him.

After hobbling to the bathroom and taking a piss, Nestor had a brief wash and snarled a curse as his mind turned to Diane. Two months before, while he was out playing football, Diane had turned up on his doorstep and told his mother that he had agreed to look after their baby while she went to London for a couple of days. His mom had tried to tell Diane that this was the first she'd heard of it but was won over by her grandson's little smile – which turned out to be only wind. Nestor finished dressing by putting on his thick gold chain and grinned at his reflection while thinking what he would do to Diane if she showed her pasty face in Wolverhampton again.

Nestor's mother was shouting something to him about taking baby Peter to the doctor as the V6 engine of his Ford Capri fired into life. He'd already told her to take the pickney to an orphanage and tell them Diane had abandoned him. There were more important things on his mind; he shouted to his mother that he and Desmond had business to attend to. She sadly compressed her lips as she watched Nestor drive away. She figured, well, hoped, that he did not really mean what he'd said about the orphanage.

Although most people thought Nestor Riley and Desmond Palmer had grown up together they had only been friends since they had both started secondary school. They had got on from the first time they'd met; they wanted the same things, had almost identical callous attitudes to life and had shared similar childhood experiences. Nestor had been eleven when his father left for Jamaica and Desmond had been only eight when his mother had walked out. But while Nestor's mother Claudette struggled to bring up all her children, Desmond had proved too much of a handful for his father Mervyn who soon packed him off to his Uncle Pernell and Aunt Beatrice in Manchester, Jamaica. In the four years he'd lived there, Desmond had picked up a Jamaican accent and a contemptuous attitude for the law – mostly because his strict uncle was a policeman.

In Desmond's lounge, Nestor saw something that disturbed him. "Wha' ppen," Desmond said to Nestor. "Me soon come," he added as Jas dropped to his knees to finish polishing Des's shoes. Nestor looked on and wondered what demeaning act he would have Jasvinder do next. He'd seen similar behaviour in a Young Offenders' Unit, when slightly built youths like Jas were bullied by bigger, more aggressive, types. He became uncomfortable just thinking about what it had been really like while he served his time (rather than the stories he'd told about how cushy it was.)

Desmond felt pleased that Nestor had arrived in time to see him exercise such control over Jas. He figured it must have crossed Nestor's mind that he too should kidnap someone to tend to his requirements. But then again there was no need: Nestor did have his mother and this made Desmond feel jealous – until it occurred to him that she could not service cars like Jasvinder. Desmond had a fleet of BMWs that were the envy – or so he reckoned – of all the guys in the neighbourhood. But they needed a lot of looking after and kidnapping an apprentice mechanic seemed the cheapest option. Jas was allowed one phone call to his family to say that he had left home and was all right before Desmond threatened him with what would happen if he tried to escape. That was four months ago and once he had serviced and valeted all the cars Des began to set him more domestic tasks.

Nestor waited until Jas left the room and then asked Desmond if Steve Patel had told him what was their next job. "Lickle ole lady in Blakenhall," he replied.

"She lived on her own?"

"Nah," said Des, unable to disguise his disappointment. "She got plenty people there to look after 'er valuables, to rasclart. Let's go pick up the van."

Walking to the Ford Capri, Nestor remembered their meeting with Courtney. "Him can wait," said Desmond, "we have to find out if Steve will settle for less. Seen?"

"Seen," Nestor said. "But, man, if he won't take less, can we really raise that kind-a cash in three weeks?" Really he was asking Desmond was this too big a deal for them to get involved with.

"Like me seh," replied Des, "this is too good a ting to refuse, this is the deal that will give us serious money. We raise wha' shekels we can an' if we don't raise enough then we 'ave to offer shares in the deal, right?"

The thought of becoming very rich very soon quickened Nestor's pulse and made all but one nagging doubt disappear. Slowly, he said, "Right." Then after a pause he went on, "Right, if we can't raise we'll have to offer some shares but that makes it risky, don't it?"

"Cha," snorted Des, "only risky for everyone else but us, right. Remember why we get away with so many skanks, once you convince people there's somethin fe nutten, or nex to nutten, them can't give you them money fast enough."

With visions of the riches they could make finally overcoming his reservations, Nestor laughed and said, "Yeah, man, risky for everybody but we . . . Let's go collec that ole lady."

4

During the previous Saturday night's celebrations of Sabina Park Rangers' semifinal victory, Mark Beckford had slipped away almost unnoticed, except for Horace who asked where he was going. Mark told his coach that he was heading home to his wife and Horace smiled as though he understood. Mark and Rachel had only been married for five months and she was an upright Christian girl who would not have appreciated the noisy company, or the flashy decor of the Star and Moon nightclub. "A'right, you can do your celebratin at home wi Rachel, no true?" Horace replied, politely ignoring the rumours about Mark and Marcia Yuell.

When Mark arrived home Rachel was asleep and he felt more like weeping than celebrating. He sat in a comfortable armchair in their lounge and surveyed all that he and Rachel had bought and wondered where, exactly, his life had gone so wrong. The pleasant house in which they lived and all the material goods inside of it should have made him content but to Mark they were a testament to the influence his parents still held over him. They had given the couple a deposit for the house and, as near as damn it, chosen the location. He had just turned twenty-three and already felt overburdened with a marriage and a mortgage – and yet he would have shouldered those responsibilities without complaint until a few minutes after the match and the moment a boyhood ambition finally crumbled into dust.

The man in the overcoat and flat cap called him over at the end of the game. His name was Bert Tomlinson and as well as filing match reports for local newspapers, he had acted as a scout for Aston Villa for over thirty years. Mark had spoken to him quite a few times over the years, firstly when he was captain of Wolverhampton schools' team. Back then Bert always had a word for him after a match but once a damaged ligament had put Mark out of the game for most of a season Bert never seemed so keen to talk as much.

After the semifinal Bert had said, "That was one of the best goals I have ever seen, at any level. That strike ranks along with Bobby Charlton's for England against Portugal in the '66 World Cup. Honestly, Mark, that's how highly I rate it."

Not knowing how good Bobby Charlton's goal had been, Mark smiled and bashfully murmured his thanks as his pulse quickened in anticipation of an invitation that never came. Scouts were full of guile and never gave away too much at first. They trawled the nation's football pitches in all weathers not only looking for talent for the clubs they represented but also doing their damnedest to find out if a scout from any other club was about to sign up a player they might have missed. Before the days of academies that bring in very young kids into professional football clubs and a heightened awareness of paedophiles, men like Bert could hang around school pitches and parks without getting arrested for it. After his initial congratulations, Bert began to ask Mark about his brother Ian, his age, if he was still at school and living with his parents and lastly (and most importantly) had any professional club ever talked with him. Ian was what was known as a late developer, once overlooked but now looking full of promise at just days after his seventeenth birthday. It was if Bert had driven a knife into Mark's heart, though he did his best not to show it. At twenty-three, he was being told he was past it to make it as a professional but there was still time for Ian – and the envy of it cut deeply into him. When Mark rejoined the rest of the team he'd said nothing to his brother or nothing to contradict those who speculated that Bert had offered him a trial with the champions of England. It was the shame, as well as his dejection, which had led him to head home from the nightclub early. All through his childhood and adolescence Mark Beckford's dreams and ambitions had centred on football. He had played for the Wolverhampton schools' team from the age of eleven and even before that he had been marked out as a player of great potential. However, his mother and father were wary that the sport would distract their eldest child from his academic studies. They had gone to the great, almost crippling, expense of sending Mark to a private school, as they later did with his sister Marianne but their youngest, Ian, went to a state school. In fact, Ian was treated completely differently from his brother and sister. It wasn't just their parents' attitude to his education, by the time he was fourteen he was allowed to make his own mind up about going to church and yet Marianne and Mark still felt obliged to attend even though they were adults.

By the time his parents finally gave Mark's footballing aspirations their approval it was almost too late. At eighteen he had got two very average A-levels and an office job at the British Steel plant in Bilston before he went to the YMCA to sign up for Sabina Park Rangers. It was during the heatwave of 1976 that he had first trained with Horace McIntosh's team and it proved to be a life-changing event. Up until then most of the black people Mark associated with were those he met at church as there were hardly any other black kids at the school he had gone to. While growing up he had heard about what the ragamuffin brethren got up to, mostly when the minister was preaching about the wages of sin, but this was the first time he had ever had any prolonged contact with them. In the changing rooms they laughed and talked about women and matters that were not strictly legal in a way he found liberating – and just a bit frightening.

On their way home after Mark's first club outing to the Nottingham tournament, Cecil Grant, who was driving the minibus, said they would head for a blues party. Mark thought he was joking when Cecil suggested continuing the celebrations; after all, the sun was up and he figured most people would have gone home to bed. But sure enough, in the blacked-out sitting room of a large Edwardian house, bodies were still gyrating to the bass thudding from the biggest speaker boxes he had ever seen. The minister had said the devil had all the best tunes. Man, this music stirred something deep within him, he'd never heard anything like it: his mother would not even let Desmond Decker play in their house as she reckoned he did indecent things with his lips as he sang about the Israelites. And as his eyes adjusted to the darkness and smoke he saw girls dancing as though they were making babies, or at least practising. One of them looked over the shoulder of the guy she was dancing with. Although he could not see her face, he knew by her eyes that she must be beautiful. Those eyes belonged to Marcia Yuell. Mark had looked away then; feeling self-conscious about the way he was dressed (in his Sunday-best three-piece suit) and guilty that even a moment's attraction was a betrayal of Rachel. Not that they were anything like a serious item back then but both sets of parents had set their minds on the two of them getting together at some point. Rachel was small, very pretty and very, very quiet; in her most sinful fantasies she would not have even imagined behaving like the girls who went to blues parties.

It had turned three before Mark went to bed. Rachel had come downstairs to find him staring blankly at the fireplace. She asked why he had not come upstairs and if anything was wrong. He looked at her in a dressing gown that would have more suited her frumpy mother and almost told her what was wrong: he was not seventeen; Aston Villa was not interested in him; and she was not Marcia. Boy, oh, boy, if only he could have those years to live all over again. But he could not say it, especially as she crouched down beside him and reminded him in such a gentle voice that he had to get up for church in five hours time. He allowed her to guide him by the hand up to their bedroom and made sure she was asleep before he let the tears trickle from the corner of his eyes.

Because of his age Ian had not been allowed to accompany the team to the Star and Moon nightclub but he did not head for home; after all, unlike Mark, he wouldn't be at the Sunday morning service. Instead, he headed for Ruth's as she had told him that her husband Harold would be away for the weekend, yet again. Ruth Martell was white with curly golden hair and sharp blue eyes; and she was ancient, she must have been at least thirty-seven. She lived in a well-to-do part of Wolverhampton called the Wergs Road. Millionaires, or as good as, lived in the big houses on the northern fringes of town. It was Ian's newspaper round that had brought them together when he was fifteen. She had opened her door one frosty morning and invited him in for a hot drink. While he sat on a high stool in the large kitchen sipping coffee, Mrs Martell went upstairs only to appear again wearing not much more than a smile. "Do you think I'm beautiful?" she asked in a voice that had turned deep and husky.

Ian slid from the stool and clumsily placed a hand on one of her bare breasts. "Easy, tiger," she said as she began to lead him upstairs. He was doing his best to get undressed as coolly as he could but only managed to pull a tight knot into his laces. "Take your time," she called from her bed, "just imagine me as Mrs Robinson," she said in reference to the film *The Graduate* in which an older woman seduces a young guy played by Dustin Hoffman. Ian immediately began reversing the undressing process and tucked his shirt back into his waistband. The only Mrs Robinson he knew was Audley's mother and the woman was six feet tall and six feet wide with more than a passing resemblance to the former heavyweight champion Joe Frazier. "I've gotta go," he said. "I'll come back when I've done my round."

"Sure," said Mrs Martell, "we'll have more time that way."

Once he had shook the dreadful vision of Audley Robinson's naked mother from his mind, Ian summoned his courage and returned after he had delivered all his newspapers. His hand was shaking as he rang her doorbell while he remembered what his spar Kingsley had explained about 'doin a ting'. It wasn't that Ian was very experienced, truth was he had no experience at all. A lot of people thought he had no problem with girls just because he was captain of the school football team but in reality it seemed all the girls were more interested in guys who were into music rather than football. Ian felt more comfortable dribbling a ball past four or five tough defenders who were aiming to break his legs rather than trying to chat up a girl. He had listened to the guys boasting in the schoolyard about what they had done with this or that girl and was always glad when they finally started picking sides for a game. Wherever Ian was on the 'gal' front, he was always first choice when it came to football. As he waited on Ruth's doorstep before that first time he told himself not to be scared because if things turned out like he hoped he too could join in the chat before the game. Most of all, he would look forward to telling Kingsley, as he was the one who seemed to know the most about girls. Ian would tell him all that had happened to check that the 'ting' had been 'ongled' correctly. As it turned out, the reporting took a great deal longer than that first event but Kingsley looked well impressed, in fact he seemed downright jealous and spurred on by the rest of the guys Ian returned to Mrs Martell's again and again. At some point, he could not remember when or why, his feelings about her changed. He was no longer excited about seeing her and didn't like all the stuff she talked about – and no, he told her, he hadn't seen that film *Mandingo* with the black boxer Ken Norton playing a slave and the white Susan George as his mistress. "What's this with you an' films?" he asked her.

There was something in the boy's voice that put alarm into the woman's eyes. Not long after that she would often talk about the time when Ian would find a girlfriend and would no longer call. She started to give him money and gifts. For his sixteenth birthday she had bought him a bike and then, persuaded by the guys at school, before the year was out – and coaxed by Kingsley – he was asking her for a car. The request did not seem to faze her in the slightest and for his seventeenth she had bought him a secondhand, but fairly modern, Ford Escort. It was only an 1100cc, she said she didn't want him driving too fast. To make up for the lack of power she had a set of fancy alloy wheels fitted to it and 'go-faster' stripes put onto its sides. The appearance of the bike had been hard enough, so how the hell was he going to explain the sudden appearance of a car to his parents?

He asked Vince Buckshot Pinnock if he could park it in his backstreet repair shop and spent the next fortnight raising the subject of buying a car with his mother and telling her he had secretly saved money from his newspaper round. She had been both surprised and pleased that he had saved so much money and said that she would ask his father to look out for a suitable car for him. "Vince Pinnock has one at his place," he blurted. "He plays for the team, Mom, there ain't no way he's gonna sell me a bad car. He says this one is jus right for me." His mother crinkled her lips and said she would mention it to his father. A few days later Clovis Beckford growled a bit but eventually he accompanied Ian down to Buckshot's place. As he inspected the car and made several disapproving noises about the wheels and stripes, Buckshot gave Ian several sharp glances. Normally, he wouldn't have put up with anything like the comments Clovis was passing, even if he were about to make money out of the deal (which he most certainly wasn't.) But he tightened his lips and silently nodded as Clovis warned him of the repercussions if the car turned out to be a dud.

"You 'ave a deal," Clovis finally said, offering Buckshot his hand.

Without any enthusiasm, Buckshot took it and told Ian he would sort out matters such as the log book when he saw him at training later that evening. On the way back home Ian asked his father why he had given Buckshot such a hard time.

Clovis explained to his son that Buckshot was a 'half-breed' because his mother, while born in Jamaica was a 'coolie', that is to say of Indian descent. "It's in the blood," his father said, "Coolies expec you to haggle, otherwise them don't get no pleasure outta the deal."

Later that day, in the changing rooms after training, Ian thanked Buckshot for going along with his deception. It had surprised him that Buckshot hadn't even asked him how he had got himself a car. Buckshot was still rubbing a towel across his back as he said, "Yout, after wha' your ole man put me through I reckon you owe me one."

"Owe wha'?"

"Owe me a favour one day. I was sayin to the guys the other day that out of us all, you're the one who can mek it as a pro. An' when you're up there I don't want you forgettin us down here. I mean I might want tickets for a cup final one day."

"Nah," Ian said happily, "I would never forget you guys."

Buckshot looked at him more seriously. "But it was that rich white woman on the Wergs Road who gave you that car, isn't it?" he asked.

Ian was shocked that Buckshot knew about her, he had only told Kingsley her name and where she lived and made him promise to keep it secret. "Who told you, was it Kingsley?"

The corners of Buckshot's mouth turned down. "I don't know any Kingsley, but I do know the guy who was asked by this woman to fit the stripes an' wheels to that car. Look, Ian, I ain't gonna tell you your business but there's been plenty young guys who had talent like yours but they never made it 'cause them got distracted, right. So here's a tip, ease out, guy, ease out now before tings get messy an' gets you all distracted. I mean, look at all this business with bringin your ole man down to my place – that's jus complication you don't need."

Ian stood trying to think of an answer that made out things between him and Ruth Martell *were* simple but as he stood there with his mouth open Buckshot laughed and slapped his shoulder. "Remember, cut the complication an' I'll be callin you one day for a few cup final tickets," he said.

5

Vince Buckshot Pinnock had to move on. His business was outgrowing the small workshop off Sweetman Street and the landlord, one of Clovis Beckford's fellow church-goers, was giving off signals that he was about to put up the rent. The crafty and flabby Rudolph Naylor would peek at the cars from underneath the rim of his hat and mutter how well Buckshot must be doing. "An' you 'ave dis place cheap, y'know," he'd always add.

When members of the congregation were speaking in tongues Rudolph was one of those who could translate the words of the "'Oly Spirit" into something that approximated to English, or more correctly *H*inglish. According to Rudolph, God was very worried that members of His flock were clinging to mammon too much, in other words there wasn't enough going onto the collection plates for the Lord's liking. Rudolph had another sort of gift that over the years had led to four members of the choir bearing his children. There was a smugness about him (and a wealth that had been explained away by his property dealings) that sickened Buckshot. Every Jamaican in Wolverhampton knew, or had heard the tales, of how he had exploited his fellow countrymen by charging the new arrivals exorbitant rents and outrageous prices for the winter coats none of them had possessed or needed back home. As he got richer, Rudolph became a part-time preacher who indulged in nearly all of the deadly sins except for the deadliest of them all: getting caught.

It was only because Buckshot liked Ian Beckford's attitude that he had not told his old man Clovis to sling his hook. Ian reminded Buckshot of himself as a teenager, always a little bit of an outsider no matter how much he tried to fit in. Clovis Beckford had started to get under Buckshot's skin from the moment he asked if he were Everton Pinnock's son. He knew damn well he was and as he spoke the corners of Clovis' mouth betrayed his pleasure that Buckshot's father was reaping the bitter harvest of his sinful sowing. "An' me hear him an' your mother split up an' ting," Clovis had remarked. He drew breath to follow up with some sort of biblical quotation but was pulled up short by the glares of both Buckshot and Ian. The break-up of his parents' marriage was the one matter Buckshot refused to talk about with anyone, including either of his parents or his sister Shannon – before she left for Hamburg. He definitely wouldn't have held his peace if Clovis had mentioned her.

Buckshot knew of several girls who had gone to Germany from Wolverhampton and figured that what he took to be 'modelling' must have been lost in the translation into German. He had warned Shannon of the possible dangers but his younger sister was too vain; and urged on by their mother who had paid for an expensive portfolio, she headed for Hamburg with dreams of becoming a model. To Buckshot's embarrassment, news of Shannon's venture quickly spread and even big Carl Hooper, who wasn't normally one for passing comment, almost said what everyone believed, "Yeah, Buckie, she modellin her pus . . ." The words died in the big man's throat as he saw the look in Buckshot's eyes.

The split in his parents' marriage of twenty-three years had been coming for some time. Everton Pinnock had been having affairs from early on and Buckshot had heard he had a brother somewhere who was only a year younger than he was. It had never been a marriage made in heaven. Buckshot's mother Susan was Jamaican of Indian descent and her family had been against her marrying Everton, not so much because he was black – although it was a factor – but because her mother had heard of his reputation around Port Antonio. "If it only was im eye that did the rovin," she had told her daughter. The marriage had lasted so long because of Susan Pinnock's reluctance to have her mother proved right. But, subconsciously at least, it did affect the way she had reared Shannon. She had encouraged her daughter to go out with white boys; they were "more respectful" and why or how she ended up with a black man the like of Danny Rankin was as much a mystery to Susan as it was a heartbreaker.

Everton did not want Buckshot sharing his house but he allowed him to do so just to spite Susan. He was still a good-looking forty-something who could pull the gals and bring them home, or so he thought. It wasn't so much that he didn't want his son seeing what he was up to but as he explained to him, "Two bull can't share the same pen. You- a big bull now, Vincent, an' it time you found your own pen. You 'ave to the end of the month an' then you 'ave to go." After Buckshot's own had disintegrated, Sabina Park Rangers had become more like his family.

On Thursday, the day after the post office robbery, the local police made door-to-door inquiries in the Newhampton Road area and got little in the way of useful information. When cops turned up at Buckshot's garage in the early afternoon, their appearance was not totally unexpected. Most times, following a robbery using a stolen car, the cops paid him a visit.

Buckshot raised his head from under a bonnet. "Yeah, wha' you want, Sergeant Boyd?" he asked, not bothering to look at the warrant card thrust in his direction. He knew the detective sergeant like he knew the answer to his own question. The detective had a reputation of being a racist and a planter of evidence if the opportunity arose. Boyd put away his warrant card and said, "Vince, Vince, what's with the hostility? I'm only here for a chat and to offer my congratulations on your team getting to the final."

He was bluffing but with the assurance of an innocent

man, Buckshot said, "Cut the bullshit, sergeant, I'm busy, okay. So to save us all time, I don't know a ting 'bout the post office job."

Boyd and another plainclothes cop began to wander around the small workshop and lifted a tarpaulin that was draped over a vehicle. "Didn't think you would, Vince," Boyd said as he continued to examine the old Mercedes convertible. "They used a 1600cc Cortina, not your style." He paused and looked over his shoulder to gauge Buckshot's reaction to his insinuation before he continued, "I've heard it was two kids, bloody inept kids at that. One of them tripped up as he backed out and let off a round. The silly bugger nearly shot someone and all he got was about ninety quid in cash and a load of vehicle tax discs. So if you get offered any I'll expect a call."

"But of course, officer," Buckshot said sarcastically, "Now if you don't mind I have to get this cylinder head finished."

"All right, Vince, I can see you're busy," Boyd said, failing to sound sympathetic. He nodded to his colleague and started to make his way out but stopped and put his head under the bonnet. He stared down at the engine as if he knew what he was looking at. "How's your sister, is she still modelling in Germany?"

Buckshot looked hard into Boyd's eyes and it crossed his mind how pleasurable it would be if he smacked him with a wrench. But he knew that DS Boyd was trying to provoke him and his interest in him was mostly because he played in the same team as Cecil Grant. Detective Sergeant Boyd suspected (but could not prove) that Buckshot had prepared some of Cecil's high-powered getaway cars. In response to the cop's question Buckshot merely sucked his teeth and got on with his work.

"Shannon's her name isn't it?" chuckled Boyd sardonically. "Very good-looking girl as I remember. Didn't think much of the company she kept . . . Danny Rankin, nasty piece of work, record for living off immoral earnings. I just hope her trip has nothing to do with him, Vince."

The sneer in the cop's voice almost had Buckshot at breaking point and at that moment he hated his sister and mother for all the humiliation they had caused him. A few years back, Horace McIntosh had once told the team that Sergeant Boyd had visited his barbershop and suggested a friendly match between Sabina Park Rangers and a police eleven. The idea was quickly shouted down; no one wanted anything to do with the police that could be described as friendly. But as he listened to the cop laughing while he sauntered his way out of the workshop what Buckshot wouldn't have done right then for an opportunity to break Boyd's legs with a two-footed sliding tackle.

The cops hadn't gone long before big Carl Hooper appeared. He usually turned up with his little three-legged mongrel he called Eastwood after his favourite film star in one hand and a curry patty for Buckshot in his other.

Buckshot was always happy to see them because he was peckish in the afternoon and the patties made by Wong the Jamaican Chinaman always hit the right spot. Once they'd eaten, and if there wasn't too much work on, Carl would get in the goal made up of two oilcans and Buckshot would have a bit of shooting practise. He also liked to see the little black and white dog as his best friend while growing up was a Labrador-cross he called Tex. "Wha' is up with Eastwood today?" he asked Carl.

The big man gently put his whimpering tri-ped on the ground and watched him squat and deposit a pile of steaming mess. "Me 'ad a good win today," explained Carl, as the little dog continued to whine, "so me thought me would celebrate and buy Eastwood two curry patties. Well, he shit an' shit an' shit, ever since, Buckie. I'm worried 'bout him."

Buckshot suddenly didn't feel hungry any more and handed back the patty as Carl asked him, "Would you 'ave somethin to put on his backside, some kind-a cream or somethin."

"Man, this a garage me-a run, wha' mek you think me would 'ave ointment for a dog's batty?"

"I just thought when you cut up your hand, you'd have somethin to rub on it."

"Yeah, well if I did, it ain't squirtin anywhere near Eastwood's rashole, me-a tell you."

"Right, right," said Carl, as his brow creased even deeper. "I'll go to the vet then."

"Probably the best place, man."

"True, true. Look, before we go, you trainin tonight?"

"Depends if me fix this car in time, why you arks?"

"Somethin I heard."

"Yeah, like wha'?"

"Somethin like there's some kind-a talk 'bout makin some big money."

"Like sponorship?"

"Nah."

"It ain't some pyramid-sellin bullshit is it, 'cause if it is I ain't interested."

"Nah, man, somethin else."

"Then wha'?"

"Not sure, I just heard that everyone is to turn up tonight an' then we find out."

Eastwood whined louder and began to drag his backside over the workshop floor and leave a trail behind him. Carl picked him up and Buckshot looked down to the streaks and then to the pile of dog shit at his feet.

"So see you later?" asked Carl.

Buckshot was mostly thinking about cleaning up the mess before he got around to figuring that he had nothing to lose. "Yeah, man," he said, "me see you later. But mek sure you get somethin done 'bout that dog's battyhole before me see him again."

6

Nestor Riley and Desmond Palmer had turned up late and missed the Thursday evening training session at Aldersley Stadium but had somehow still managed to get two tickets off Horace McIntosh for the 'beauty contest with a difference' at the Star and Moon club the following night. The two men went to the changing rooms to find their team-mates showering and drying themselves and as usual all of them refused to shake either of the men's hands while they were in their work clothes. Still dressed in black suits and white shirts they would have passed for nightclub doormen but they actually worked for a funeral director named Steve Patel who had set up a company specialising in services for the ethnic minorities in the West Midlands area. Steve had tried his hand at several businesses and thought he found a niche in a market that would never run out of customers. It was not long before he spotted other opportunities, especially if the deceased had no relatives around the place but he needed personnel who had no respect for the dead – or as he put it, "Graverobbers who don't want to go to the trouble of burying their victims first." He had known Nestor Riley and Desmond Palmer from the days when they used to steal from his father's shop on their way to school and they were the first people who came to mind. Normally their belief in duppies (ghosts) would have made them reluctant about taking up this line of work but the opportunity to remove items of value and cash along with the corpse helped them to overcome their reservations. The deal they had agreed was that Steve got antiques and jewellery and the two guys kept the cash.

"Listen up," Nestor called out to his team-mates, "me an' Des have a way of you guys mekin some serious money.

An' before any of unno arks, it don't involve sellin soap or shit like that, right. Our spar Steve Patel has a contact in India an' he wants to import some high-class caskets, you know serious mahogany an' ting. Man, these tings are so comfortable once you see one you jus wanna 'urry up an' die. Now these caskets from India are half the price any funeral director can buy in this country so Steve is gonna buy in a few thousand an' sell them wholesale. But there's a catch, for the best price he's gonna have to buy a shipload, to rasclart. So now he's havin to raise some serious shekels an' the deal is this – anyone who puts in at least a grand will have his money doubled in one month. So put in two grand an' you get back four, put in twenty an' you make another twenty . . . fe doin nutten."

Nestor Riley braced himself in the expectation of the rush that never came. Most of the responses were made up of loud suckings of teeth and several cuss words directed at the two guys. Some told Nestor and Desmond they must be insane if they seriously thought that they had that sort of money (who in turn would also have to be insane to hand it over to the likes of Nestor and Desmond). "You guys must be crazy," snorted Norman Longmore, "since when does a coolie cut a black man into a deal that's any good. No, sah, if the coolie 'ave a good deal him tell only coolie. You too fool, man, the two-a unno, too fool to believe dat, or to see any of my hard-earned money, to rahteed."

Several players followed Norman and shouldered their way out while shaking their heads scornfully. "If you need money for ya coolie spar," Audley Robinson said to Desmond as he left, "why don't you go arks ya daddy fe some-a im t'irty-five grand winnins?"

By his puzzled expression and the way he kept silently mouthing "t'irty-five grand?" it was obvious that Desmond Palmer was one of the few people in the town who had not heard about his father's pools win. Both he and Nestor stood with their mouths open as Courtney Wright explained about the win and Mervyn's purchase of a brand new Austin Princess for five grand. Desmond's mind was filled with questions of how so much money could be so close by without him knowing about it and he exchanged a disbelieving glance with Nestor.

"Me know, man, me know wha' you're thinkin," said Nestor. "A rasclart Austin Princess. The man jus go waste five-rasclart-t'ousand pounds!"

"Well, that too," Desmond muttered. But he was thinking more about his greedy older brothers and sisters who had probably already got their share. But it only took a second or two for him to rethink that: his old man was too mean to start sharing. The one lesson Mervyn had taught Desmond was to look after yourself first . . . second . . . third . . . fourth . . . and you only do someone a favour if you know you will get more back.

With their minds busy with thoughts of thirty grand they didn't notice how few were left in the changing room until Cecil Grant spoke. "Now the *h*upstandin members 'ave gone," he said, "you can cut the foolishness 'bout coffins from India an' tell us wha' the real deal is."

Nestor's eyes refocused and surveyed those who had remained. Besides Cecil the bank robber there were the usual guys who were up for any dodgy business. Courtney Wright, who traded in herbal matter; Buckshot Pinnock, a man who dealt with the odd stolen car; Bryce McBean who was currently selling stolen goods in the Birmingham area and had done his fair share of robbing; and lastly (and most surprisingly to Nestor and Desmond) Mark Beckford. "No offence, church-bwoy," Nestor Riley said to him, "but these men here 'ave ways an' means of raisin serious cash, if you know wha' I mean. That's unless you're gonna rob them teefin pastors you see every Sunday. Bwoy, there's not a man here who can get near them men fe skanks an' robbery, to ras."

"To ras," mumbled the others.

"Yeah, well I do have a way of raisin a stake," said Mark, "but that's all you gotta know until we hear wha' the real deal is." Unbeknown to anyone, Mark had finally decided he wanted to leave Rachel and break away from his parents' influence to start a new life with Marcia. The dejection he felt when the Aston Villa scout asked about his younger brother Ian had been that final straw of misery that had made him want to get away. But with the constant threat of redundancy the only way he could do it was to steal the money that paid the wages at his factory. It had started off as an idle fantasy as he watched the wages truck come and go every Thursday but as the weeks went by he had come up with a plan that could not fail. At first he thought he was mistaken but now his mouth went dry just with the thought of what he had stumbled across: a very short time in which bags of money were left unguarded in a safe that, contrary to directives, remained unlocked for long periods in the day.

Cecil Grant was the key to what Mark would do with the money he was planning to steal, if Cecil went along with what Nestor and Desmond were proposing then Mark and everyone else present would do too. The logic was simple: Nestor and Desmond would pull every skank imaginable to make money but the one man they would not dare to double-cross was Cecil Grant as they knew only too well what he would do to "dem greedy clarts".

"It's true that a heap-a coffins are comin from India but it's wha' inside dem that is gonna make the money," Desmond explained. "Steve is doin business with some Pakistani guy in Birmingham. The more money he puts in the more he draws. Now, Steve wants to make out that he has more money than he's got so the Pakistani guy thinks he's loaded. It's the way these kind-a coolie go on, dem only respec money."

"Yeah, well I got somethin you an' dem will respec if this

turns out to be a skank," growled Cecil. "Where an' when are these coffins landin?"

"Couple-a weeks," said Nestor. "but Steve ain't stupid, he ain't sayin anythin 'bout where the stuff lands in case any-a unno want to rob it."

Cecil looked over and swapped smiles with Bryce McBean. Beanie preferred to work on his own, stealing the takings from supermarkets mostly, but Cecil had often thought they would make a good team if the prize were big enough. "So when do we get our money back?" he asked.

"Steve says that everythin is lined up an' you would 'ave the money you put in two weeks after it lands," Desmond answered, "an' two weeks after that you get the same amount again. This is a one-off opportunity, 'cause once Steve makes this deal him'll 'ave so much money him won't need the likes of we again, unnerstan?"

"Then what's in these coffins," asked Courtney, "ganja?"

Nestor rolled his lips momentarily before he answered, "Nah, man, ganja don't raise this kind-a money, it's heroin these guys are dealin with."

Courtney sucked at his teeth. "I don't know if I wanna get involved with brown, man, that narsty shit, seen?"

Nestor could sense that Cecil and the rest were now losing interest and looked over to Desmond for help. "Hey, Courtney," he said, "wha' black man you know who do anythin but ganja? Heroin is a white ting, man, like coke an' ting. So let the white man 'ave im habit but at a price 'cause since the Russians go into some place me never 'ear of, Alf-ganja-stan or somethin, the price has gone sky-rakstone-high."

All eyes were now on Cecil Grant as he was the guarantor for everyone's investment. For extra drama he looked up to the ceiling and let a forefinger slide up and down his throat. Finally he lowered his chin and held Nestor and Desmond with one of his diamond-hard stares. "This is a big decision to make . . . Me say that we meet up nex trainin session an' by then we'll 'ave made our minds up an' will know exactly how much cash we can raise. An' you guys can let Stevie Patel know, though you nah mention my name, what's gonna happen to him an' you two, if me come into this deal an' then don't get every penny that me due."

Nestor was going to ask for a more definite answer but all those standing in front of him were already nodding their heads in a manner that told him to try and get any more of a positive commitment would be a waste of time. "Right, right," he said disappointedly, "so nex week, yeah?"

Once they were alone Desmond asked Nestor what he thought the chances were of them raising the one hundred grand they wanted. Steve Patel had promised them that if they could come up with that sort of money he would only then let them in on the deal that would see their investment at least trebled. "Cha," sighed Nestor, "it's all down to Cecil, if he comes in then the rest-a dem follow. But wait, your ole man, him still good fe t'irty grand if we get to him quick."

"But look, Nestor, you know me an' him are like poison. The man never do nutten fe me except sen me to Jamaica so a bunch-a crazy people could beat me an' . . . an' . . ."

"An' wha'?"

". . . There's some tings best lef unsaid, me-a tell you."

"Well, that's why we should go check the man right now, the man owe you fe all the tings him didn't do fe you when you was a bwoy. The man, owe you big-time, to ras."

Nestor said nothing else for a while as he watched Desmond go through a flashback of his Jamaican experience: he knew it was happening by the way Desmond's eyes had turned blank and the muscles at the edges of his mouth had started to twitch. He had first witnessed this happening to Desmond after playing a joke and locking him in a cupboard of a recently deceased old man when he had gone in search of his money. A high-pitched howl went up from inside and when Nestor's fit of hysterical laughter subsided he opened the cupboard door and found Desmond mumbling about his grandmother's dress. "What's that you seh, Nestor?" Desmond now asked, as if unaware that several seconds had elapsed since Nestor had spoken.

"Me seh, we go an' see your ole man right now 'cause him owe you big-time."

"Big-time," muttered Desmond angrily. "Yeah let's go see him right now."

7

The evening had turned out to be a very disappointing one for Nestor Riley and Desmond Palmer. There were enough guys playing for Sabina Park Rangers who were making money through illegal means to have made the pair think that their team-mates would have jumped at the chance that had been offered them. The trouble was, at least in their opinions, there was no one else around who was as smart as they were. It was this belief in their superior intelligence that allowed them to think that they would always come out on top no matter what and they would never have to face the consequences of their skanks. To add to their frustration, there had been no answer when Nestor and Desmond had called to Mervyn's house. To make sure he wasn't just hiding from them they went around the back and broke in through a kitchen window. There was no sign of him or, come to think of it, his new Austin Princess. When they checked his wardrobe and saw he had not packed they decided to stay for a while. Nestor figured that he was out celebrating and only wanted to take advantage of Mervyn's drunken state to persuade him to part with most of his winnings but Desmond had thoughts of torture crossing his mind. They found a couple of cans of *Red Stripe* and settled down but by the morning all they had to show for their troubles were horribly coated tongues and stiff backs from sleeping in the badly-sprung armchairs.

As he woke, something about Mervyn's recent purchase occurred to Nestor Riley. "Hey," he said while shaking Desmond's arm, "I jus thought 'bout your ole man's money. I bet he didn't buy that car with im winnins. I bet he ain't even collected it yet an' he's got a stash-a cash some place."

Mervyn Palmer was not the sort to trust a bank with his money and the idea that he might have some hidden in his house immediately roused Desmond. They had searched enough houses of the recently deceased to know if there was any money around they had a good chance of finding it. Over the months they had found money secreted in tea caddies, disused fireplaces, toilet cisterns and under loose floorboards. Only once had they found anything hidden under a mattress. Desmond went upstairs and it wasn't long before he found rolls of money in a pair of shoes and in the lining of a navy blue suit.

"How much?" asked Nestor.

"Six grand."

"Not bad, that means we got nearly twenty. Another eighty, man, an' we're cool," Nestor said. The thought about what sort of money Desmond's fleet of BMWs would bring in had crossed his mind. He had yet to raise the subject as he knew how much they meant to Desmond – if only because he had taken the trouble to kidnap and enslave Jas just to look after them; although he was beginning to wonder if there was more to their relationship than that. Desmond pushed the banknotes deep into an inside jacket pocket. "Let's hope the guys come forward with the dunsai nex week, or some lonely millionaire dies real quick," he said.

This was as good a time as any, thought Nestor. "We're gonna have to consider doin everyting an' anyting to get that money, y'know, 'cause this is a once-in-a-lifetime ting, Des."

Desmond sucked at his teeth as if he had just been told the obvious for the thousandth time. "But me know already," he said, "an' me ready to do it – as long as it don't include sellin mi batty or any of mi BMW."

They had previously talked about setting up some sort of pyramid scheme; defrauding the DHSS on a large scale; and even trying to rig one of the poker games that happened late at night in the room below Horace's salon – but they would all take too long to produce the amount of money they wanted. Selling shares in "coffin importation" seemed a good idea that would bring in those who were naive and desperate and, at the same time, the reality of the deal attracted those who were neither scared nor had any scruples about getting involved in funding a massive narcotics deal. "You could always buy the BMWs back when we made the money," Nestor ventured.

Desmond's face contorted with real disgust at the idea. "Oi, behave yuhself, man," he said without a hint of irony, "if we don't 'ave some standards we're jus goin on like beasts, isn't it?"

Friday mornings were always busy in Horace's barbershop but it was especially busy because of the beauty pageant that was to be held at the Star and Moon nightclub that evening. Whatever the attitudes about such contests in the wider world, they were very popular amongst the West Indian men of Wolverhampton and very good for business too. In order to continue with the prosperous line of enterprise, the club's management had done their best to come up with variations on the theme. Once they had got the Miss Star and Moon competition out of the way; there was

Miss Swimsuit (minimum covering of the cratchies required); Miss Wolverhampton Afro-Caribbean; Miss Black West Midlands (although the lighter the skin the better the chance of winning); Glamorous Grannies (proof of grandchild must be produced); and Moms and Daughters (minimum age 17). It was therefore intriguing that they merely advertised tonight's event as a 'beauty contest with a difference'. Word had got around that the contestants would be nude, or at least topless, but could not be advertised as such because of some old law about keeping a disorderly house – or some other "rasclart ting".

Most of Horace's customers were young men who wanted to look their best for the weekend. Before the wet-look curly perm became socially acceptable on a man's head, as well as on a woman's in the mid-eighties, a generation of fashionable black men had to go through the rigmarole of combing out, oiling and finally plaiting long hair prior to retiring to bed with stockings on their heads. Once the hair was combed out it was essential that the young black man always carried an Afro comb with him to ensure his head looked perfectly symmetrical at all times. It was such a nerve-wracking process to get from the home to a club with prefect hair, that many a man developed the Afro-hump, which came about because of the permanent stoop some of them had to adopt to avoid the bigger Afro brushing the roof of a car while driving. Sticking your head through a sunroof was not an option. For men of Frank Grant's generation the Afro belonged on a woman's head. For younger guys who didn't want to run the risk of being stigmatised as "'avin a 'ead like a gal" a simpler solution to the hair problem was to get a big woollen hat or turn Rasta.

Horace McIntosh was cleaning his electric razor before lunch when he asked Frank Grant what he had thought of Mark Beckford's attitude during the training of the night before. "Him look a'right," said Frank, "him say im 'amstrings are sore but him'll be fit fe de final."

Horace was not convinced, he thought his star player seemed distant and he had avoided giving a direct answer when he was asked if he'd heard any more from Aston Villa. "Me was tinkin more about im mental *h*attitude."

"Im mental *h*attitude?"

"Yeah, man, like him distracted."

"Look, man, dem was all distracted last night. Dem was waitin fe Nestor an' Desmond to turn up, de two-a dem 'ave come up with some get-rich-quick ting, Norman was tellin me about it. Steve Patel is bringin in t'ousands of coffins from *h*India an' dem talkin some foolishness about doublin money in a month."

"Doublin money, eh? Well, you know we all gonna need a coffin one day, for true."

"Yeah, well Audley tell Desmond to go see im daddy an' arks him fe some-a im money."

"Maybe dat's why we nah see Mervyn today, him out now doublin im money."

"Cha, Horace, man, one ting Mervyn nah do is give im money to Desmond, whatever de plan. Him don't like de bwoy an' de bwoy don't like im father."

"But money talks an' no one makes money like a coolie."

"Yeah, well if you tink dat go give dem a t'ousand of your money. But me? No, sah, me-a go de bookies first, at least me 'ave a chance of seein it again."

Frank went for his lunchtime trip to the bookies and for the first time in days he left Horace preoccupied by something other than football. Horace often thought that too many West Indians, particularly Jamaicans, had got into the habit of other cussing other people's entrepreneurial talents and were too ready to make accusations when the aptitude for business had reaped its rewards and they had missed out. Horace knew that his barbershop had once drawn the same sort of resentful comments. Back in the fifties he had seen his opportunity and was now beginning to figure that there just might be another opportunity coming along that was too good to refuse.

At the Bilston steel plant Mark Beckford sat at his desk thinking about money and Marcia. He hadn't mentioned anything to her about his plans for the two of them, he thought he would not say anything until he had counted out the proceeds of his thievery. It was difficult to concentrate because, try as he might, he could not help but try to figure out how much he could get away with. He could not be greedy; it was one of the deadly sins whereas stealing was more in the line of simply breaking a commandment. He could only risk taking the contents of one cash bag. In six days time he could be a rich man and felt excited but not scared by the idea. Then it would be down to Nestor and Desmond to double his ill-gotten gains before he would finally set off for a new life with Marcia.

The teeth-grinding boredom had him sliding his newspaper from the drawer and placing it on his lap so he could read the back page. It was mostly about the Wolves team and if they could avoid relegation to the Second Division after suffering a demoralising defeat to Tottenham Hotspur in the replay of the FA Cup semifinal. But it wasn't long before the newspaper was back in his desk and Mark was staring out of the window replaying his favourite fantasies. They used to be dreams of glories on the football pitch. When he was a kid he would go to bed wearing a football jersey rather than a pyjamas and dream of walking out from a tunnel and onto the turf of Anfield, Old Trafford, Highbury and even Wembley. He had scored his greatest ever goal to get Sabina Park Rangers to the final and it should have been one of the highlights of his career. But the memory of it was now clouded by disappointment: not even that example of brilliance was good enough for him to be wanted by a professional club. His mind turned back to the bag of money he planned to steal; football no longer seemed so important.

8

Like blood in the water, by Friday night the scent of money was wafting around the nose-holes of many in Wolverhampton's West Indian households. News of the double-your-money scheme had spread rapidly once Nestor Riley and Desmond Palmer had put it to the players of Sabina Park Rangers in the changing room at Aldersley Stadium. Fierce arguments were already raging about if it could be true or not. For some it was just too good to be true and they were already threatening violence to anyone who tried to skank them but there were others who countered that the proposition made perfect sense as coffins were always in demand whatever the economic climate of the time.

"Who involve?"

"Some coolie."

"Cha, you can't trust no coolie in dis country."

"Him runs de funeral home in Sweetman Street."

"So 'ow much him want?"

"Minimum a t'ousand. Him 'ave customers lined *h*up so you get yuh t'ousand an' annoda t'ousand back *h*in a week."

"*h*In a week?"

"*h*In a week, to rasclart!"

"Mi ras! But wait, me nah 'ave no t'ousand pound."

"Well me 'ave five hundred if you can find a lickle raise."

"Yeah, man, me can raise five hundred. So wha' happen then?"

"We go see Mervyn's son, the one wid all de nice cars who works for de coolie, him tekin care of the runnins. 'Ow you tink him an' im farda buy so many nice cars, man, dem 'ave money long time before him win the pools, to ras."

"To ras."

As Nestor and Desmond entered the Star and Moon club it quickly became obvious to them that they were at the centre of attention. At first they were nervous but then they relaxed as several women – the sort that would normally cuss their ras if they came too close – were smiling in their direction. All became clear once Lenley Greene sidled up next to them. "This coffin ting," he said while pulling anxiously at his little goatee beard, "is it for true?"

Nestor exchanged a glance with Desmond before he said, "Yeah, man. 'Ow much you 'ave?"

" 'Ow much you want?"

"A grand minimum."

"Yeah, that's wha' me 'ear. An' the money comes back double in a week?"

"Nah, money back in two weeks an' whatever you put in comes back again a week, or two weeks after that."

"Me 'ear it come back double in one week."

"Then you 'ear wrong. But don't fret yuhself, Lenley, plenty people want in an' there's only a couple-a grand lef to raise. If you don't want it there's plenty who do."

"Wha' if I call aroun your yard tomorra?"

"We's busy tomorra, we 'ave bisniss in Nottingham."

"You mean the football ting?"

"Yeah, the football. Check me Monday an' if there's space me let you in on it 'cause me know you a long time."

"Thanks, Nestor, man, me appreciate it. Me see you Monday."

The club was starting to heave under the weight of the hot and sweaty crowd as Nestor and Desmond used their newly found popularity to ease themselves to the front of the stage. Horace McIntosh was seated at the judges' table and beckoned them over. "Dis ting you were tellin de guys about last night, is it some kind-a skank?" he asked them.

"Horace, man, we might do some tings," protested Desmond, "but we ain't gonna skank our own spars, are we? I mean the team is like family to we an' there's certain tings we nah do fe money," he went on, as though thoughts of torturing his own father had never crossed his mind.

"An' it Steve Patel who's bringin in the stuff?"

"Stuff?"

"The coffins."

"Oh yeah, man, the coffins. But the minimum is a grand."

"Me might raise a lickle more than dat. Me know me don't 'ave to remind you guys about Nottingham."

A hand came onto Desmond's shoulder and he looked around to see the club's manager. "Horace," said Uriah Cunningham, "is dis fine young man one of your players who 'as done so much fe black footballers in de town?" Horace nodded proudly. "An' is dis de same young man who 'as de *h*interestin business plan?"

"Yes, dis is Desmond an' im friend Nestor."

Uriah Cunningham searched the two faces looking for some sign, eyes too close together, or a pair of horns, something that might give him a clue about their true character. He saw nothing to dissuade him. "You two men mek sure you come to my office before you leave an' we'll 'ave a lickle chat about some business, okay?"

"Don't keep dem long," said Horace, "we 'ave a tournament in Nottingham tomorra."

Desmond was smiling broadly, but it was the realisation that he and Nestor were about to make the easiest money of their lives, rather than the thoughts of comely Nottingham girls, that was bringing copious amounts of saliva to his lips.

With the air conditioning switched off and the beauty

contest running more than an hour late, the audience began to get restless. The warm-up artist was having a hard time drawing anything but abuse. After he had finished his third song the MC came onto the stage and asked for just one round of applause only to be met with more abuse and shouts for him to "Bring on de gal dem!" Wolverhampton had a reputation of having audiences that were the hardest to please in the whole country. Many a famous artist had been met with icy silence – if they were lucky. The not so fortunate, whatever their reputation or record sales, were often told to remove "dem clart" from the stage after one or two songs into their act.

In amongst the crowd two predators remained silent and nodded in acknowledgement to each other. Cecil Grant and Bryce McBean were at the club for the same reason – and it wasn't the allure of scantily clad women. The possibility of big money had them making their own separate plans. Neither man was thinking of giving Nestor and Desmond much of their own money: they planned to take it away from them and Steve Patel once the transaction had taken place.

Uriah Cunningham, mopped his brow and came back to where Desmond and Nestor were and asked them to come to his office to discuss some business. The young guys frowned: they were waiting to see a parade of almost naked women and thought the business could come later. Uriah dabbed his forehead again and explained there were some difficulties with a few of the contestants and it might be some time before they appeared. Reluctantly, they followed him and within two or three steps there was a surge in the crowd and their places were taken. Uriah sat behind his desk and gestured for the two to pull up chairs for themselves. "First tings first," he said, "is dis ting a skank? 'Cause me is willin to put in five grand but me is also willin to pay a man to kill unno if me nah see mi money again."

He felt comforted by the way Desmond and Nestor

laughed so easily, it communicated that they had no fear of reprisals. "Look, man," said Nestor, "we ain't skankin. We need a lot more money than five grand to buy into the coffin ting an' that's the only reason we's offerin the people we know a chance to come in on it, seen? Believe me, if we had the money none-a you guys would know about it until you see we drivin in our brand new cars."

It was the perfect answer for Uriah Cunningham as he immediately identified with Nestor's admission of greed and selfishness. He unlocked the cash box he had taken from his drawer and pushed five bundles of notes across the desk. "Me wanna receipt but count it first," he said. The bundles were of single and five-pound notes but Desmond and Nestor would see it as a labour of love. They were only halfway through their first bundles when there were the sounds of uproar from inside the club. Alarm spread across Uriah's broad face. "Stay deh an' carry on countin," he said as he rushed for the door. It was only the texture of the money on their fingertips that stopped the two guys following Uriah to see what was going on.

He had been gone almost half an hour and the money had been long counted before Uriah unlocked his office door and re-entered. He flopped down onto his chair muttering to himself, seemingly oblivious to the men sitting opposite him. "Receipt," he said vaguely. Once it was written and Uriah had repeated his threat to have them killed if this turned out to be a skank, they filled their pockets with banknotes and left his office to find a scene of utter devastation.

It turned out that the 'beauty contest with a difference' was far more different than any of the punters had imagined. The women were fit, some said crisp, and when they got into their swimwear they were, if anything, even a little more forward than most of the crowd had hoped for. Every one of them had come to the front of the low stage and jiggled their batties; and when hands made a grab for their loveliness they had responded with smiles rather than the usual cursing. Although Horace was one of the three judges it was the audience who picked the winner by giving the loudest cheer to their favourite. The winner was a statuesque black woman called Grace; her face wasn't the prettiest but most of the crowd agreed that her figure was way more attractive than that of any of the other women's. And this is where the problem lay. A guy who was sweeping up the broken glass explained to Nestor and Desmond, that the contestants weren't women at all but drag queens. Those who had groped their batties became enraged by the questions that were instantly raised in their own minds once the contestants had lined up and taken off their wigs. The thoughts that friends had witnessed them feeling up another man filled them with horror and despite Uriah's intervention to say it was all a joke, the only way they felt able to reclaim their masculinity was by way of that old tried and tested method of mindless violence.

"So all we missed was a load of battyman dressed up like woman," laughed Nestor as they drove home.

Desmond remained quiet for a few miles. "Them guys mashin up the club," he said, "them *h*insecure an' need to mature themselves, to ras. Them drag queens are entertainers, man, dressin up like a woman don't mek them battymen."

Nestor Riley had never before heard his friend give such a considered opinion that challenged the conventions of the day – and that worried him. "Er, right," he said. "Is Jas still workin on ya cars dem?"

Not picking up on what lay behind Nestor's enquiry, Des proudly said, "Yeah, man! Him like mi slave, him do anyting me want."

Nestor thought it best that he asked no further questions about Jas and turned the conversation to the money they had raised so far.

9

The tournament in Nottingham had started in the 1970s after a number of black football clubs from across the Midlands had got together with the idea of setting up a black league or cup competition. The experiences of Sabina Park Rangers being subjected to racial abuse, having their minibus stoned and biased refereeing were shared by all too many teams that were made up of black players. But any idea of a separate league was eventually dismissed because of logistics, too few teams and, most importantly for several coaches, such a move would only confirm the racist notions in some minds that black players were neither mentally nor physically tough enough to play the 'English' game. The Nottingham cup came about because it was thought it would be a good idea if black teams could play for at least one day in a friendly and relaxed atmosphere. The theory may have been a good one but it was not a tournament without hostility just because it was black teams playing each other.

The players of Sabina Park Rangers were the ones who seemed to have most problems getting out of the way of the hard tackles that were flying from the first whistle. After the wrecking of the Star and Moon nightclub several of them had gone straight to a blues party and had turned up for the tournament without having any sleep at all. With the cup final so close Horace McIntosh had intended to leave many of his best players on the sidelines for long periods but he soon found that he had to employ them as substitutes as his players continued to be fouled with an increasing frequency. At one point the referee halted a match and called the captains together to get them to tell their players to cool down before a mass brawl broke out. Horace turned to the coach of the host club and wondered out loud if the other clubs were jealous of his team's success in the more prestigious Watney's cup. The man snorted and replied it had nothing to do with what the Wolverhampton men had done on the pitch that was provoking the rough play but rather what they had got up to at last year's dance.

It was the arrogance of the SPR players, as well as their notion that they were coming with the purpose of chatting up the local females that had the Nottingham footballers well and truly vexed. As usual, the Wolverhampton players had spurned the use of a minibus so they could turn up in their highly polished cars. Still pulling Afro combs through their hair, many of them stepped out of gleaming BMWs, Ford Capris and Granadas and a sporty Toyota Celica – the sort of shiny stuff designed to mesmerise and then steal away the women the Nottingham guys thought 'belonged' exclusively to them. There had been talk before the tournament that they would not allow it to happen again.

True to form, the Nottingham women had turned up in new hairdos and clothes that accentuated their feminine forms. They were there to supposedly cheer on their boyfriends but their presence only served to provoke the local players into even more aggressive attempts to wipe the knowing leers from the faces of the SPR team, who were quite certain that the female presence was all down to them.

Nestor Riley and Desmond Palmer were doing more talking than playing. Suddenly it seemed everyone wanted in on the deal, even Norman Longmore and Audley Robinson who had previously been the most vocal in their scepticism. Once it had got around that businessmen like Horace McIntosh and Uriah Cunningham were prepared to invest their money no one wanted to look foolish by refusing the chance to have their money doubled. The talk went back and forth to reinforce the opinion that the idea was a good one: people died every day, they all needed a coffin and it was one of the few things in life (or more correctly, death) that everyone was going to use. It seemed so simple that it had to be brilliant. Even as Nestor and Desmond took pledges of cash that were to be handed over at the next training session there was feverish activity going on back in parts of Wolverhampton: areas of poor housing; poor job prospects; and, most of all, poor judgement. Those who had only a few hundred pounds to their name were trying to find a friend or relative to come up with enough cash to bring it up to a thousand. Groups who were running 'pardna' saving schemes met to see if they should invest the money they pooled every week. Around the town there were pockets of something approaching hysteria.

"Hey," Desmond said to Nestor, "if only there was a way we could keep this money without gettin killed." The same thought had crossed Nestor's mind. He was busy thinking if there was any place they could hide if they did go down that route just as Cecil Grant shoved an opponent off the ball and began to make a run towards goal. Cecil had once shot and wounded a man over a video recorder worth about four hundred pounds and even though he had yet to hand over any, Nestor figured he knew the lengths Cecil would go to if they ran off with his money.

"Put it out your mind, Des, 'cause me already give it serious thought an' it's the kind-a ting that could put me an' you in a couple-a Steve's mahogany boxes."

"Yeah," Desmond said regretfully, "but it was a nice thought while it lasted though."

On the pitch the sliding tackles that were catching the Sabina Park players earlier on were now being avoided. Retaliation took the form of 'accidental' falls onto the tacklers that normally left them prone and needing the trainer's wet sponge. Now the SPR players were only thinking about football – and not the pleasurable activities that might follow during the evening. The deft touches returned for the final match and Ian Beckford began to show the sort of skill that had so interested the Villa scout. Horace had told them that they had to prove that they were the best black football club in the Midlands now or else, whatever happened in the much more prestigious Watney's Cup final, there would be a few players in Nottingham reckoning that their achievement was not up to much.

The first half was a scrappy affair and it was one-all as the referee blew his whistle to bring it to a close. The Beeston Caribs scored shortly after the restart and began playing with an intensity that revealed how much winning the tournament meant to them. SPR responded by bringing on Mark Beckford and Bryce McBean to start winning more of the ball in midfield. With only five minutes to go Beanie threaded a free kick to Ian Beckford who then passed the ball to Cecil Grant. He shrugged off a feeble tackle and slammed the ball into the corner of the net. Even though the game had restarted, the Beeston players were still arguing amongst themselves about who was to blame for the goal as Ian Beckford began a run that took him past three opponents. As a fourth closed in he released the ball to his brother. Mark had been forced wide as the goalkeeper came off his line to close down the angle but Mark kept cool and forced the ball through the gap between the keeper and the near post.

When the final whistle blew and superiority had been restored (at least in the minds of the Wolverhampton side) the more belligerent amongst the Nottingham men tramped off the pitch shooting glares at the female spectators that dared them to even applaud Sabina Park Rangers.

As was the custom, the teams showered and changed before making their way to a nearby church hall where there would be food, speeches and presentations before those who were young and willing enough would spend the rest of the night – and following morning – at a dance.

The remnants of fried chicken, rice and peas and a variety of green salads were gathered from the long tables as the players and officials waited for the speeches and prize-giving. As with weddings, baptisms and funerals, the speeches at many West Indian functions are noted for being excruciatingly long – and in anticipation of the ordeal backsides shuffled impatiently on the plastic seats. Horace McIntosh anxiously looked around for those of his players who were absent from the meal (as they prepared for the dance by chatting up what girls they could). As the guest speaker was about to take the podium, SPR's missing players walked in – just in time to make a 'bad bwoy' entrance and receive any prize that might be going their way. Tournament organiser Sammy Sterling finally said, "Ladies an' gentlemen now dat unno belly full I would like to *h*introduce unno to Brotha Joseph. Not only is him a member of de Jamaican Footballers *h*Association an' de Midlands Afro-Caribbean *h*Association of Football Clubs but also him a cherished member of dis church dat 'as kindly given us de use of dis hall. Come on, put your hands together fe Brotha Joseph Swaby."

The applause was less than enthusiastic for the tall man with the bald and bulbous head. He smiled appreciatively at the effort that had been made by those seated closest to the podium and showed off a mouthful of gold teeth that made him look the epitome of a sixties gangster. He waited for Sammy Sterling to stop clapping before he said, "I'm 'onoured that I was axed 'ere today to wha' really is a celebration of young black talent. Talent that 'as been bestowed upon you by God Almighty . . ." He had played his 'God card' much too soon and most of the audience immediately stopped listening as he launched into the parable of the servants and the talents. By the time he had come to the end of his speech several had fallen asleep and had had their snores halted by an elbow to the ribs. ". . . An' finally, you are all pioneers. A great scientist called hIssac Newton said he couldn't 'ave done the tings he done if it wasn't for the people who 'ad gone before him. He said he was standin on the shoulders of giants. Well, all of you are giants because of wha' you do. Because of wha' you put up wid to play football means that black men play for Englan' now. An' I'm proud it was a Nottingham Forest player, Viv Anderson, who became the first black man to become a full English international. He is a real credit to black people an' I know more young black players will play at the top level an' become a instrument of God Almighty because of the foundation that 'as been laid by clubs like those playin here today."

Although most people who were listening liked the idea they were giants, the rapturous applause was more for that Joseph Swaby had finally finished. Medals to the losing and winning finalists were quickly dispensed before the award to the tournament's 'outstanding player' was handed out. Sammy Sterling went through a brief list of players including Mark Beckford who had scored most goals. "But," said Sammy, "wha' we were lookin for was de most improved player, a player to use Brotha Joseph's words, who is makin the best of im talents . . . An' dat haward goes to Ian Beckford of Sabina Park Rangers!"

Ian went up to collect his trophy and Mark did his best to look happy for his younger brother. But as he applauded Horace had looked him straight in the eye and immediately saw the pain brought about by a dream that was coming true for someone else.

More cheers went up as three young men entered the hall hauling enormous speaker boxes, and in doing so ended of the formal part of the evening and signalled the beginning of the much anticipated night-time activities. Horace McIntosh (with the rest of his generation) had headed for home by the time the dance had started really swinging in the early hours. But the number of revellers had swollen and not decreased as more locals turned up. Nestor Riley and Desmond Palmer patrolled the edges of the darkened hall. There was no need for verbal communication between the two of them; not that it was possible anyway with the thunderous bass of the music that was threatening their eardrums. They had mastered the art of gestures; sometimes all that was needed was a simple look – and they knew who they were looking for. The year before they had met two sisters that were so accommodating they were even enticed to make the journey to Nottingham several more times, until the girls' father threatened to show them what his machete could do.

But in the months since they had last met Marlene and Maureen, the two girls had become part of the sound system. The problem was the two MCs – Sir Dread and Judge-I – viewed the sisters as much as their property as their records and other sound system paraphernalia. Desmond soon spotted Marlene – then again he could hardly have missed her as she had drawn most of the male gazes by the way she gyrated in time to the thudding beat. He stepped in between her and a guy who was just about to get acquainted and she smiled at him as if to ask what had taken him so long. Once he had captured his prize he looked around for Nestor and saw that he'd already found Maureen, who had him propped up against a wall. They exchanged smug smiles, unaware of the malevolent stares shooting their way. There were threats that were overheard by the other Wolverhampton guys who now reckoned that they had overstayed their welcome. They gestured to each other and headed for the exit; the only ones who did not see them leave were Nestor and Desmond. Marlene and Maureen were giving it large, so large in fact that Desmond was glad he had brought along one of his bigger cars with the reclining seats. The music halted abruptly but it took a few moments for the two dancing couples to realise something strange was going on.

"Somebody turn on de lights," barked Sir Dread, "so we can see 'ow many is still 'ere. 'Cause if any unno out deh see one of dem Wolverhampton men me want you to chop dem clart . . . Yes, run dem men who come 'ere an' disrespec we . . . Kill dem blo . . ."

By the time the lights came on Nestor and Desmond were already heading out of the door, an instinct for self-preservation had them running as soon as they heard the 'W' in Wolverhampton. They were running across the pitch for Desmond's BMW only to see that their team-mates were well ahead of them (for once) and were already throwing themselves into their cars. As they sprinted full pelt Desmond pulled his keys from his pocket but they slipped from his fingers. He stopped to find them and caught his first glance of their pursuers. They were closing in fast and he had to make the split-second decision to leave the keys in the grass and run for his life. Nestor was standing at his car with Courtney Wright. Courtney had been left behind by Donovan Brown who had driven away in his Ford Capri with its passenger door still open. "Run!" screamed Desmond as he ran towards them, "Me seh run!"

Nestor and Courtney started running, although they didn't know to where they were heading. Desmond quickly caught up with them and then passed them out before jumping over a garden fence. They followed and jumped another seven fences before a big dog stopped them jumping number nine. No one had followed and they took the opportunity to try and force some air into their burning lungs. In between gasps Desmond said they should wait a while before heading back to the car: the guys chasing them had a dance to return to after all. After twenty minutes they decided to go back to the car and this time the fences were a lot harder to climb. Desmond had been right; the lure of the dance meant the guys who had chased them had not hung around. But before returning to the hall they had smashed every piece of glass and dented every panel of his cherished BMW. The angry tears in Desmond's eyes prevented him from finding the keys that had been trampled under foot. It was Courtney who found them, just as it started to rain.

It would prove to be a slow, cold and wet journey back to Wolverhampton.

10

Marcia Yuell liked Mark Beckford, liked but not loved him. Her mother Ida had once warned her to only love the things she didn't have to depend on loving her back. Marcia knew that her mother had been talking from experience because she had seen her give love to men and not receive anything but misery in return. For a while Ida and Marcia tried devoting themselves to the Lord at the church the Beckfords attended. Both of them were looking for guidance but Marcia's churchgoing had come about after she had seen Mark that first time at the blues party. She'd asked around and heard he was a footballer destined for greater things. Rudolph Naylor offered both Marcia and her mother private bible instruction but by then their zeal was already on the wane; the way their lives were turning out so bitterly disappointing, it seemed the Good Lord also wasn't returning the sort of love they had hoped for. All the talk about bounteous gifts rang hollow when all their money had been spent by Wednesday and the Giro cheque did not arrive until Friday. Maybe it was because she saw so little of it while growing up that, like her mother, Marcia gave her love to money, or at least the things money could buy. It was the way of the world: a 'good' house was an expensive house, the same went for a 'good' car or a 'nice' piece of jewellery – the sort of things Mark was never going to be able to provide her with, especially as he had his *nice* little wife to keep in their *nice* little house. She as good as told him that; well, not the bit about only liking and not loving him and she hadn't told him about loving money either but she had said the rest, more or less.

He'd rang her from Nottingham and said he could travel back and spend the night with her but she had told him it wouldn't be possible as she had a girlfriend staying over. She could hear his disappointment and then the rapid bleeps that were telling him to put more coins in the box as he called out he would have some exciting news next week and something about Rachel, something about leaving. Were they leaving town together? Was she was leaving him? Marcia was tiring of the game she had played with Mark and wasn't bothered about what he had to tell her.

She went to the bathroom of her seventh-storey flat and as she looked into the mirror she thought it funny how feelings change. There was a time when she wanted Mark so badly, in a time when there was talk of him becoming rich and famous like Cyrille Regis. It was a nice dream while it lasted but once Mark's parents saw that she had a child they did everything they could to make sure their precious son married Rachel. It made her glad that he never became a professional and that Rachel would not be benefiting from Mark's career as a footballer. Marcia had only continued to see him after he got married to prove that he really wanted her and not prim-and-proper Rachel.

Marcia smoothed a crease in her dress and went to the bedroom to make sure Tania was still asleep. She stroked the little girl's hair and whispered she would be back before she woke. Perhaps out of everyone she had ever known Tania was the one person she truly loved and sometimes the thought of it scared her. There was always the nagging doubt that Tania would not continue to return the love as she grew older and found out what her mom was really like.

Marcia was about to go out clubbing with some friends at the Rialto in Birmingham after earning some good money the night before. She had been on her way home from a netball match when Mervyn Palmer slowed his new car and asked her if she wanted to come for a drive. She knew of the old lech's reputation and his cow-cock soup that was the stuff of local legend. Marcia had also seen his photo on the front page of the *Express and Star* and figured that this fool and his money might be easily parted. They drove around the West Park before heading out along the Tettenhall Road to a more gentrified area where there were houses even Mervyn could not afford. He laid it on thick about how he had so much money after his pools win and no one to spend it on. After he returned to the loneliness theme for a fifth time Marcia grew impatient and told him that he did not have to be lonely but they would have to book into a hotel. He immediately began to sweat and crashed the gears a few times as his foot slipped from the clutch. "Blouse an' skirt," he kept muttering while laughing to himself in a high-pitched whine. Mervyn could not believe his luck until she added she would want two hundred pounds to cover childcare expenses. "Mi ras!" he exclaimed, "dem *h*expensive baby-sitters in Blakenhall." But as they headed back in the direction of town they arranged where and when they would meet up.

She wasn't going to do anything immoral; Marcia was just going to provide company for a lonely old man. It wasn't like what the two white girls from Manchester, who lived on the floor below her, got up to. Whatever the inclement weather they were on street corners and putting themselves at risk to feed a drug habit. Marcia thought she would act like an escort. Escorts were women like her friend Lorna who earned up to two hundred pounds a night (plus tips) and they didn't even have to kiss, never mind do *it*.

Once they'd had dinner, Marcia and Mervyn retired to their hotel room. He was almost falling asleep as Marcia finally emerged from the bathroom after contemplating how far she would go to alleviate Mervyn's feelings of loneliness. She was wearing a pair of pyjamas and a stocking-foot on her head as a means of communicating where the boundaries lay. The boundaries got a bit blurred once she got into bed and Mervyn made an attempt at a kiss that was abruptly curtailed by his loose dentures (which he then placed on a bedside table). After a little indecent fumbling in the dark and Mervyn cussing he collapsed into a heavy sleep. Within minutes his snoring reached such a level that Marcia spent most of the night with her head under a pillow regretting that she had not insisted on the money before they went to bed. When Mervyn woke in the morning, seemingly refreshed, he made another attempt at seduction which again was unsuccessful and provoked Marcia into demanding that he also pay for her taxi home.

It was only when she was out with her friends in the nightclub did she hear about the double-your-money scheme Mervyn's son Desmond was running with Nestor Riley. She wished she had asked Mervyn for more when she heard that the minimum was a thousand pounds. Still, all was not lost, she could see Mervyn again; it would be money for old rope.

Bert Tomlinson, the Aston Villa scout, thumbed his index cards looking for Mark Beckford's old telephone number. He knew Mark had married and moved on but he did not want to speak to him, just his parents and his talented younger brother Ian. It was always a matter of regret for him that Mark had never broken through to the professional ranks but it was his injury as a youngster that had blighted his chances with several of the clubs who, up until then, had been very interested in him. And then there was the fact he was black. For although with every passing season there were more black professional players, a big proportion of scouts were still stuck with a mind-set that informed them that most black players did not have what it took to play at the highest level in the English game. "It's all about British fighting spirit that they can't ever have," one of them explained to Bert. But as the myths and fallacies were gradually broken down, other, more commercial, reasons were given for not taking on black players. Attendance figures had slumped by over two-and-a-half million during the 1980-81 season as unemployment grew and fans were increasingly unable to afford to go to matches. "Let's say they are as good as white boys," a fellow scout had said to Bert, "but two or three in a team is the max. A little bit of colour is tolerable but do you really think that thirty-odd thousand people are going to turn up every week to watch twenty-two nig-nogs playing? They might for a couple of games just to make some monkey noises but after a while clubs would go bankrupt because the crowds just wouldn't relate to what they're watching."

Bert had seen the future for English football and it was going to black and brown as well as white. And it was also going to be foreign. There would be two Argentineans playing in the FA Cup final in little more than a week and Frans Thijssen, a Dutchman playing for Ipswich Town, had just won the Football Writers' Player of the Year. As crazy as it sounded, there might be a time, though surely not in the twentieth century, when there would be even 'arrogant' French and 'temperamental' Italian players appearing in the English League, although the idea that there would also be European managers was way beyond even Bert's imagination.

Research was the secret of Bert Tomlinson's success. He

already knew that the Beckfords were a religious lot and had found out that Ian had another year at school before he took his A-levels. He was confident that if Ian was taken on as an apprentice he could continue with his education, even if there was an attitude in some parts of the Football League that too much education had a negative impact on the ability to play good football. Aston Villa were a bit more enlightened in that regard and had a reputation for taking good care of apprentices and Bert reckoned he could persuade Mr and Mrs Beckford to allow their youngest child to attend the upcoming trials.

Two days after he had made a call, he was sitting in an armchair in the rarely used front room of the Beckford household, amongst one of the largest collections of glass ornaments he had ever seen. Bert started off with a hint of his own religious beliefs, he looked to Clovis and Mona Beckford seated on the sofa and said, "Your son has obviously been blessed with many talents."

Ian, who was in the other armchair, was positively beaming. Ruth Martell had often said that he was blessed all right. Bert said to him, "I suppose Mark told you how impressed I was with your display over Fowler's Park."

"Nah, he didn't," said Ian, suddenly angry.

"Ah well, I suppose he was still on too much of a high after that great goal he scored to take in everything I was saying. But as well as congratulating him I did say that you had a great game."

"An' I helped make the goal."

"That was the cherry on top."

"What, exactly, are you offerin Ian, Mr Tomlinson?" asked Clovis Beckford.

"A trial with the new First Division champions, Mr Beckford. If he gets through, and I'm pretty sure he will, he'll be offered a year's apprenticeship with the top club."

"Him 'ave A-levels an' maybe university to look forward

to, why should he give up all that?"

Bert smiled, pleased that he had done his research. "I know that, Mr Beckford, and the club's Youth Development Officer has given me an assurance that Ian will be able to continue with his studies. His contract will be for a year so if neither party is happy with his time at the club he can continue with his academic studies at university if he so wishes. What we're offering, providing he gets through the trials, of course, is a widening of his opportunities and not narrowing them in any way. He'll also have a wage, not great, but more than he's getting at school and if any of you can think of something negative I haven't thought of, then please tell me."

Clovis looked to his wife, who in turn looked to Ian who just shrugged his shoulders. "All I ask," said Bert, "is that Ian comes and sees what Aston Villa has to offer, even if another club makes an approach."

"You have my word," said Clovis Beckford, "Ian will go to Villa first, no matter who else arks him to go to their club."

Bert shook hands with Clovis and then Ian and his mother, who was quite taken aback by the gesture as she had felt invisible and unable to make any contribution; it was man's talk about a man's game and she was only there in case anybody wanted tea. Bert thought the meeting could not have gone any better until he enquired if Clovis had passed on any football ability through his genes. There was a subtle change in Clovis' face, a tension around the mouth and Mona stiffened and looked embarrassed.

"Mus be on Mona's side," said Clovis, "I'm a cricket man."

11

Something had changed about the town Horace McIntosh had left on Saturday morning, not the whole town but the parts in which a lot of Jamaicans lived. By the time he opened his barbershop on Monday morning rumours about the double-your-money scheme were spreading but not everyone who had heard about it was impressed. As Horace knew all too well, there is a dour streak that is part of the Jamaican makeup that made some of them instinctively put a dampener on the rumours. There had been a collective suck of the teeth and many became argumentative as though the person who had mentioned the scheme had asked them to part with *their* money. But there were people who believed the scheme was a genuine chance to make money, perhaps even get them out of the debt and the misery in which all too many found themselves. Their belief was more of a pot-of-gold-at-the-end-of-the-rainbow sort rather than anything based on reality. It was turning out that the fewer the people who knew the hard facts about the scheme the more certain others became that this was their opportunity to make money. While some swore that they had heard it on pirate radio station that a music mogul, as a means of black empowerment, had started the scheme, others said it was coffee and not coffins that was being imported. However, everyone was certain that the minimum figure required was one thousand pounds. The bitter letdown felt by those who had no hope of raising that sort of money spawned other rumours that the whole business was a fraud. Those rumours did not get much of a hearing – there were just too many of the other sort circulating around the town. As for the identities of those behind the plan, the mere mention of "some millionaire" reinforced the notion of those who were ready to part with their money that they were onto a winner. While for some the mere mention of the names Nestor Riley and Desmond Palmer was enough to confirm that this whole business was a skank which would end in tears.

Because Horace and Frank had been away the previous Saturday, Mervyn Palmer turned up at the barbershop Tuesday morning with his blackened dutch-pot of cow-cock soup as well as that morning's edition of the *Daily Mail*. He sat in his usual chair in the corner and raising his voice above the buzz of Horace's razor gave the customers his take on events as they waited for their turn. None of Mervyn's comments provoked much of a reaction except for a few grunts as the majority of the men waiting for a haircut were feeling resentful that Mervyn did not have to concern himself with whether the double-your-money scheme was genuine or not. He'd had the cheek (or feistiness as Jamaicans call it) to win thirty-five thousand pounds and put himself on the front page of the *Express and Star* and now sit there and go on as if nothing had happened. The very least he could have done was to head to his local (which he had avoided since he found out he'd won) and buy everyone two or three rounds of drinks. Of course, if Mervyn had mentioned his pools win at all they still wouldn't have talked to him because then he would have been showing off. If Mervyn was aware of the hostility he didn't let on and continued to read out loud and amuse himself, if no one else.

Mervyn's chuckling was getting on everyone's nerves more than usual and Frank Grant took it upon himself to bring it to a halt. "Oi, Mervyn," he said, while sweeping away the fresh cuttings from the red lino floor, "Are you puttin any money into dat double-your-money ting?"

"An' wha' dat?"

"You nah 'ear? De coolie who runs de unnertakers in

Sweetman Street, him bringin in coffins from *h*India an' anyone who can raise a t'ousand will get two t'ousand back."

"Nah, me nah 'ear."

"Well it's your son who's collectin de money."

"Desmond? Ras . . . clart, if it anyting to do wid him, me seh it mus be a skank." He saw the glances exchanged by those on both sides of the argument and went on, "You know me sent him to Jamaica an' mi brodda seh him never know a pickney so bad. Dem beat him, you see, but dem couldn't beat de badness outta him. Desmond don't tell me 'bout it 'cause him know me would run im clart if him did."

The mere mention of Desmond put Mervyn in a sour mood but at least he'd stopped laughing to himself and annoying everyone. In fact he said nothing much until lunchtime when he announced to Horace and Frank that he would prepare the soup. "Man, dis stuff good, me-a tell unno," he said referring to his dalliance with Marcia Yuell. "It strengthens a man's back for true . . . Me found *h*out de odder night dat me still like a li-on."

He was a bit disappointed that when his laugh faded neither Horace nor Frank had bothered to ask for any details about his so-called night of passion. He went downstairs to the small kitchen to heat up the soup, muttering to himself as he went. Both Horace and Frank had other things on their minds. They had heard only snippets of what had gone on after they left Nottingham and were still wondering how many of the squad would turn up for training at the YMCA later on. Three of the players had been picked up by a patrol car as they walked along the A5 in the early hours of Sunday morning, while heading in the direction of home. Horace had spent most of Monday ringing around but had still failed to make contact with nearly half of his squad. His feelings that something bad was going to befall his team before the cup final had grown by the hour. He thought he was about slide into depression until he heard the news that Aston Villa was interested in Ian Beckford and not his brother Mark. Ian may have had more potential but Mark was still his best player – and he knew for a fact that the both of them had safely returned to Wolverhampton.

The other thing on the minds of Horace and Frank was the double-your-money scheme. It had caused some friction between them as Frank, like Mervyn, was still of the opinion it was a skank, despite Horace ringing Steve Patel to ask if it were true that he was bringing in a shipload of coffins from India in the next couple of weeks. Steve confirmed that he was but had refused to let Horace in on the deal directly and said that he'd made an agreement with Nestor and Desmond that they would get a cut if they could raise a certain amount of money. "And if you can't give me a number with six digits, Horace, we will have to do business through Nestor and Desmond. Thanks for calling."

"See?" said Horace, "Nestor an' Desmond would not skank us."

"Okay," replied Frank, "you 'ave it your way but me nah give dem my money."

Besides young Ian Beckford, it was no coincidence that those who turned up first for training at the YMCA were the married members of Sabina Park Rangers: Norman Longmore and Audley Robinson. Horace had rang around and left messages with various girlfriends and baby-mothers, at three and four numbers in some cases, to try and make sure that there would be a good turnout. Mostly, the young women had not seen the men Horace was leaving the message for and he spent a lot of his time being on the receiving end of a good deal of vexation. The phrases "good fe nutten" and "wukless" featured frequently and Horace felt it inappropriate to counter that the young men were at least good for something on the football pitch.

Nestor Riley arrived in his work clothes again. It was clear that his season had finished as far as he was concerned due to his sending off in the semifinal. He told Horace that Desmond was still working and was at the Royal Hospital collecting a 'customer' as he spoke. "So, 'ave you the dunsai?" he asked.

Horace did indeed have the dunsai, two grand's worth of dunsai to be precise. There was a moment's hesitation before he finally forced himself to place it into Nestor's hand. The money disappeared so fast that it could have vanished down one of Nestor's sleeves. In all his dealings over the years, it was one lesson Nestor had learnt quite early on: never flash the cash. He produced a small receipt book and took time to carefully insert the blue carbon paper in between two pristine white sheets. "Mr Hector McIntosh," he mumbled as he wrote, "received the sum of two t'ousand pounds . . . Wid tanks an' praise."

"So when are these coffins landin?" asked Horace, while silently praying he had not just blown his hard-earned money.

"Nex week. They'll go to a warehouse in Birmingham; get sorted an' then go out to customers Steve 'as lined up, right. So in about a fortnight's time me come see you an' give you this money back an' anodda couple-a weeks me come see you again an' same ting." When Horace still wore a worried frown Nestor added, "By that time you'll be manger of the cup holders, yeah?"

"Me hopin," replied Horace, still thinking about his money.

Norman Longmore and Audley Robinson then came over. At the last moment they had decided against giving Nestor a thousand pounds each and thought it best to give a grand between them. "An' wha' dis?" asked Nestor in a voice that shook with disdain. These were the two that were only too ready to dismiss his idea and now they were creeping back with a miserable five hundred a piece. "Minimum a t'ousand."

"Dat's a t'ousand, spar," said Norman.

"A t'ousand each, man. If me let you do this, there'll be ten people comin to mi yard sayin they 'ave a hundred each an' that meks a t'ousand. If you want in, come in but it'll cost you the *h*admission fee, right? A t'ousand pound me-a talk. Seen?"

Norman and Audley trotted back to their bags and after the briefest of conversations came back with another thousand pounds. When Courtney Wright arrived he had fifteen hundred; Buckshot Pinnock had brought three grand. Carl Hooper brought his three-legged dog and five hundred. Nestor didn't feel able to refuse and told Carl, as a favour, he was putting his money in with Courtney's to keep things simple and rewrote Courtney's receipt. He wouldn't call Mark Beckford's non-appearance a disappointment as he had already said he wouldn't have the money until later on in the week but Cecil Grant certainly was a letdown when he turned up. He made a great show of slapping a brown envelope into Nestor's hand, as he knew how many of his team-mates were looking on hoping to see that he too was in the scheme. By the weight Nestor could tell either the money was in larger denominations than the Bank of England recognised as legal tender, or that Cecil was only putting in the minimum amount. "'Ow much?"

"A t'ousand," answered Cecil.

Nestor was doing his best to keep his smile in place for the benefit of the onlookers. "Cha, man, me thought a guy like you would be good fe ten times that."

"Recession, ole man. Beanie reckons he might raise two by Thursday."

Nestor felt hot and uncomfortable as he wrote out Cecil's receipt as he had been counting on him producing a lot more. A week before he thought it would be impossible –

but even though he now had ten grand in cash in his pocket, he could only feel disappointed. He would have been feeling something other than disappointment if he knew Cecil had got together with Beanie and had decided that this was just too good an opportunity to miss. But they had no intention of putting in their own money – except for the minimum amount so as not to raise suspicion about what they were really up to. It seemed obvious to the pair of them that those who were involved at the Wolverhampton end of the operation were hopelessly out of their depth and they should take any proceeds off them before someone else did. To Cecil and Beanie, Desmond and Nestor were only mere youths; and Steve Patel was not the sort to survive in the nasty, double-dealing world of illegal drug importation. He'd had a privileged upbringing due to his father's chain of stores and spice importing business that had funded his private education at a posh school on the Penn Road. During the evenings, after homework, his father insisted that Steve (whose actual name was Anil) helped out at his shop on the Newhampton Road so he would get to learn the business. It was there that he had met Nestor Riley and Desmond Palmer. Steve liked the way they would stop and chat, even if they were filling their pockets at the same time. Later on, as he grew more resentful of his father, Steve gave them a small proportion of the stock every time they called. With profit margins being so tight it wasn't long before the Newhampton Road shop became a loss-maker and so his father moved him out and put his cousin in – along with an expensive CCTV system.

Horace McIntosh, normally not a man for cussing, began to utter several bad words as the JA City netball players left the court. So few of his squad had turned up that he could not even have them play five-a-side. He was wondering out loud how many of them realised how big a game the cup final was, not just for Sabina Park Rangers but for black players in general, when a young Rasta bounded towards the court. From a distance it looked as though he had a black octopus hitching a lift on his head but as he got nearer Horace could tell by his expression that he was the bearer of bad news. "Audley!" he gasped, "come quick. Babylon 'ave your brodda!"

12

A large and noisy crowd had gathered outside the Dunstall Road police station. From the steps of the main entrance, a couple of dozen cops looked on from behind their riot shields. In one masterful stroke, the cops from Birmingham had managed to bring most of the young black population of Whitmore Reans out onto the streets with the arrest of Devon Robinson. It was obvious to the cops that if they allowed this misdemeanour of riding a bike on a pavement to pass Devon could well be committing more serious crimes by the following week. And, of course, the cops just 'knew' that the bike had to be stolen.

Devon had continued to cycle as the police van pulled alongside and did not react kindly to being referred to as 'Sambo'. His failure to comply with the order to stop had the driver mounting the van onto the pavement and colliding with the rear wheel of Devon's bike. As he rolled on the ground, Devon was more concerned with his buckled wheel than the cops who were already swarming from the van. Following the riots of the previous year, particularly in the tabloid press, the young black man had been depicted as a very dangerous man, so therefore it was only reasonable for eight cops to descend upon Devon with truncheons drawn.

Rumours were circulating that Devon was lying dead in a cell, or at least had been very badly injured and a few at the edge of the crowd had already left to get petrol and find some empty milk bottles as Horace pushed his way through to the front. "I wanna see Chief Inspector Forbes," he shouted at the cops on the steps. "Someone go tell him Horace McIntosh wants to talk to him right now." Close up he could see the fear in the policemen's faces. As yells of "sell-out" came up from the crowd at his back, Horace shouted out, "Get me in to see Devon right now or dis ting is gonna get outta hand."

A cop to the rear went inside and within seconds he had reappeared and ordered those in front of him to let Horace through. Chief Inspector Forbes was waiting in the foyer. He knew of Horace and Sabina Park Rangers and immediately bestowed upon him the title of 'community leader', which was unknown to most black people in the town at that time (and used by very few who did.) "Good to see you, Horace," said Forbes, as if they were friends. "I need you to go out there right away and tell those people to disperse. Reinforcements are on their way and a lot of people could find themselves arrested fairly soon if they don't move away from here."

The naivete of the request brought about a deep, dismissive chuckle from Horace. "Man," he said, "if you've gone crazy then I haven't. De only way people are gonna move is when dem see Devon Robinson come out wid me."

"That cannot happen, Horace, he's being processed at the moment."

"Process him tomorra, I'll bring him 'ere miself. Word is out dat de police 'ave either hurt or killed him. If none-a it true then let him walk out wid me . . . Now ridin a bike on de pavement ain't worth dis whole ting blowin up."

"Is that a threat?"

Horace sucked at his teeth in exasperation. "T'reat? Man,

look out there, dat's de t'reat. You really tellin me you can't let tings cool down an' sort dis out in de mornin?"

After a moment or two of rocking on his heels the policeman said, "We'll bail him to appear back here at eleven o'clock tomorrow morning."

"Good," said Horace, "but do it quick."

It didn't take long for Devon to be brought from the cells and sign the forms presented to him by the custody sergeant. A cheer went up as he and Horace made their way down the steps and although it took another twenty minutes, the crowd did break up after a little coaxing from Horace and members of the Robinson family. Those who had found the crates of empty bottles and had bought petrol arrived just in time to see the last of the crowd heading for home. They cussed their missed opportunity but knew that it wouldn't be long before another came along.

When Horace returned to the YMCA there were even less players there than at the start of the session. The ever-dependable Norman Longmore put the few who were there through a series of drills while Horace rubbed his troubled brow. He figured that most of his players had intended to turn up for training but life outside of football had intervened and directed them elsewhere; and that was just about what he feared most.

On his way to the YMCA, Mark Beckford encountered a police car blocking the road and diverting traffic away from the area. He turned his car around and once he had found out what was going on he headed for Marcia's flat. After travelling in the lift that smelled of piss – and worse – he arrived on the seventh floor still holding his breath. He hissed a cuss when he discovered that Marcia had not returned home. Hoping that she had not got caught up in the trouble, he took the stairs back to the car park where he sat in his Hillman Hunter and waited for her. No one could even guess at the turmoil in Mark's head. It felt like it was about to explode sometimes. Disillusion: he'd often heard the word but did not know what it really meant until now. It would not matter to him if he never saw his wife or a football again. He used to think that he had once loved both of them but Rachel had come to embody the misguided duty he felt to his faith and his parents; football epitomised all that was unfair in his life. It still stuck in his craw that even though he was the Nottingham tournament's top scorer it was another player who had received the best player award. That it was his brother Ian who had taken the prize away from him only intensified the pain.

They had never been close, more than six years of an age difference meant that they were always at different stages of development and other than playing for Sabina Park Rangers they had little in the way of a shared experience. Even the way they had been raised was different. When Ian had rebelled and made it clear he was no longer going to church, to Mark's surprise, his father did little more than shrug his shoulders. Mark figured there would have been a very different reaction if he had done the same. Now he was hurting, it was easier to believe that rumour he had heard all those years ago was true.

After attracting one stare too many from the young black guys going to and from the tower block, Mark thought he had better move on. On the way home a pulse of excitement went through him as he imagined what he would do in two days time. It was the sort of excitement he used to feel before a match, but now the only thing that stirred him was his plans to steal money from the wages office and the life he would then lead with Marcia.

Nestor Riley had moved decisively and made sure that he kept the cash both he and Desmond had collected. It was approaching sixty grand and he knew that his friend might be tempted to 'borrow' some of the money so he could repair the beloved but battered BMW he'd had to leave on the A5 in the early hours of Sunday morning. It had taken until Tuesday evening before the car was towed back to Wolverhampton, at an exorbitant rate, and Desmond had wept and swore vengeance as it was deposited outside his place. He had once beat up a man who had accidentally dented one of his cars with a bicycle and luckily for the populace of Nottingham, in 1981 firearms were a great deal scarcer than the present day. So it was Jas who became the object of Desmond's rage. Jas had been out all day scouring breakers' yards to find replacement glass and lenses for the BMW and when he returned empty-handed Desmond threatened to beat him with a length of rubber hose.

"Irie," said Nestor, as he walked in to see Jas cowering in a corner of the sitting room. Although he was not normally one to flinch from violence, he told Desmond that beating Jas was not going to get his car fixed. "Look, man, in a few weeks time you'll 'ave the dunsai to get everythin brand new an' pay fe the best paint job money can buy. It ain't Jas's fault there ain't a lot of BMWs in the scrapyard, is it?"

Des put down the hose and put Jas scuttling to the kitchen to cook some food. "So wha' happen?" Des asked Nestor. "Did the guys produce the readies?"

"Yeah, even Norman an' Audley come forward with a grand each. Cecil only come up with the same though. I thought he'd do more than that . . . You 'ave money?"

Desmond pulled two thousand pounds from his pocket. "Rudolph Naylor jus give me that. Him collectin it in hundreds from im congregation an' promisin them one-fifty for every one hundred that them put in, so him mekin im cut fe Jesus already. Him seh he'll be back with more."

"That's how him make so much money already."

"So 'ow much do we 'ave now?"

"Includin this, sixty-one. That still leaves a heap to find, thirty-nine grand."

"Steve's bluffin, man, he ain't gonna turn down wha' we raise," said Desmond.

"Nah, he ain't but he ain't gonna give us the same deal either if we don't come up with the hundred grand. Still, come Thursday Beanie an' Mark will 'ave produced. The good reverend might come up with more but we still might 'ave to do somethin to raise the rest."

"Me tell you already, as long as it don't include sellin mi batty or mi cars dem."

"I was thinkin more about your ole man. Him still 'as to be good fe thirty."

"Yeah, but we'd 'ave to kill the bastard to get it."

"Nah, *you* would 'ave to kill him but if we still short with the dunsai, I'm gonna go check him an' like the Godfarda give him a *h*offer him can't refuse."

"Man," laughed Desmond, "the *only* ting him don't refuse you, or any guy, don't 'ave . . ."

13

Frank Grant read the afternoon edition of the *Express and Star*. "Wha' did me say de odda day, eh? Black people front page news again. Mi ras, Horace, since when did you become a community leader?"

Horace sucked at his teeth. "Never mind dat, 'ow de Wolves get on last night?"

"Win one-nil so dem scrape anodda season in de First Division. Dem lucky this time but me can't see dem doin any better nex year. Down, is the only way dem-a go. Me 'ear there's big money problems. Watch it now, dem build a fancy new stand an' there'll be no one it, to ras."

"To ras," sighed Horace. Frank had done his best but getting words out of Horace had been like pulling teeth. Sabina Park Rangers had been all about giving the local youth opportunities but the faces Horace had seen in the crowd outside Dunstall Road police station had stayed with him and he felt powerless in the midst of so much anger and hate. Frank ambled over to the bookies for the three o'clock race at Ascot and left him alone with his thoughts.

As he did with an increasing frequency, Horace was staring blankly out his window looking at the traffic on the Newhampton Road when the sound of footfalls on the stairs roused him. Courtney Wright and Carl Hooper had come to why say that they had not made it back to the training the previous night. They had left Dunstall Road to look for projectiles, only to find that the police had cordoned off the whole area by the time they tried to return. Horace's reaction, or lack of it, concerned Courtney. His coach seemed tired; it was if a spark within him had dimmed. "Are you all right, H?"

"Jus wonderin if anyting me ever do in dis damn place 'as made any difference," Horace said. "Me used to think football is more than a game, dat it mek a difference to 'ow young guys can live dem lives. But, when de final whistle blows, unno still 'ave to go back to livin de same lives. So me start to think dat all me ever do is provide a distraction fe ninety minutes."

Courtney was about to offer some encouraging words about all Horace had done for young guys like him when Carl said, "Mi dog's battyhole is better now so I ain't gonna miss any more trainin, Horace."

Horace tried to smile but there were too many other matters, besides the state of Eastwood's battyhole, on his mind. "So, is dis town gonna blow, Courtney?" he asked.

"Jus a matter of time, man. Wha' happened to Devon last night happens all the time. You know the Robinsons already, respectable people but when I called around to their yard this mornin it was one house full of angry people. Even, Audley, an' you know him don't look fe trouble or nutten like that. But him a changed man now, H, if somethin kicks off Audley will be at the front of it."

A heavy breath escaped from Horace; if someone as law-abiding as Audley Robinson was now thinking of rioting he figured that there was no chance for the town. He shepherded the two men out of his salon and put the 'closed' sign on the door. "So see you tomorrow at Aldersley?" asked Courtney as they went downstairs ahead of him. At the foot of the stairs Horace gave a tired nod of his head and went into the gambling room.

Clovis Beckford was waiting at the school gates for Ian. There had been a call from Bert Tomlinson that afternoon to ask if Ian would turn up at Aston Villa's Bodymoor Heath training ground that evening for a trial. Bert apologised and said it was such short notice because someone had dropped out and he was anxious that Villa should see Ian's talent as soon as possible. Mona thought that was very considerate of him.

"Problem is, Mrs Beckford, the training ground is situated near Tamworth and it's not an easy place to get to from Wolverhampton using public transport," explained Bert. She called her husband at his workplace to tell him the news. Clovis did not sound greatly enthused – and when she mentioned the problem with Ian getting there he said, "So you want me to stop work early so me can tek him?"

"It's his big chance," she said. Clovis put down the phone without saying anything else but Mona took heart by the way he had not refused point blank to take Ian to the trials.

The dressing room was full of the smells of liniment and just a little fear. Ian had tied his bootlaces twice and tried to avoid making eye contact with any of the other players. Some of them were the size of grown men, complete with five o'clock shadows and the odd tattoo. Out of the thirty or so that had turned up for the trial game, there were only three other black players besides him. A man in a tracksuit entered with a clipboard and began to call out names. When they answered some got numbered green bibs and others got red. He told them they were about to go for a jog around the ground's perimeter to warm up and get the nerves out of their legs before they would have a game. Ian noticed that another black player collected a red bib like he had while the other two had got green ones. As they started to jog the other black player in a red bib came alongside. "First time?" he asked.

"Yeah. An' you?"

"Nah, this is my third. I've done Walsall an' Wolves so far. Who do you play for?"

"Sabina Park Rangers."

"Oh yeah, good team, man. In the Watney's final ain't ya? I'm Priory Green, we're in the Walsall Minor League." Ian grunted as if he had heard of them and his jogging companion went on, "You gotta fit in, like you're playin in a proper team, right. Thing is, some-a the white guys won't give you the ball. So when I get it I'm gonna look up for you, okay? . . . Give you a chance to show them wha' you can do . . . The name's Conrad, by the way." Nervous energy was making Ian short of breath but he managed to give his name. "Right, well have a good game, Ian. At least you'll have someone on your side, okay."

Ian started the game out on the left side of midfield but failed to get a touch of the ball in the first five minutes except for a fifty-fifty tackle, which he lost. There was a residue of nervy feeling in his legs that he was sure would disappear once he got a few touches. True to his word, when Conrad got the ball he looked up for Ian and made a thirty yard pass to him which, unfortunately, ended up going out for a throw-in. When he finally received a decent pass Conrad immediately shouted out for the ball and Ian laid it back all of five yards so Conrad could aimlessly boot it up field. The game seemed to be drifting away from Ian, or at least drifting over to the right side of the pitch, and he found himself being drawn out of position towards the middle of the field in the hope he might get more involved.

After several fruitless runs and shouts for the ball, it bobbled out from a group of players and went straight to Ian's feet. Within an instant he was taking it up field with a player clipping his heels. Ian stopped, pivoted, sold a dummy and continued his run and easily got past the lumbering centre half. All he had between him and the goal now was the goalkeeper and the other central defender rapidly closing in from his right. He was about to make his move for glory when the hoarse screaming filled his ears. It was Conrad shouting for the ball as he ran toward the eighteen yards box. "C'mon, man, pass me the ball!" A moment's hesitation about what he should do preceded Ian's pass back and across the pitch. Conrad scuffed the ball as he came under pressure from a challenge and it tamely rolled into the goalkeeper's hands. Conrad shook his head. "You held on too long, guy, too friggin long!" he snarled. Ian barely had the will to run back from the box, such was his disappointment: he'd had his chance and blown it.

The first half flew by; it seemed as if they had only played twenty minutes when the players were called to the centre circle. The panting became tremulous as names of those who were to be substituted were read out. Unlike Conrad, Ian had survived for another forty-five minutes and he was so relieved that he did not hear his name being called from the sideline at first. It was Bert Tomlinson who was shouting to him and he did not look very happy. Ian ambled over to him. "You're a lucky boy," said Bert. "You were about to be taken off but I had them take off bloody Conrad instead. Whose idea was it?"

"Wha' idea?"

"The bloody stupid idea that you two would pass the ball to each other, no matter what." Ian looked down to his boots and Bert continued, "I thought so. You've another forty-five minutes, Ian, so don't let yourself down. No one out there has played with each other before, so use that football brain of yours. Look up, look for the options and use that ball best as you can. Have you got that?"

Ian grimaced as he nodded, knowing that he had made a big mistake in listening to Conrad. He trotted back to his position with a determination not to mess up a second time. The second half went by as quickly as the first but he'd had two good shots at goal, made enough runs and completed a reasonable amount of good passes to feel that he had done himself justice. After the final whistle the man with the clipboard called out the names of those who would be coming back for a second trial. Ian's was the last name to be called.

14

Every football team has within it a diverse range of characters. Cecil Grant had the build of a John 'The Bash' Fashanu and the attitude of a Vinne Jones (except that he did not have to *play* at being a bad man with a shotgun). Mark Beckford, on the other hand, had more of an Ian Wright physique but was a more saintly type on the pitch, something of a Gary Lineker, and like him had never even received a booking. He was the sort who would stop at a red light at three in the morning, despite no other traffic being around, and would wait patiently in his Hillman Hunter until it turned green. And yet, as he drove to work, it was on his mind to steal thousands of pounds from his employers.

He had hardly slept the previous night. Rachel snuffled as he got out of bed to get himself a drink. There were conflicting forces at work in his mind, the pastor would say it was down to choosing between God and mammon. Ironically enough, it was while doing God's work that he had first glanced over and seen the open safe. The turmoil and strife in the inner cities of 1980 had prompted a few Christians at the works to get together during the week to pray for peace at lunchtime. The prayer meetings took place in the wages office and it was as Mark had raised his eyes to heaven that he'd caught sight of the open safe door and temptation entered his heart.

Leading the prayers was lay preacher George Rowley whose conspicuous support (demonstrated by his continual scarf-wearing at work) for West Bromwich Albion was somehow supposed to convey that he was a regular guy and not a religious nut. But he *was* a religious nut – it just so happened that he was also an avid football fan. Wolves fans throughout the factory detested George, particularly since WBA had just finished fourth in the league, a place above the mighty Liverpool. Mark had got an invite to come to the wages office as George knew he was a Christian as well as a footballer. George didn't want to give the impression that the meetings were all about white people praying to the Lord to aid the police "to subdue the revolting black people." Of course, he meant black people who were in revolt.

News of the confrontation outside of Dunstall Road police station had brought George to Mark's office to ensure he would be there for the Thursday prayer meeting. Both agreed some serious praying was required to prevent a replay of the riots of the previous summer. A police chief at George's church had mentioned praying for rain, saying that rain cools tempers and a hot sun shining down on black people tended to have a negative effect on them. George replied he was going to ask The Lord for it to be nice and sunny, as well as peaceful, as he did not want black people being held responsible for any miserable summer weather.

George's reminder to Mark about the meeting could be interpreted as a sign from God, even if he was using the self-serving Rudloph Naylor's method of interpretation. The Lord, reckoned Mark, owed him big time, mostly because of all the wasted prayers about becoming a professional footballer since he was a child. The contents of the safe would only be some meagre compensation.

Frank Grant arrived at the barbershop with a parcel tucked under his arm. He had been drinking at the Three Crowns the previous night when he had heard talk about Horace McIntosh that had him fretting. Devon Robinson had returned to Dunstall Road police station to be charged with assaulting a police officer as well as stealing a bicycle and Horace was now getting the blame for him facing the trumped-up charges. At least Devon had a solicitor with him to lodge a complaint about the injuries he had sustained during his arrest but because he had left the station (with Horace) before a doctor could examine him, the cops were claiming the injuries happened after they had let him go. Frank listened as the more hot-headed in the bar alleged that the police had arranged for Horace to turn up so they could get Devon out before a doctor arrived. It could have been the drink talking but Frank thought he would wrap his machete in an old copy of *The Weekly Gleaner* and take it with him to the shop the following morning. For men of Frank's generation the machete (pronounced by

Jamaicans as 'mash-ate') was a constant presence in their lives since the age of eleven or twelve. It had been bestowed with almost mythological powers (that could chop off parts of the anatomy doctors had never heard of) and symbolised Jamaican manhood. Many of the machetes around Wolverhampton had travelled from the West Indies (sometimes via the plantations of Florida) with men who were not sure what to expect in England. It was a regular event for Frank and his friends to meet in a back garden, roast a few breadfruit and gather around a sharpening stone to hone their blades and swap stories of hard times, severed limbs and hot blistering sun. The lack of sugar cane around the place did not mean that the machete became redundant; it turned into a utility tool that chopped, levered and hammered; in some cases it was even used in food preparation. A man's dexterity with the blade was a source of pride. A friend of Frank's called Herbert Walker had a wife who once complained that their front door was sticking. Rather than go to the expense of hiring a carpenter Herbert said he would run his machete down its edge. There then followed some considerable chopping and quite an amount of cussing before he produced a door that no longed jammed in winter – but unfortunately it also produced a hallway that became known as the draughtiest in Whitmore Reans.

"So wha' happen?" Horace asked Frank as he put his machete down.

"It need a sharpen, man. Me take it to Walker later on."

Horace, who had already been made aware of the same kind of talk Frank had heard in the pub, nodded in the direction of his own machete and laughed quietly to himself.

Mark Beckford was not laughing, he was crapping himself. He had visited the toilet three times during the morning period, each time quite certain that he had completely emptied himself and any subsequent visit would lead to him flushing vital organs down the pan. And he did pray: if by chance George Rowley had chosen this day, of all days, to follow proper procedure and re-lock the safe after every time he opened it, Mark would take it as a sign from the Lord. But if it were left open . . . well, that would be a kind of sign too.

Though he had first denied it to himself, Mark had planned the robbery for some time; it started off by pretending it was just a sort of intellectual problem he had set himself to pass away the time. Because his office was the nearest, he had always been the first to turn up at George's, usually two minutes before a draughtsman called Tom and a further minute before anyone else arrived. Upon Mark's arrival George would disappear for a few seconds to wash his hands in the toilet that was adjacent to his office. It was if the ablutions were part of the religious service and George had made a ritual out of cleansing his fingers that had been soiled by the dirty banknotes. For the last four weeks Mark had turned up with his sports bag and informed his fellow Christians that he was running during the lunchtime to increase his fitness for the semifinal and then the final. George thought it was a praiseworthy sign of dedication and had even asked for prayers for a Sabina Park Rangers' victory in the semifinal. After that match he had promised Mark he would ask his congregation to have a word with The Lord about winning the cup. Following the prayer meetings Mark would change in the showering room close to the foundry and walk out to the car park where he would then deposit his sports bag in the boot of his car. Though he was tempted to spend his lunchtime sitting in the park, he always ran for around fifteen minutes just in case any of his co-workers saw him. On his return to the works he would retrieve his bag and have a quick shower before changing and getting back to his office. Today he had two identical holdalls in his car boot.

At five-to-one he began the walk to George's office. He

tried to look relaxed but every muscle in his body had seemed to tense, he could feel the blood pumping through his veins. "You're early," said George.

Mark didn't want to be too early, he didn't want to be seen doing anything out of the ordinary. "I'll come back in a minute then."

George checked his wristwatch. "Actually, you're not that early. Time has flown, we had a problem with the wages this morning, the truck had a puncture and turned up late, so we're a bit behind schedule." He got up from his desk and looked down at the bag between Mark's feet. "Running again, eh?"

Making sure he didn't let his gaze drift towards the safe, Mark said, "Keepin myself fit for the final, George. Jus one more game an' then I can relax."

"Right, well I suppose I'd better give the old donnies a wash before the rest turn up."

Once George had disappeared from view Mark's heart began to thrash wildly against his rib cage as he saw that the safe door was slightly ajar. He looked to the office door and thought it was now or never and that he had to go to the safe. Now he could hear his heart drumming in his ears as he pulled the safe door open. There were bags of various colours sitting in it, coins at the bottom and notes on a shelf. He reached over towards the back and took hold of a bag and thrust it into his holdall without even looking to see what denomination of note was in it. Resisting the urge to take another bag, he quickly got back around George's desk just as someone stepped through the office door. It was Tom the draughtsman. He laughed and said, "I thought I'd beat you to it today."

In less than ten seconds his life had utterly changed and Mark could feel his jawbone shaking. He smiled, "Jus by two seconds, didn't you see me come in?" Before Tom could reply George returned and Mark had regained enough composure to swap a bit of banter about Wolves' lucky escape from relegation to Division Two. For the first time, that Mark had noticed, George went behind his desk and locked the safe before the prayer meeting began. Mark felt comforted that his crime hadn't been discovered right away and closed his eyes and silently gave thanks to whoever was up there. The prayers seemed to go on and on until George said that Mark had to go for his run and that he had to get to the canteen for a sandwich. They were running a little late and Mark was grateful that he now had the excuse to rush and get changed. As he ran along the streets, feelings of elation, fear and guilt took turns to make him feel queasy. The fear of getting caught would remain until he drove for home with the money in the boot of his car. And then there was the guilt that he had betrayed the trust of a man like George but he looked for some comfort in that he had robbed the company and not him personally. By the time he had got back to the car park and retrieved the second holdall he was back to feeling excited again. He had often imagined how it would feel once he had got his hands on the money and it didn't feel good – it felt way better than that.

15

Mervyn Palmer may have been sixty-three years of age but he hadn't got past the stage of thinking that just saying something (loud and often in his case) made it true. It may have been a minor miracle that he had travelled along life's bumpy road with this notion intact but his capacity for self-delusion seemed limitless. For example, he figured he could pass for a man of forty-five (with his teeth in); that he was a popular man around the town and the pools win had made him more popular; that he had been a good and loving father to all his children, even Desmond; and his Austin Princess was a gal-magnet and the powers of cow-cock soup had made him a formidable lover-man once again. All of it was ridiculous but now he had the idea that his new car and aphrodisiac soup had made him into Wolverhampton's Casanova. It was Marcia's arrival at his front door that had served to reinforce Mervyn's fantasy that she had had the time of her young life and was back for more.

She sat on his sofa and crossed her long 'creamed' legs. "I was jus passin," she lied, "an' thought I'd pop in an' say hello . . . an' thanks for the other night, Mervyn."

He liked how she said his name, so soft and suggestive. "Like a rum?"

"Hmm, that would be nice."

Excited by her response, he went out to the kitchen and found two small glasses that could pass for clean and poured the drinks. "Pop in an' say 'ello, to rahteed," he muttered while laughing to himself. It was well known by men of his generation that a woman who came to a man's yard and accepted a drink was really looking to "forward the punnani". He gave her a drink and sat beside her. As he took a sip of rum he let a hand wander over her thigh. She laughed and put some space between them. "Wha' sort-a girl do you think I am, Mervyn? Behave yourself, I did only come in to say hello."

"Glad you did, glad you did," he said, not believing her. "I was tinkin of you the odda day when me was out shoppin."

"Oh? An' wha' were you shoppin for?"

"Finish your drink an' me'll show you. It *h*upstairs."

"Now you've got me rushin my drink, Mervyn."

"No, man, don't rush, we 'ave plenty-a time."

"Then why don't we jus take our drinks upstairs?"

Mervyn laughed that whiney high-pitched laugh of his

that betrayed his excitement. He'd always thought that young women would not be able to resist the charms of an older man once they had been persuaded to take that first sample. He led her to his bedroom and let her gaze at the magnificence of his purchase. "King-size waterbed, wid it own 'eater, to rahteed. G'wan, man, try it out."

Marcia looked over the rim of the glass as she took a slow drink before she sat primly on the corner of the bed. "Yes, I imagine it mus be very comfortable," she said.

Mervyn was about to suggest that she lay down and found out how comfortable just as his troublesome bladder signalled that it needed emptying again. "Blouse an' skirt," he muttered, "me 'ave to go to the bat'room. Me soon come."

When it finally started, the piss seemed never-ending: he thought he had finished twice and he gave 'de bwoy' a good shake only to find out there was a little more emptying to do. Mervyn peered down and saw the large stains on the front of his trousers. He cussed for a few moments while figuring out what to do: his other trousers were in his bedroom and he did not want to spoil the moment by going back to Marcia with two big piss stains on his legs. The only thing for it was to take off his trousers and wrap a bath towel around his middle. While he was at it he might as well take off the rest of his clothes: they both knew what the woman had turned up for.

Marcia stood up as soon as she saw his almost-naked form (if it wasn't for the towel and his socks) come through the door. "Hey, mister lover-man," she said, "I thought we'd jus have a chat . . . about us . . . see if there's any future, see if we want the same tings, you know?"

Mervyn inflated his chest. "Well, me know we want same tings, 'cause dat's why you come to mi door. Me *h*unnerstan dat you nah get wha' me can give you *h*enywhere else, to rahteed."

There was a moment in which Marcia thought she was going to be sick but she took a deep breath and cleared the feeling of nausea by thinking of why she had come. "Yes, that's true an' I came here because I know you are a very sweet man . . ."

"True, true, many people say the same ting to me."

". . . Sweet an', erm, attractive . . ."

"Yes, yes, many-a ooman tell me dat too."

". . . Sweet, attractive, in a distinguished sort-a way. A man with a good heart, the sort-a man a woman can turn to when she's in trouble . . ."

Suddenly suspicious, Mervyn asked, "Trouble? Wha' kind-a trouble?"

"It's, erm, money trouble, Mervyn, erm, not much . . . an' I'll pay you back within a month."

"Not much, 'ow much is not much?"

Marcia paused as the figure changed rapidly in her head, spinning like the symbols of an one-armed bandit until it came up with the jackpot. "Five thousand," she said. "It's not like you don't have it, or it's gonna leave you short."

Mervyn let out a disdainful snort. "An' 'ow you gonna give me dat back in a mont'? Blouse an' skirt, you mus tink me's daft. Is it you gonna pay me when Desmond gives you it back *h*after dem coffins come in? It a skank! . . . Otherwise me put mi own money in it." Perhaps he'd misinterpreted her motives but he'd managed to get her into his bedroom without too much effort – and it would be a shame to waste the chance. He knew what he had to do to get her to stay. "But look," he said as he whipped away the towel so she could see the entirety of his manliness, "me will tink about it, right, an' give you mi *h*answer over breakfast."

"Lend me the five grand," she said, determinedly staring into his eyes, "an' we'll share more than one breakfast together."

"Get on mi blasted bed an' me tink about it."

"If it turned out to be a skank I would pay you back in

other ways, Mervyn, you know that."

"Yes, yes, well let's 'ave de first down payment."

"It's *re*payment when there's a loan involved. Mervyn, I need this money an' I promise I will come round to you any time you call."

"Mi ras! You tink me-a jus get off de boat? Look, me is prepared to nice you up again an' ting, give you lickle treat an' ting, but me nah give no ooman five grand to see 'er cratchies! Cha, man, get outta mi yard 'cause you too damn feisty!"

Marcia knew it had been a long shot to get any money out of Mervyn but felt that even a slim opportunity was too good to pass up. She tilted back her head and swallowed the rest of the rum and thrust the tumbler at Mervyn's bare chest. "Nice me up *again*?" she sneered. "Man, the only ting 'bout you that make me feel nice was the two hundred pound."

As she left Mervyn shouted from the landing, "Two hundred an' ten pound! You feget de taxi fare, you *h*ungrateful, gravelitious bitch!"

Horace sent his players out to do four laps of the athletics track at Aldersley Stadium. He watched as they jogged past a group of female athletes from the Wolverhampton and Bilston club and was momentarily concerned that they would be distracted, trip over one another and injure themselves. It was a good turnout for a Thursday night; nearly every member of the squad was in attendance. Even Nestor Riley had decided to put on his tracksuit even though he had no chance of playing in the final, which was now only eight days away. Horace wondered how many coaches in the country had his worries. Not only did he have the usual concerns about injuries and team selection but he'd also had to fret over possible arrests because of the real possibility of riots in the town and most of his squad getting caught up in the violence. He watched them laughing as they ran; life at one level seemed so easy and carefree for them.

Instead of circuit training with weights, Horace thought he would have them concentrate on stretching and ball skills on a piece of ground adjacent to the stadium. As he watched the likes of Cecil Grant, Audley Robinson and the Beckford brothers juggle the balls, he could not help but marvel at their skill and regret how their gifts would never be seen by more than a few. Sabina Park Rangers was supposed to be their platform to greater things but perhaps with the exception of Ian Beckford, it would be the one and only showcase for their talents.

Horace knew that his team had many other attributes besides ball skills. He was aware of how many of them were involved with downright illegality, as well as just the usual slightly dodgy business that a lot of people indulged in, just to get by. He made allowances for them, turned the proverbial blind eye, because he felt partly responsible for their plight. Horace and Agnes McIntosh had come to England with all sorts of ambitions for themselves and their children. His two kids had done well, against all odds, mostly because their mother had an education to pass onto them. Like a lot of his generation, Horace thought he had done right to tell his kids as they grew up that they could do anything, that there were no limits for them. Now he thought it had been crazy, unrealistic talk: the land of opportunity had turned into a country of limitations and unforeseen prejudice. On reflecting on all the angry faces he had seen outside the police station, he pondered over how much people like him had unwittingly added to their rage. He asked himself to who did they really aspire to be equal: the likes of the white kids in Low Hill and The Scotlands, known in polite circles as 'sink estates', or the middle class prosperity of the Tettenhall and Castlecroft areas? Truth was, no people in their right minds wanted to live like the unfortunates in

Low Hill where there was lots of unemployment and crime and little in the way of facilities or education. Houses on Low Hill were only just getting inside toilets; and there would be few, if any, doctors or bank managers coming out of the secondary modern school that was supposed to educate the local kids. It was on Horace's mind that he and his friends had a stoked the frustrations of black working class kids by giving them unrealistic expectations. Maybe the criminals like Cecil and Bryce had it right when they had taken what they could in some of the few ways that were open to them.

Cecil and Bryce had seen their latest opportunity all right. Bryce had asked around the people he knew in Birmingham about the man who was the Mr Big when it came to heroin importation. He had then hung about close to a sportswear factory in Balsall Heath and on the second day he'd caught sight of Steve Patel's Mercedes pulling into the car park. He then told Cecil what he had seen and they decided it was best if they spent their time watching Steve. The money collected in Wolverhampton was small change in comparison to the eventual sum that was to be handed over. They also had found out that at some time over the weekend Nestor and Desmond would give the collected cash to Steve and it would be only a matter of days before the really big money started to change hands. It would be then that they would make their move.

Bryce McBean handed over two grand to Nestor after the training session and noticed how Mark Beckford had hovered in the background until he had moved on. From a distance he watched Nestor look into Mark's car boot and start laughing. Desmond joined them and shook Mark's hand. It seemed as though church-bwoy had just bought himself a piece of the action, maybe a big piece. Bryce thought that was a pity, he did kind of like Mark, more like felt sorry for him because as a footballer he had never got the break his talent deserved. Bryce didn't want him losing too much. He and Cecil had already talked about (once they had carried out their plan and made serious dunsai) reimbursing some of their relatives and team members. Norman Longmore and Audley Robinson would be among those to get nothing back – those two were too full of this preachy-preachy nonsense and would have to learn a hard lesson. Maybe he was going soft but he'd have a word with Cecil about giving Mark's money back too.

16

That Thursday night Marcia Yuell went to bed well vexed. She had sold herself too damn cheaply. It was bad enough that she had gone to bed with a man, if only to sleep, for two hundred lousy quid (plus taxi fare) but because that man had been Mervyn Palmer her vexation grew because she had not asked for more money in the first place. The only silver lining was that old Mervyn's soup made from 'cow-cock' turned out to be more 'cock and bull'.

Mark Beckford had slept soundly. He had been relieved to hand over twenty thousand pounds in cash to Nestor and Desmond. He'd watched enough of *The Sweeney* on telly to know he would have had a problem with getting rid of so many new banknotes as their serial numbers would have been recorded and easy to trace. There was a brief regret he hadn't kept just a few pounds as he stopped for petrol on the way home but he figured that people like Nestor and Desmond were the best at 'washing' the money and making sure it was not traceable back to him in any way. Now there was no evidence to link him with the stolen money and in a fortnight's time he would receive a different stash of cash. He wasn't greedy, he was not sure how much he had stolen until Nestor counted it out and called Desmond over to tell him that they had almost reached their target. Mark felt strangely disconnected from the money and if he didn't receive another twenty grand on top of his initial investment he didn't think he would feel too hard done by.

When he got home Rachel was fretting about a leak coming from their washing machine. Only the day before her words would have twisted through his skull like a metal drill but now he felt able to handle her incessant whining. He would give it another month before he broke her the news that their marriage was over, mostly because he had to wait for the money to return and that he did not want to draw suspicion on himself by handing in his notice too soon. With a bit of luck, he might receive a redundancy notice before too long – and then his tracks would be well and truly covered.

Driving to work the next morning Mark was relaxed, elated even, about returning to the scene of the crime. He felt comforted that the works had not been swarming with police before he clocked out the previous afternoon and that he had been able to collect his wage envelope as usual. He'd listened to the likes of Cecil Grant and Bryce McBean and their contention that cops were not great detectives and the West Midlands force had got most of their arrests through informers, or stupidity on behalf of the criminals, or they simply fitted up people. Perhaps the money's disappearance would never be noticed, or it would be put down as an accounting error. It did not take long for those flights of fancy to vanish from Mark's mind as he clocked in. A man in a grey suit approached him and flashed a warrant card. "Mr Beckford," he said, "my name is Detective Sergeant Ray Boyd, Red Lion Street CID. Would you follow me, please?"

Mark did not have to pretend he was shocked but he had enough presence of mind to say, "What's wrong, sergeant, is it my wife? . . . I only left her minutes ago, she was . . ."

"No, Mr Beckford," said Boyd, "it's nothing to do with your wife. It's another matter, if you would just follow me."

He followed the detective to a ground-floor office that had large panes of glass in its metal partitions which were painted dark green. Mark could see George Rowley sitting ashen-faced in another office and could not help feeling a twinge of guilt. He found out later that George had not gone home and had been at the office all night with senior management and the police. Boyd offered Mark a seat and introduced him to his colleague, a constable with an oily complexion and a notebook in his hand. He started off by asking if Mark had noticed anything out of the ordinary during his previous day at work. Mark stuck out his lower lip and slowly shook his head. "No, it was jus a borin day like every other one."

"What about around George Rowley's office, anything unusual there?"

The movements of Mark's lip and head remained the same. "No."

"Say, at the prayer meeting?"

"No, sergeant."

"Bit unusual, a prayer meeting at work."

"Depends on if you've accepted the Lord Jesus Christ as your personal saviour, Sergeant Boyd. If you believe then every day is a day to give thanks an' praise."

"Not yet, Mr Beckford. Funnily enough, some of the biggest crooks I've come across have taken the Good Lord into their hearts, usually while they're doing bird. Goes down well with the prison governor and the parole board if they think you've seen the light. When you arrived at Mr Rowley's office was anyone else in there besides him?"

Now Mark's heartbeat started to accelerate. George had obviously given the cops his version of events and probably said he had left Mark in the office on his own. "Erm . . . not that I can remember. No, erm, I think George was there on his own."

"And what happened then?"

"He went out to wash his hands an' Tom Howard came in."

Boyd frowned, as if disbelieving, or perhaps he now was already wondering how accurate George Rowley had been. "When did Mr Howard come in?"

"Two seconds after George went out. We had a chat, George came back, gave me a slaggin because I'm a Wolves fan an' he supports the Baggies."

"West Brom," Boyd muttered under his breath, as though that was enough to put George Rowley under suspicion. "And then?"

"We had our usual prayer meetin . . . an' that's it, really. Nothin else."

"Do you remember anything about the safe, Mr Beckford?"

"Safe? Nah."

"Are you sure?"

"Yeah."

"Only Mr Rowley says he locked it while in your presence."

Mark was about to say that wasn't right and it had been locked while he and Tom were there but that would put the pair of them in the office while the safe was open. It was as he was about to give his answer that Mark instantly recognised that George had put him in the clear. "Oh, yeah, now I remember," he blurted. He took a breath to slow himself down and added, "Yeah, erm, I came in, we exchanged a few words, George locked the safe an' went out to wash his hand an' Tom came in a couple of seconds later."

The constable looked up at his superior and then frowned as if to declare that it wasn't the greatest line of questioning he had ever heard. Boyd ran the tip of his tongue over his back teeth, he was never good in the mornings; he was more of an early evening person. "I hear you're a footballer, Mr Beckford, with Sabina Park Rangers, no less," he said while staring hard into Mark's eyes. "A veritable rogues' gallery. Put it this way, if any one of several of your teammates worked here I would be questioning them down the nick. A piece of free advice, find yourself a new team for next season or you might find yourself becoming a focus of our attention. That's all, Mr Beckford . . . For now."

"Okay, sergeant. By the way, what's happened, I mean why are you here an' why all these questions?"

"Somebody's been breaking the eighth commandment, Mr Beckford. You'll find a whole list of them in Deuteronomy, chapter five, I think."

Mark then spent most of the day moving from office to office acting shocked by events and swapping gossip. When he heard that George Rowley had been taken to a police station for further questioning he was unable to eat as remorse put his stomach churning. It could have been just his imagination but he thought Tom Howard had looked at him with accusing eyes.

The elation he had felt driving to work was well and truly dissipated by the time he got home. Rachel had the dinner cooked and waiting on the table for him. She had a strange smile on her face and he hoped to God that she was not about to tell him the last sort of news he wanted to hear.

Claudette Riley called up to Nestor to keep an eye on the baby and that she was going out to the shops. Nestor hadn't been listening; he was busy counting money in his bedroom. Rudolph Naylor had just produced another eleven grand that he had extracted from his flock. Nestor and Desmond had discussed amongst themselves why such a tight-fisted and normally suspicious man was so keen to hand money over to them. They figured it was because he had presided over a number of funerals in which he had thrown dirt over many polished hardwood caskets and had seen just how much money was going down a six-foot hole. What they didn't know was that he had already worked out a deal regarding the funerals with Steve Patel. Rudolph would receive a commission for every deceased member of his congregation he put Steve's way; and he had notions of going into partnership in the box-'em-and-bury-'em business at some in the near future.

Nestor had just counted his one-hundred-and-second wad of notes when the baby started crying. It wasn't until he had counted his one-hundred-and-fourth that he decided to go and see what was wrong. Baby Peter was almost purple and bawling loudly despite being told to shut up. Nestor tried putting a dummy in the baby's mouth but he would not take it and at that moment all Nestor felt was hatred for the writhing little mass of purple flesh in the cot – and for Diane and how she had dumped the pickney on his doorstep. And just like Diane, the baby wasn't listening to a word he was saying. He picked up baby Peter cussing the little bastard and his bitch of a mother. He would make him quiet one way or another. "Nestor! What are you doin?"

He looked over his shoulder to see his mother. She had forgot her purse and had heard the racket before she opened the front door. He thrust the baby into her arms. "Quiet him an' then get rid, or else I'm movin out. Right?"

Nestor went back to his room and started to count the money again. The muscles in his neck were stiffening by the second. It wasn't only the baby's bawling that was making him tense, it was the thought of handing over the most serious amount of dunsai he had seen in his life to Steve Patel on Sunday morning. A bird in the hand and all that. He had mentioned to Desmond the possibility that it could be all one gigantic skank by whoever Steve was dealing with and if it all went wrong they would have a large proportion of

Wolverhampton's West Indian population arming themselves with machetes before hunting them down. Desmond laughed as he raised his arm – the one with the ugly scar – and reminded him he had been through a similar experience already, while Nestor had been banged up in the Young Offenders' Unit. When Desmond was fifteen he had talked a cousin into driving him to Sheffield with one video recorder and a vanload of boxes filled with various bits of electrical rubbish he had picked out of a skip. He had conned almost dozen people when a machete-waving mob rounded the corner. Both he and his cousin did get out alive – but only just. "Jus remember, Nes," said Desmond, "we're too smart an' too fast for the people aroun here. Them could never catch we, right?"

17

Possession of a sliding hammer was a criminal offence. It only had one purpose: to break the steering locks on motor vehicles. Carl Hooper had one in his bag, along with his strip and goalkeeper gloves, just in case any of the keys Buckshot had given him would not fit into the ignition. Getting in would be easy enough, the car Carl was about to steal was a Ford and throughout the 1980s, locking even the most expensive models was a largely a futile gesture as it was possible to get into most of them with a nail file or a screwdriver. He was about to steal a Ford Escort RS 2000, to be even more precise the Ford Escort RS 2000 in the car park of the *Wolverhampton Ad News* that belonged to the photographer. It still vexed Cecil Grant that he had not taken that photo of the JA City netball players bending over and showing off their beautiful batties. He'd said then that the man didn't deserve such a nice car and that was why he had asked Carl to steal it.

Cecil and Bryce McBean wanted a fast getaway car for when they robbed Steve Patel and a man named Khan who was at the Birmingham end of the heroin operation. They had decided not to let Nestor and Desmond know what they were planning until they had handed over the dunsai to Steve Patel, otherwise they might pull out of the scheme and consequently Steve would know something was going down. "True," said Cecil, "once them give Steve the money either them fall in with us an' mek some money or them gonna get nutten an' 'ave half-a Wolverhampton chasin them clarts."

"Exactly," said Bryce, "once all that dunsai is handed over, them 'ave no choice but to do wha' we tell them, to ras."

"To ras."

The photographer was gazing blankly out of his office window at an unseasonable grey summer sky when the throaty roar of a two-litre engine drew his attention to a car speeding from the car park. For a few moments he was only clucking at the irresponsible waste of tyre rubber until he realised it was, in fact, *his* tyre rubber being left as black streaks on the tarmac.

Carl Hooper headed for a lockup garage in Whitmore Reans. Buckshot had already left a pair of false numberplates there which he would fit immediately. By the time he was strolling to Buckshot's repair shop the whole operation had taken less than twenty-five minutes, which was still five minutes less than it took the cops to respond to the photographer's frantic phone call.

"It done?" asked Buckshot.

Not a man to waste words, Carl nodded and handed him a bunch of keys.

"You 'ave to break the lock or anythin?"

Carl snorted and shook his head. "It a Ford, Buckie, wha' do you think?"

"Good, good. So check me tomorra, okay?"

It was back to nodding from Carl.

"An' Eastwood's sore batty, it still a'right?"

Another slow nod.

"Then cool, man, me see you later."

If only they knew then that "later" in this case would be five months later. Carl Hooper went back to the house he shared with his mother, Jamaican stepfather, two half-sisters and Eastwood his three-legged dog. It was not a happy household, probably never had been but Carl knew he had never been happy there since the day he'd landed from Grenada at the age of thirteen. As time went on Joseph Dean's resentment of his wife's child increased with every inch he grew. Carl would have left long before but for his mother, he did not want to abandon her after she'd had a stroke. For the last two years she had been mostly confined to bed and was no longer able to get in between the two men when the arguments started. All she could do now was bang on the floor with a stick when they raised their voices – which meant Carl was always at a disadvantage as he would be the first one to quieten down.

When Carl arrived home from Buckshot's workshop he used the back door as usual and saw little Eastwood was curled up and shivering in his basket as though he was very scared. Carl could tell that he had been hurt and knew who had done the hurting. Joseph came into the kitchen and sucked at his teeth as he saw Carl examining his dog.

"So wha' happen to Eastwood?" Carl asked in a voice full of anger and accusation.

"'Ow de 'ell would me know?"

Eastwood was wagging the little stump of a tail furiously as he licked Carl's arm, nervous that he would be touched where it was hurting. Carl could feel the fury building up inside of him. Six years of grumbling about another man's 'small island pickney'; six long years of resentment; six years of not one damn good word to say. He put Eastwood back into his basket. "Did you 'urt mi darg?" Carl asked. Joseph sucked at his teeth again and carried on making his cup of tea. "Did you 'urt mi darg?"

Joseph spooned in his sugar and began to stir. "You too fool, bwoy. It a Hinglish ting to let darg into a 'ouse, you know. Me trip over the flippin ting. It was a *h*accident."

That was all Carl needed to hear: Joseph had hurt his dog and he was not going to believe any lies about it being an accident. Joseph was taking his first slurp as Carl lifted the heavy kettle from the stove. A blow to the back of Joseph's neck had him pitching face-first towards the floor. He was later to claim in court that he did not remember what happened next and reckoned he must have been knocked unconscious. This didn't square with the statements of his neighbours who had heard him begging for mercy and screaming out in pain before they rang for the police, convinced a murder was taking place.

As Joseph had only sustained cuts and heavy bruising and the judge was probably something of a dog lover, Carl was sentenced to only four months. He should have been released after two but he ended up serving five months because of another assault in prison. At the start of his sentence Carl had been sharing a cell with a stocky, multi-tattooed skinhead of around his own age. As Carl wasn't much for talking he didn't say as much as 'hello' to this man as he'd been in prison once before and knew it didn't do to get too friendly. For ten nights the skinhead had howled long into the early hours before he finally fell asleep. The bawling was so loud and went on for so long, that it not only made Carl wish that he hadn't had that operation to fix his hearing, it also put his imagination running overtime about what serious crime the guy had committed and what sentence he was doing to be bawling this way. On the eleventh night Carl was laying in his bed as the blubbering started all over again. Exhausted by the lack of sleep, curiosity got the better of his natural reserve. "Hey, mate," Carl called out, "wha' you in for?"

The man wiped his eyes. "Twenty-eight days," he sniffled, "non-payment of fine."

Carl had expected to hear about a gruesome murder and a life sentence. Enraged he had lost so much sleep over such triviality he got out of bed and snarled, "Right, now me gonna give you somethin to cry for!"

Word of Carl Hooper's arrest had reached Horace McIntosh almost as soon as the police van had driven him away and Joseph Dean had been loaded into the ambulance. As usual, Friday afternoon was busy and he had a shop full of customers when Chief Inspector Forbes appeared at the door. "Can I have a word please, Horace?"

A row of suspicious eyes silently questioned the nature of the visit as they flitted from the cop to Horace and back again. Horace continued shaving a young guy with his cutthroat razor. "Wha' do you want, Chief Inspector?" he asked, as his eyes turned to the row of customers shifting uncomfortably on their seats. "You can see I'm a busy man."

"It's private," and for the benefit of the onlookers he added, "I think you must know that it has to be very important as this is the first time I've had to come and see you, Horace."

Frank Grant let out a few cuss words with a heavy breath. He wanted to let the young men who were waiting for haircuts know that the barbershop was not a place where cops were welcome: a rumour like that could be very bad for business. "So wha' happen now," he sneered at Forbes, "you arrest another black guy for ridin im bike on de pavement?"

Not to be drawn, Forbes said to Horace, "It is urgent. I'll only keep you for a few minutes."

Horace slapped a few drops of *Brut* onto the freshly shaved face and followed the cop to the landing before he showed him into a musty room he used for storage. "As a matter of courtesy," Forbes began, "I thought I'd come and tell you personally that we've had to arrest one of your players, Carl Hooper, for a serious assault on his stepfather at their home this afternoon. Mr Dean is on his way to hospital as we speak. Only, the way things are at the moment, with rumours flying around the place, I thought it best to let you know exactly what happened. There was a dispute over a dog and Mr Hooper took a rather heavy kettle to Mr Dean."

Horace had never liked Joseph Dean's carry-on and thought he had probably deserved whatever Carl had given him. It was only surprising that it had taken so long. "Well let me tell you," Horace said, "I don't appreciate your call. Dat business at de station de other night, word is goin aroun dat de police call me to get Devon out before a doctor could examine him. You turnin up now ain't doin me no favour. An' don't tink if rumours start goin aroun about Carl any of de yout is gonna listen to me. After wha' happen to Devon, Maggie Thatcher at a CND meetin 'as more credibility than I 'ave."

Forbes shuffled his feet. "There's some things out of my hands, Horace, all I'm trying to do is defuse a possible tricky situation. I have information there are agitators in town, militants who are trying to exploit the present difficulties. I just want you to know what has happened so at least there's an informed voice in the community who can speak out against the people who are doing their best to stir things up."

"Man, go talk to these race relations people who get paid fe talkin an' don't tink I'm gonna stand up in front of a group of angry guys an' tell dem it all a'right because Chief

Inspector Forbes 'as told me wha' really happen."

"Maybe not young men you don't know . . . but I have come by information that some members of your team have links with race militants and the like. All I want to do is avoid anyone getting into serious trouble."

Whatever else Horace would call any of his players, 'militant' was not one of them. "Who are you talkin about?"

"Courtney Wright, his brothers Oliver and Patrick have links with a black militant group; Audley Robinson, his sister is living with a man who is a committed Pan-African; Donovan Brown travelled all the way down to London to go on the Deptford Fire march and was seen talking to known extremists. All I'm trying to do is help, Horace. And if you hear anything that makes you feel alarmed and think I could help . . ."

"Hol' on, man, dis sounds like you want me to start informin on mi own players." Enraged, Horace opened the door. "Get out! G'wan an' don't come back!"

Chief Inspector Forbes stood his ground for a second; he was not used to being talked to like that. Before he left he said, "I hope you have a team by the time the cup final comes around, Mr McIntosh."

Forbes went out to the waiting police van as heads peered out of the gambling room and it wasn't until it moved away did the scramble begin for all the ganja that had automatically dropped onto the floor upon its arrival.

"So wha' happen?" Frank asked Horace.

"Dem arrest Carl for beatin up Joe. Me tink he was tellin me to find a replacement goalkeeper for de final."

Frank Grant took up his brush. "Nestor suspended, Carl arrested," he grumbled, "let's 'ope dem-a de only two who 'ave to be replaced, to ras."

"To ras," sighed Horace. He picked up his razor and to the row of customers he called out, "Who nex?"

"Yeah," Frank mumbled to himself, "who nex?"

18

Lorna Ruddock had a head full of green and yellow hair rollers. She was halfway through her beautifying routine, not that she needed that much beautifying, when Marcia Yuell rang. She had only an hour before she had to go out but Marcia had sounded so low and in the need of some good friendly advice that she invited her around to the flat. They had been friends ever since Ida and a seven-year-old Marcia moved into the same street. Their lives had taken similar paths; they had even both got pregnant at around the same time, at barely sixteen years old. But Lorna's baby was never born and the more she saw Marcia struggle with her child the more she was certain that she had done the right thing.

It was only when Marcia told her that she had spent a night with Mervyn Palmer for just two hundred quid (plus taxi fare) that Lorna realised how low her friend had sunk. "Mervyn Palmer, the ole guy who win the pools?" Lorna gasped. "Wha' was he like?"

"If you mean did we do anythin, the answer is I only let him have a kiss."

While the coffee was being made, Marcia looked all around her and saw just how well Lorna had done for herself. She was the girl Marcia should have been more like, according to her mother, a self-made woman who not only knew the cost of everything but also knew her own value. In the flat was a white leather three-piece suite; a big colour TV, three feet wide and almost as deep; underneath it was a state-of-the-art video recorder – it even had a remote control attached to it by six feet of wire. Marcia let her bare toes feel the depth of the white shag pile carpet and figured that she should have become an escort when Lorna had first mentioned it. She made her money by accompanying men to dinners, shows and various social functions and Lorna assured Marcia she had done nothing more than look pretty and make polite conversation to make her money.

Lorna put the coffee cups on the low glass table and sank into an armchair. "You have to wise up, Marcia. You're gorgeous an' should have all this too you know."

"That's why I'm feelin so down, Lorna, 'cause I do know wha' I should have. You've always had the knack of seein opportunities an' makin the right decisions but me, I only see them when it's too late. I heard about that double-your-money ting but . . . Well, I don't have a thousand pounds anyway. Have you put any money into it, Lorna?"

"A couple-a thousand."

Marcia compressed her lips regretfully. "I should have a lot more, for Tania."

"Of course, we gotta do everythin to look after our kids. They deserve the best. You an' me went through the same kind-a things, Marcia, an' when I have one, I ain't never lettin a kid of mine wear any second-hand clothes, sleep in any second-hand bed. That's why I'm doin all this, gettin all this stuff together, so when I do have a kid, at some time in the future, it'll be brought up in the right way, wantin for nothin."

"But I'm not sure wha' to do."

"The first thing you do is ditch that footballer, 'cause he's a waste of time. Start datin some guy with a future an' then sign up with the agency an' you'll get wha' you need for little Tania."

Marcia wanted what Lorna had but she didn't know if she was that brave. Lorna saw what was running through Marcia's mind and said, "Now, I ain't sayin you can do wha' I do straight away. But I'll arrange an interview for you an' tell you wha' to say an' wear. By nex month you can be earnin yourself some serious money. The agency mostly deals with businessmen, rich guys. They take you to a nice restaurant, you arks them about their work an' make out like you're impressed an' stuff. They don't even put a hand on you without arksin permission first. You can do it, Marcia, you deserve the chance, Tania deserves the chance. But can you ditch the footballer?"

"Him already ditched, him jus don't know it yet."

"Well that's good, because he owes you. Wha' you gotta learn Marcia, is your worth, you gotta love yourself more, realise the time you gave this guy is very valuable. He's a married man who's been usin you. So you ditch him on your terms. Jus think wha' you've been givin this guy for free an' all he ever did was take an' take. Now it's your turn to do the takin."

Courtney Wright went to his parents' house in Blakenhall to find his brother Oliver and see if he would play in goal for Sabina Park Rangers' most important game. Oliver had the talent but not quite the size to make it as a professional but he had played semi-pro for about fifteen quid a game, which was fifteen quid more than any of the SPR players had ever received. In amateur teams there is rarely room for more than one goalkeeper and once Carl Hooper became a regular Oliver went and found another team. Even though it was such an important game, Courtney wasn't certain if his brother would play again for the manager who had rejected him.

Courtney sat down at the kitchen table with Oliver chatting about Carl's arrest when their younger brother Patrick walked in. "Wha' happen," he said to Courtney, "I hope you ain't come here to try an' get Oliver to play for that sell-out's team as well."

It was going to be a hard enough job for Courtney to persuade Oliver even without being side-tracked by Patrick's unwelcome intervention but he couldn't let what he had said go unchallenged. "Shut your big mouth, Patrick. Horace ain't no sell-out. I was there when that Rasta turned up at trainin, the one who looks like he got an octopus on im head . . ."

"Them call him Octopus."

". . . Yeah, him. Him say Devon arrested an' Audley an' we all dash down to Dunstall Road. Me an' Carl went to look for some stuff to fling an' then we saw how the cops had the whole area closed off. If anythin had kicked off then a lotta people would-a got mashed up an' arrested. Horace saved a lotta people an' all this business about the cops arrangin for him to go in an' get Devon is bullshit, pure bullshit."

Dismissive, Patrick said, "Well, me hear different."

"Then you hear wrong," said Courtney.

"But it don't change wha' them do to Devon." said Oliver.

"No one said it did, I'm jus tellin you two wha' happened an' I know it's true 'cause I was there, right. Anyway, back to wha' I come for. Are you interested in playin in the final, Oliver?"

"He ain't interested in football no more," Patrick interjected. "Man, you're the oldest but you're the one still goin on with kids' games. Us two have moved on, us two have grown up an' know we have to start to fight for our rights an' not waste our time kickin a ball around the place."

Courtney Wright thought of himself as a 'roots man', a man who was proud of where he was coming from and who bucked the system, in every way he could. But the atmosphere around the town had become so poisonous following Devon Robinson's arrest – and attitudes so polarised – that, as crazy as it seemed to him, he was in danger of being labelled a betrayer of his own people because he played football. "Hol' on," he said, "Sabina Park have jus reached the final, the first time a black team ever do it, we're goin out there an' provin somethin."

"Provin wha'?" snorted Oliver, "that black people are good at sport? Man, it time you made yourself aware. You think Laurie Cunningham, or Viv Anderson, pullin on an Englan' shirt has done anythin for us? Did it get us a job? Did it stop the police makin up all sort-a false charges an' oppressin black people? All them doin is givin white guys a chance to make monkey noises an' fling banana an' not take a beatin for such liberties. Me see the light, any black person takin up sport when there's a war goin on out in the streets is helpin the white man by distractin the black yout from wha' them should be really doin. An' any black person pullin on a Englan' shirt, Englan' athletics vest, should should be strung up from the lampposts an' then chopped up as an example."

"The word you're lookin for is lynched," said Courtney. "Wha' the hell, man, now mi own brothers are talkin about lynchin black people. It's crazy talk, guys, an' the more you talk it the more crazy it gets."

"It figures you'd say somethin like that," retorted Patrick. "Ain't you the one who had all those white friends at school? An' where were they when all those white guys jumped you at the Molinuex, eh?"

Courtney got up from the table. Hating people because of the colour of their skin played no part in him being proud of who and what he was. "Check me if you change ya mind," he said to Oliver. But Oliver wouldn't be changing his mind. His brothers' attitude towards him had been taken as an insult and Courtney had thought briefly about punching the two of them. But after a moment's reflection he realised that just the idea of fighting his own family was a sign he too was becoming infected with the sort of madness that was spreading all over the town. It was only going to take one little spark and the whole place would blow.

19

On Sunday morning Nestor and Desmond were sitting in Nestor's Ford Capri outside the West Park and didn't notice Ian Beckford's car had pulled up alongside them. They were too busy reassuring each other that they would be doing the right thing in handing over one hundred and six grand to Steve Patel. He had seemed confident enough that they would see it again very soon. "Everything is in place," he had told them, "the stuff will be with me by the end of the week. I have already lined up customers. There is no problem, I have guarantees that nothing will go wrong."

They asked each other what the guarantees were worth while they waited for a group of black guys to finish practising karate in the park before they would go in and play football. The karate guys had a reputation for being as mean as they were tough and most of them didn't like Nestor and Desmond, who had once dabbled in the martial arts and quickly found it wasn't for them. There were two who were particularly nasty and worked as doormen at the Star and Moon nightclub. One had kicked Nestor in the head and said he was just playing, otherwise he'd be in hospital. Thankfully, none of them had put any money into their scheme.

While the rest of the Beckford family spent their Sunday mornings at church, Ian went to the park for a game of football. Once the football season had finished players from Punjab United and Afro as well as Sabina Park Rangers would meet up and have a game. There was even a referee: a small white guy in his mid-forties who turned up with the kit, whistle and the whole caboodle his mother had bought him. Everyone chipped in twenty pence to pay his fee and he seemed more than delighted to be amongst so many pairs of muscular brown legs.

News of Ian's invite to a second trial at Villa had got around and the Punjab United captain shook his hand and promised that none of his players would be sliding in on him with their studs showing. "Play the way you play here and there's no way they won't sign you up," he said. It seemed everyone, even the ref, wanted to congratulate him and for the first time he thought he knew what it would be like to be famous. His friend Kingsley wanted an assurance he wouldn't be forgotten after all the favours he had done for him. Ian had given Ruth Martell Kingsley's phone number so messages could be received without his mom and dad knowing. Just lately Ruth had been calling Kingsley's number quite a lot and then had him making up stories for his parents about why a fraught white woman was ringing him so many times.

Ian had told Kingsley to make up some excuse why he couldn't see her; he realised that he had to concentrate on his football and he didn't want her distracting him. Kingsley, never the coolest under pressure, had snapped on the fifth call and told Ruth Martell that Ian was about to break into the big time with Aston Villa and he didn't need to be calling on a white old bag any more. "Did he say for you to tell me that?" she'd asked, her voice all trembling. "More or less," Kingsley retorted before cutting her off.

The sun was breaking through the clouds and making the air muggy. The play slowed down to walking pace and the passes were getting longer as the legs became leaden. Courtney Wright had made a special effort to make it to the park so he could have a game in goal. He was having some difficulty judging the out-swinging crosses but his reflexes had helped him to pull off several spectacular saves. Ian enjoyed the attention he was receiving on the pitch; every time he got the ball he found himself facing two opposing players, he figured it would be good practise for his next time at Villa's Bodymoor Heath training ground.

It was the wolf-whistles that took his mind off the game and turned it toward the woman approaching the sideline. She was blonde and dressed in a low-cut blouse, bright red trouser suit with shoes and lipstick to match. Man, the closer she got the more she looked fit, and then, to his horror, the more she looked like Ruth. When Ian saw it really was Ruth he ran toward her, panicked that the guys on the pitch would find out he had been dealing with such an old woman. "Ruth," he said in a low hissing voice, "wha' the hell you doin here?"

She took off her tinted sunglasses so he could see the fury in her blue eyes. "Your friend, Kingsley," she said, "is it true what he's been telling me?"

"Wha' has he said?"

"That you don't want to see an old bag like me because you're going to make it big with Aston Villa."

"Shit! I never told him to say anythin like that!"

Ruth Martell's expression did not change until she satisfied herself that he was telling the truth. She put her sunglasses back on and let her lips move with a smile. "I didn't think so, you're too nice a boy to even think anything like that. But was he telling me the truth about Aston Villa?"

Ian looked back over his shoulder and saw the game had virtually come to a halt as the players gawped at the pair of them. "Yeah, that bit's true," he whispered. "Look, Ruth, I gotta get back to the game."

"Then when are we going to see each other?"

"I've got to go back for another trial Wednesday an' I can't see you before then."

"Thursday then?"

"Nah, that's when we got our final trainin session. Is your husband around Friday night?"

"Don't worry about Harry. I know how to get rid of him. So let's make it Friday and let's make it special."

"Okay, Friday. I've gotta go."

Ruth leant forward to kiss him and sent him scurrying back to the cheers coming from the pitch. Later on Ian told them Ruth was the mother of a girl he was seeing.

Before they had gone to church, Mark Beckford had warned his wife not to say anything to his parents about the pregnancy.

"But why? I'm ten weeks gone, I'm sure it'll be all right."

"No!" he snapped, "I – I'd like you to wait jus a little longer. Call me superstitious but I don't want to tempt fate. Let's wait for a while." Like wait until I've gone and left you, he thought. News that he was about to become a father had convinced Mark that he had to leave – and soon. It had also made him superstitious: around the time Rachel had conceived he had noticed that the safe's door was open and the first thought of stealing the money entered his head. He was now sure it had been an omen.

Come Monday morning he might find himself arrested and heading towards a prison sentence or he would have an indicator he had got away with it and could plan his future with Marcia. One way or another he would not be around for the birth.

When the game at the park had finished, Desmond told Nestor to head for his place for something to eat while they waited for a call from Steve Patel to find out where they were to meet up. They had figured they were just going to give the money to him at the funeral parlour but Steve told them there were people they had to meet and it was for the best if these people were not seen in town.

Nestor sat in the lounge watching a favourite video of Desmond's called *Shogun Assassin*. Desmond had told him it was about a little fat Jap guy pushing his pickney around the country in a little cart chopping off the head of almost "*h*every-rasclart-one" he met. Nestor figured that his friend should have been a film critic as he had summed up the whole film so well. The fat guy had just killed the three Brothers of Death in such gruesome ways he had Nestor calling out a variety of cusses with every sword stroke when Desmond shouted out the dinner was ready. Nestor followed the aroma that put his belly rumbling only to be met with a sight that almost killed his appetite immediately. Jas was in an outfit that Nestor would later describe as: "some sort-a blouse an' skirt."

He lowered himself slowly onto a chair and stared at Desmond's grinning face. He feared the answer but he had to ask the question. "Des, wha' the bloodclart is goin on?"

It took a while for Desmond to get his breath after laughing so hard. "Cha, Jas was bawlin the other night that him want to go back to im family in Bilston 'cause some skinheads attack them 'ouse. When me tell him he ain't goin nowhere he kept bawlin like a gal, so me dress him up like a gal, seen?"

"Nah, Des, me don't see, me don't see! Anyone come in 'ere now an' them think somethin-a go on, man. A man dressin up another man like a gal . . . Man, them would mek out we's the batty-men! Cha, tell Jas go put on proper clothes or I'm outta 'ere. I mean it, Des!"

Desmond nearly fell off his seat; he was laughing so hard. "It a joke, Nestor," he said wiping his eyes. "Jas, go put on your clothes before this man gets all emotional."

Nestor sat with his arms crossed and refused to start eating until Jas reappeared in more masculine attire. He could take Desmond's physical cruelty to Jas but he was starting to wonder what sort of twisted mind could even come up with this sort of degrading treatment. If it ever got found out, Nestor was worried that he would get labelled a sexual deviant by association. After they had sorted out business with Steve Patel, Nestor thought he'd mention that perhaps it would be for the best of everyone concerned if

Desmond let the apprentice mechanic go home. The whole thing was getting too weird for him to handle.

They spent the rest of the afternoon watching *Shogun Assassin* again, this time with Desmond giving a running commentary until the phone rang. It was Steve Patel telling them to bring the money to a pub in Willenhall – which was just about the only place lower than Wolverhampton in their estimation.

20

Willenhall, a place of vague boundaries between Wolverhampton and Walsall, was mostly famous for lock making and as the birthplace of Alan 'Sniffer' Clarke of Leeds United and England, when Leeds was one of the best two teams in English football. Willenhall was a town of divided loyalties. To the north they had the fairly consistent, Plain Jane, dull-as-dish-water fourth, sometimes third, division football (as they were called in the days before the Coca-Cola Championship and Leagues One and Two) of Walsall FC. To the south there was the unpredictable, once glamorous and fast-fading leading lady in Wolverhampton Wanderers. Nestor and Desmond did not like Willenhall, they felt intimidated because they had never seen a lot of black people around the town. As they met Steve Patel in a car park of a small town-centre pub their discomfort grew. It was bad enough that they were going into unfamiliar territory but having one hundred and six grand in a bag made the experience more intense. But again Steve surprised them when he did not take the money but instead said they would go into the pub.

All the men at the bar were white and middle-aged. A few of them glanced suspiciously at the new arrivals before they turned back to their pint glasses of Banks' mild. Steve led the way to the snug at the rear where two hard-faced women sat on one of the benches that ran the lengths of three walls. It was part of the Black Country etiquette of the time that no 'decent' women drank in the bar with their menfolk: they had their own enclosure in which they drank beer, served in supposedly more feminine half pint glasses.

Steve Patel bought three halves of lager and immediately brought the three men's sexuality into question. Neither Nestor nor Desmond could see any good reason why Steve should have arranged for the delivery to happen here of all places; they were hardly blending in. The strain of handing over so much money finally got to Nestor. "Wha' are these guarantees you're supposed to have, Steve?" he hissed. "We got a heap-a dunsai here an' there's plenty-a people with mash-ates back in Wolves waitin for us if them nah see wha' we've promised them."

"Knowing you guys, the hardest thing about this is handing over all that money," said Steve. He lifted the glass to his lips and added a little class to the proceedings by extending his little finger as he did so. He smacked his lips and said, "Don't worry, lads, my guarantees will be here any moment." The glasses were half-empty, or half-full, depending on your viewpoint, when two men came into the snug. They went over to the women whose smiles turned brittle and then disappeared altogether before they gathered their handbags and quickly left. Nestor and Desmond exchanged sideways glances as the two guys strolled over in the way hard men do: as if they had a pair of melons hanging in a string bag between their legs.

"Thought we'd have a bit of privacy," said the white guy with a criss-cross pattern of scars all over his shaven scalp. Worse still, in Nestor's mind at least, he was a Scouser. They drew up two stools and sat down. The other one was a mixed-race man with a pair of hollow, dead eyes. Scar-head put out a hand towards Desmond. "The name's Nigel. A puff's name, I know, but I think my old man was doing the Johnny Cash bit, y'know, that song he did called *A Boy Named Sue*, like. A name like Nigel tends to get you into plenty of scraps around Bootle. My mate here's called Psycho, that's not short for psychotherapist by the way."

Neither Desmond nor Nestor had a clue about who Johnny Cash was or anything about his songs but they did their best to look as though they understood as they shook hands with Nigel. Psycho didn't offer a handshake. Nigel did the talking: he let them know he had watched them and knew all about their scheme; the football team they played for; that Nestor still lived with "mommy"; and Desmond shared a home with "the pretty Indian boy". He then gave a potted history of his and Psycho's criminal, and violent, careers. "Psycho hasn't been too well lately, change of medication, and don't take this personally but he kind of hates black men, something to do with his black father murdering his white mam. I just thought I'd let you know why he isn't talking much."

Psycho's face didn't flicker and Nigel then pulled out an automatic pistol from his waistband and put it onto the small round table as he described the weapon as the guarantee of his guarantee. "Don't worry, boys, Stevie here has told us how your arses are on the line due to you collecting this money from members of your community. Personally, I like the idea that so many black people are gonna make a bit of money for a change. And rest assured, we will have no hesitation in shooting anyone who tries any funny business . . ."

"Like, shoot them dead, like," said Psycho, in a distant voice.

". . . See, I was worried when I heard how you two fellas raised your stake just in case any of those who contributed might have got around to figuring there isn't that much money to be made out of the coffins and got curious. Two spades were following you here in a red Escort RS 2000 . . ." Nigel allowed himself a smile, ". . . until a car rather stupidly pulled out in front of them and blocked their way."

Nestor had always been quick to pick up on things; that's how come he had survived a lifetime of pulling skanks. He reckoned a good proportion of what Nigel had told him was bullshit to put the frighteners on. Well, it was working because the two Liverpool men were definitely frightening him. But to pull skanks you have to be able to bullshit too and Nestor thought now was a good time to give a bit back. "Yeah, well that was our security, Nigel. A bit like you, we got a bit worried that people knew we had collected so much money. So we had two friends of ours, tooled up friends, cover us for the last few days. They must 'ave done a fairly good job if you hadn't spotted them before now. I think we'd better conduct our business real quick in case they find us an' get the wrong idea when they see your shooter."

Nigel begrudgingly appreciated Nestor's front. "How much did you raise?"

"A hundred an' six grand," said Desmond, feeling as though he should let it be known he was no silent partner like Psycho.

Nigel put his gun back into his waistband and nodded. "That's not bad. People around here must be very trusting, or very desperate. I take it it's all in the bag. Let's have a look then." He opened the bag, took out random wads to check they were all notes and not bits of newspaper and then zipped it shut again. "Right, lads, me and Stevie will count it out later but you two look honest sorts, I'm sure it will be all there."

"I can vouch for them," said Steve, "if they say there's a hundred and six grand, we'll be counting a hundred and six grand, no problem."

They all strolled out of the pub; Psycho in front and Nigel last out carrying the bag of money. At the car park he said, "Thanks for coming, lads. Oh, and good luck with the cup final next weekend."

"Yeah," said Nestor, "an' I hope your guys win the European Cup after such a crap season in the league. You know it's been crap when you finish behind West Brom."

"Our team's not playing in the European Cup," snarled Nigel, "I think you're referring to another Liverpool team that neither me or Psycho think very much of."

"Right," Nestor said quickly, "I mean I hope Everton do better nex season."

"We couldn't do much worse . . . unless we were Wolves." Nigel scanned the vicinity and added, "And I used to think we were living in shite."

Nigel and Psycho headed to their car and Steve told Nestor and Desmond that he would see them at work tomorrow. On their way back to Wolverhampton, the pair kept a look out for any sign of a red Ford Escort RS2000. "Who do you think it was?" asked Desmond.

Nestor snorted, "Who you think? It 'as to be Cecil for one an' I guess the other one was Bryce. That's why them didn't forward the dunsai we expected, them were plannin a big draw whatever them put in."

As they pulled up outside Desmond's place they saw the red Ford Escort parked up. Cecil didn't look happy as he came over to them and said that they had better go inside for a chat. At first Nestor was just relieved that Jas was not in a dress again but as they entered the sitting room he became angry at what Cecil and Bryce had been up to. "You guys are lucky," he said.

"Oh?" said Bryce, "an' 'ow you reckon that?"

"'Cause that car that pulled in front of unno was no accident. 'Cause Steve 'as gone an' hired himself two professional gunmen," said Desmond. "You think the guy's stupid, that once we 'anded over the dunsai you could jus come in an' tek it? Gosh, man, unno should-a seen these two guys him 'ave. Them call one Psycho, an' like the one wid the scars all over im 'ead said, that ain't short for psychotherapist, to ras."

"To ras," said Nestor, as a vision of getting caught in the crossfire flashed through his mind.

"Nah, you got us all wrong," said Cecil, "we were jus checkin that our investment was gettin to where it had to go."

Nestor sucked at his teeth. "Show some respec, guy, an' don't tek we fe damn fools. We know you two a long time, right."

Cecil and Bryce laughed like it did not matter they had been found out, after all for them robbing was all about never having to say sorry. Bryce said, "Look, guys, we wasn't gonna stick you up today or nutten like that. Why would we, you only had a hundred grand an' the deal that's goin down is costin Steve half a mill. He's buying the stuff off a guy named Khan an' then he's sellin to some Liverpool crew for a cool million. The man will double his money in a few days. It's the million me an' Cecil want to share wid you two. It's when he's got the cash from these guys up north we wanna mek our move."

"Cha," huffed Desmond, "Steve's a coolie, him don't even trust his ole lady when it comes to the dunsai. Him was never gonna tell us when this deal is goin down."

"Well, you guys 'ave gotta mek sure you go wid him when him go north with the gear," said Cecil. "If Steve gives you nonsense about handlin it alone then he's plannin a double-deal. You're im partners in this deal an' you say he ain't goin nowhere without you, right? Once the dunsai's collected you call us. Who else beside unno who's workin for Steve knows about the heroin?"

"Are you mad?" asked Nestor. "No one but we knows

what's goin on. There's two deals, him cut im two cousins called Gully an' Sunny in on the coffin bisniss but as far as them are concerned everyting is legit, they don't know nutten about no heroin."

Cecil and Bryce began to smile broadly. "We're gonna keep an eye on tings," said Cecil, "an' you guys get ready to head north an' mek some serious money. We're talkin a hundred grand to cover the money you raise an' then another hundred grand a piece."

Greed overcoming his fear, Nestor asked, "So what's gonna happen to the other seven hundred grand?"

The smile disappeared from Cecil's face. "This deal is non-negotiable," he said.

21

There had been a lot of wailing going on in the Robinson household. Devon had collapsed during Sunday afternoon and was rushed to hospital. It was soon discovered that he had suffered massive kidney failure and had to be hooked up to a dialysis machine after being transferred to the Queen Elizabeth medical centre in Birmingham. The hospital management had even specially brought an Indian consultant in to break the bad news. They figured his colour might make a difference to how the family would respond to what he was saying – but none of the Robinsons were going to believe it was due to a disease and not the beating to the body the cops had given him.

The rage within Audley that had slowly started to cool was burning fiercely again. On his way home from the hospital he took a left turn to call into the Wrights' house in Blakenhall to tell them what had happened. Oliver and Patrick were there. He told them he had previously stood up for Horace McIntosh and said the man's motives had been the right ones, even if what he had done might have been a mistake as far as Devon was concerned.

Oliver was never going to be even-handed when it came to Horace and said, "Audley, I was sayin to Courtney yesterday that black people in this town had better start buckin up them ideas, 'cause we is too easily controlled, man. Anyting Horace do has been to help control black guys. Look, over the years him tek grants off the council, him even try to arrange a friendly match wid the cops an' you guys still go on as though him do you a favour. It's the white man him do the favours for but you don't see it yet."

Horace had been cutting Audley's (and Devon's) hair since they were small kids and the kind of stuff Oliver was saying was akin to describing an admired uncle being caught doing something very embarrassing in a public toilet. It put a sick feeling in his stomach. "You're a grown man," said Patrick, "with wife an' family so why are you still playin football? You don't mek money from it, it teks up a lot of your free time, don't it?"

"I play because I like playin football," said Audley, "I like keepin fit. Wha' are you sayin, I shouldn't 'ave some kind-a hobby?"

"Nah," replied Oliver, "it's a good ting to do, I play it miself, when there ain't nutten else to do. But this is wartime, black guys are dyin, maybe Devon's dyin, an' you're tellin us playin football is helpin guys like him? It's a luxury that none-a we can afford right now."

"He's right," said Patrick, taking advantage of Audley's hesitation. "Even Donovan says he ain't playin no more."

"Are you talkin about Donovan Brown?"

"Who else? He was down London the other day at the inquest for all them black people who got killed in the

Deptford fire. He's already tellin us the verdict before it gets started properly. Look, man, there ain't no justice in this country for the likes of we."

It embarrassed him but Audley's mind was immediately full of thoughts about the team and its chances in the final: if Patrick was right about Donovan it was now three players down. He was confused: about his feelings toward the sport; toward Horace; and about if it was such a bad thing to be distracted sometimes when life was turning out to be a heap of shit. "I gotta get back home," he said.

"You gotta get even, for Devon," said Patrick. "In twenty years time do you want your baby goin through the same shit? Think about it, Audley, your family 'as suffered enough. If you don't think that violence an' gettin even with the cops is your ting then 'ave a think about who you're playin for. Mek a stand, yeah? For Devon."

He thought he was like a man travelling that final mile to a place of execution. Mark had looked in the mirror before he left home and wondered if he looked like a guilty man. Driving to work he had stopped trying to figure out what he should wish to find as he arrived at the plant. If George Rowley was back at work it would mean the cops were happy with his version of events and they were looking for someone else; if he wasn't there then Mark could be in the clear – but an innocent man would be taking the rap for him. Either way he was not going to feel good about it and wished then that he had not taken the money.

Hardly any work was done during the morning. Mark had put himself behind his desk and stayed there, wanting to ask colleagues if they had heard about what was going on but scared to hear their answers. He was deliberating about what he should do at lunchtime when Tom Howard appeared in his doorway. "Not running today, Mark?" he asked.

Mark wondered if there was some sort of insinuation behind the question. Maybe Tom had spent the weekend pondering over what had really happened in the office, and what the sports bag had been all about. Maybe he had worked out there was no way Mark had arrived at George's office only "two seconds" before he had; and that George had locked the safe *after* he had returned from washing his hands. A little baffled by the lack of an answer, Tom went on, "Only if you're not, we're going to have a short meeting in my office to say a few prayers for George. I suppose you've heard."

"Heard wha'?"

"That George was charged over the weekend."

Mark felt himself turn weak, he had imagined it was the best news he could hear but now it was a reality he thought he was going to be sick. Tom was talking but he couldn't make his brain decipher what was being said. "Sorry, Tom, I'm so shocked that I didn't catch wha' you jus said."

"I said that George admitted to everything. He'd been siphoning off money for years, they think he took well over a quarter of a million. He gave most of it to the church and good causes. He was in court this morning and at least they have given him bail, I don't think he would last in prison."

It was at that point Mark almost slid off his seat and fell to his knees to give thanks. He was in the clear, the twenty grand he'd taken was small change in comparison to the sums embezzled by George. Sweet Lord, what he'd done wasn't even stealing, it was a reward for uncovering a crime. This was the best possible outcome, one he could never have imagined. It was a sign, the omen that he had made the right decision. He went along to Tom's office and doubted if anyone there could have said more heartfelt prayers.

He was walking on air for the rest of the afternoon, his car as good as floated home; it was just a pity it was Rachel waiting for him rather than Marcia but it wouldn't be long before that changed. However it wasn't just Rachel who was waiting for him to return home, Ian was in his lounge, sitting sullen-faced in an armchair. "He won't tell me what's wrong," explained Rachel, "he's been sitting there for half an hour without saying a word."

Mark surmised there had been bad news from Aston Villa and instantly all the envy he had felt vanished. Although his own attitude toward football had changed radically over the last few days, Mark was not about to give Ian crap about it not being the end of the world. Because he knew that football was the world Ian still inhabited, it was still so easy for Mark to recall his pain when his own had shattered. He went over and put a hand on Ian's shoulder. "So what's up, bro'? Is it about Villa?"

Ian dropped his head. "In a way," he mumbled. "Dad found out I drove the car to the West Park yesterday an' went crazy. He says he ain't gonna take me on Wednesday because of it. Then when Mom tried to talk him round he lost it completely. Man, he was sayin some strange things, callin Mom some . . . some bad things, you know, Mark."

"Like wha' strange things?"

"Like, 'none-a my family good at football, dem get it from your side, so you tek the bwoy'. So I took the car, it was quiet an' I've done it before so why is Dad actin like this now? Why is he tryin to spoil my chances?"

Ian let the question hang, as if he suspected his older brother should know. Mark did have his suspicions. He'd heard his mom and dad argue when he was younger and he'd also heard something just once and it had led to a fight. Until Ian had raised the question he had erased the incident from his memory but now he recalled how the boy he'd beaten up had said something about Ian not having the same daddy and that his mother had taken Rudolph Naylor's 'holy seed'. "I don't know," Mark said softly. "You know

Mom, she's always quotin the pastors' sermons an' that, Dad is probably gettin sick of it. An' he did tell you not to drive that car unless me or him are with you, didn't he? By the time you go back he'll have cooled down, he'll feel bad for blowin his top an' will probably arks if you wanna go for a drivin lesson later."

A big globulous tear dripped from Ian's chin. "Yeah, you're right. I just wish I could tell him some stuff, you know, about how I appreciate everythin he's done for us 'cause I know he thinks I take it for granted. I know he's mad about me not goin to church but I love him an' I feel embarrassed jus sayin that to you but he's never given me an openin so I can tell him. It's like he knows I wanna say it but he don't want to hear it."

"That's 'cause of the time an' place he's comin from. He ain't the sort-a man who would know wha' to say if his big son started talkin love. Anyway, if he's still in a sulk Wednesday I'll knock off work early an' take you myself."

"Yeah?"

"Sure. I was gonna come around to you later to find out if you wanted to go over the park for a bit of practise. Work on that right foot of yours so you can do more than jus stand on it."

When Ian went home Rachel told Mark that she had overheard some of the things he had said. "I thought it was really lovely that you offered to take him to the trials, it sort of reminded me of why I fell in love with you."

She slipped her arms around his waist and he drew her close. While staring over her head he thought about Marcia and about how many more days he would have to pretend with Rachel. But it was bearable because soon he would have forty grand and a way out. Still hugging her, he thought he would count to ten before easing her off him so he could get changed into his tracksuit.

22

Business in the barbershop had been slow, even for a Tuesday morning. Mervyn Palmer hadn't stopped long; he had put his cheque from the pools company into a bank the previous week but they had given him some nonsense about having to wait for five working days before he could make a withdrawal against it. "Mi rahteed," he'd sighed, "it a pools company, you know, dem good fe de money." It was difficult to believe but banks elevated even Mervyn to a moral high ground and, from that lofty position, in his estimation they were a bunch of crooks. "Usury is a sin, you know," became a favourite saying of his. Today was the day he was going to remind the bank of its sinning ways again and take every penny of his winnings home. Before he went, Horace McIntosh thought this was about the best time to ask Mervyn for a little sponsorship, just a few pounds towards the pre-match breakfast he had planned. Mervyn said yes too quickly to be believed, when a Jamaican responded like that he usually meant 'no' and Horace doubted if he would see Mervyn again until after the final had been played.

Horace didn't say a great deal after that, he seemed preoccupied and Frank Grant thought he had something other than the approaching final on his mind. As there were no customers about, Frank sat down and read the newspaper Mervyn had left behind. "Look like that IRA man on 'unger strike is gonna die any time now," he said. "Problem is dem gonna be showin all dem riots in Ireland an' givin de yout 'ere ideas." It was his attempt to let Horace know that there were matters beyond their control and if Wolverhampton erupted with violence and mayhem there was little either man could do but to sit tight and watch it happen.

It was since Courtney Wright had ambled over from the

bookies to tell them the news about Devon Robinson that Horace had become more withdrawn. He sat in the red swivel chair in front of the mirror, as he again mulled over if he had done the right thing in getting Devon out of the police station. Perhaps the police had fooled him; that they knew they had hurt Devon and Chief Inspector Forbes was going to release him anyway if Horace hadn't mentioned it first. The early edition of the *Express and Star* had Devon's hospitalisation on the front page. There was a quote from a doctor saying that the kidney failure was down to a long-standing, if previously undiagnosed, illness. A woman who said she was a spokesperson for 'Black Defence' said she believed that the violence that had been meted out by the police was a contributing factor and announced that there would be a peaceful vigil outside Dunstall Road police station. Both sides were gearing up for conflict and a pattern of behaviour was emerging: the only evidence that was going to be accepted on either side was that which backed up their own viewpoint. A police representative retorted that the woman from Black Defence was from outside the area and said agitators were coming into town to stir up trouble between the police and "the local West Indian community".

Frank tried to bring the conversation around to football with reminiscences of the Jamaica versus the Caribbean All-Stars match in 1950 at Sabina Park in Kingston. "Me was jus tinkin last night about Gil Heron, man, wha' a player . . ."

"An' Lindy Delapena," Horace responded spontaneously, "he was a bit better than Gil."

"Nah, man, Gil was a better player than Lindy. Blouse an' skirt . . ."

And so it went on. They'd had this conversation many times before, swapping statistics and anecdotes and stuff they just made up. Frank could keep it up, sometimes with outrageous fabrications, until he felt he had won the argument. But this time he would keep Horace talking just for the sake of it. For Frank it was a bit like treading water next to his friend to stop him from drowning in a deep pool of depression.

Buckshot Pinnock had been out most of the morning looking for spare parts around the various scrap-yards in Fox's Lane. With so many of his customers unemployed there was often a lot of haggling over the price and most of them took the option of using second-hand parts. On his return to his repair shop he saw Sergeant Boyd and his sidekick waiting for him. "Hello, Vince, I thought I'd just make a social call."

Buckshot opened up the padlock on his double gates and went in without replying. Boyd and his oily-faced colleague made a quick scan of the yard, just in case Buckshot had slipped up and left something incriminating around the place. "Why don't you get yourself a search warrant an' waste some more people's time?" Buckshot asked Boyd as he started to replace a rear brake disc.

"Are you trying to tell me that I've grounds for applying for a warrant, Vince?" Boyd turned to the constable and said, "That's a result, I count it as almost an admission."

"I'm busy, sergeant, I'm very busy, so why don't you get to the point, arks your questions an' let me tell you that I don't know one damn ting."

"And they say there's bad relations between the police and black people, if only they could hear us two, going at it like two old mates."

"Yeah, well that's one ting we'll never be."

"I tell you what, Vincent, you know how to hurt a man's feelings. You got a big match the weekend, haven't you? I was wondering where it's being held as me and a few friends might come and cheer you on, seeing as we know most of the team in a professional capacity. Pity about Carl Hooper finding himself on remand, I don't think we'll be seeing the big man for quite a while. Funnily enough, the same day he banjoed his old man a bloke fitting his description was seen in a car park just before an RS2000 went missing."

"I'll keep an eye out for you."

"I'm sure you will, Vince, I'm sure you will. Saw another of your mates the other day, a Mark Beckford at the steel plant. Seems a very nice lad, makes me wonder how he fell in with a group like you lot. But I'm delighted to say that, on this rare occasion, a member of Sabina Park Rangers was not the prime suspect."

Buckshot didn't bother with a reply; he was too busy straining to undo a rusted nut after pouring a little diesel over it. He gave it a little more torque and with a final heave it suddenly came away, as did the skin from two of his knuckles. The blood oozed from beneath the layers of oil and grease. "As I thought," said Boyd, "scratch us and we're all the same underneath."

In an exemplary exercise in self-control, Buckshot kept his lips squeezed shut and went looking for the antiseptic cream. As he applied it to his hand he couldn't help but think of a little dog's battyhole. "Are you still here, Mr Boyd?" he asked as he was about to resume work.

"You're making us feel so unwelcome, Vince, that I nearly forgot what I came here for."

"Yeah, an' wha' was that exactly?"

"Picked up some info the other day. There's this girl, she took a hell of a beating off some pimp but of course she won't press charges. We went and had a chat with him anyway, turns out it was Danny Rankin. And guess who was with him, only your sister Shannon. Now this isn't bullshit, Vince, she didn't look great, in fact she looked bleeding awful."

The mention of his sister's name froze him for a split-second but the memory of the pain she had caused him sent a pulse of hot anger through his veins to get him moving again. "She mek her own bed."

"Then she's lying in a bed of shit. She's in Franchise

House, number 67 if you're interested. I think she's in need of help. If you don't want to maybe someone else in the family might. And don't think I'm telling you this because I want some favour back, Vince, as far as I'm concerned it's an attempt at crime-prevention. I told you before, Danny Rankin, like any of his brothers, is a nasty piece of work. If you'd seen what he'd done to this other girl's face I don't think you'd be here now, you'd be straight up to Blakenhall to pull her out of that flat. But it's up to you. Put it this way, if Rankin fell down a few flight of steps there would be some happy people in Wolverhampton, a lot of them in the place where I work. Take it from me, if he tried to make out someone pushed him down those stairs there are very few of my colleagues who'd believe him."

The constable had turned away, as if to say he had heard nothing of what Sergeant Boyd had just said. "When you say awful," said Buckshot, "do you mean as in beat up awful, or drugged up awful?"

The constable looked over his shoulder at Buckshot and then at Boyd as if to caution the sergeant about how he should answer the question. Boyd rubbed a thumb against his chin and then said, "Let's say, she looked awful in more than one way."

23

It was gone. It had disappeared. Mervyn Palmer checked again and then tried to think if he could have put the money anywhere else. He screamed curses and blasphemed more than once as he checked all his shoes and the lining of his navy blue suit one more time. He sat down on his waterbed with thirty-five thousand pounds but all he could think of was the six grand that had gone missing. His stash had meant more to him than the pools win because of the time and trouble it had taken to accumulate. Many a woman and child of his had tried to trick him out of it with their hard-luck stories but he had always been too sharp for them, or so he had thought. He put away his winnings in a place he had specially prepared behind a skirting board in a partition wall of his bedroom while cussing every single one of those he suspected until his mind fixed on the one he thought the most grasping and greedy of them all.

Replacing the brake cylinder on the Ford Cortina took much longer than Buckshot had first estimated but he knew how difficult it would be to try and get more money for the job so he would put it down to being just another part of a bad day. The worst part was the visit of Detective Sergeant Boyd with news of his sister.

Shannon was twenty, a grown woman and it was no longer any of his business what she did with her own life, or so he told himself. When Shannon had first gone to Germany he did not want to think about what she might be up to and went along with the modelling story. At first he found comfort in that she had been signed up with an agency in Birmingham when she was seventeen. They did find her work with a hair products company – but that was about all: in the 1970s there was little demand for black models outside of the 'ethnic minority market'. As more girls travelled from the West Midlands to Hamburg for 'glamour work' it became increasingly hard for Buckshot to even mention his sister, never mind go along with the charade about what she was doing. A lot of those who had gone the 'modelling' route were emotionally vulnerable young women and that's what made Shannon's actions harder for Buckshot to understand, or accept. It was if she were broadcasting to the world that she too had a troubled family background and that there was something wrong with the Pinnocks. Even the other SPR players had stopped bringing her up in conversation because *they* felt embarrassed for him. Now, if Boyd wasn't just winding him up, she was back in town and her presence threatened to increase his shame.

With the exception of Nestor and Desmond, hardly any of the team mentioned Danny Rankin either, even though he had spent part of a season playing for Sabina Park Rangers. He had talent, so much so that The Arsenal had signed him as an apprentice, but he had no discipline and they let him go after a few months. And even Horace McIntosh, who was normally the most tolerant of coaches, had been driven to tell Danny that there was no longer a place for him in his team. Danny had just shrugged his shoulders and told Horace he didn't care. One of the reasons behind Danny Rankin's apparent indifference to the premature halt of his football career was that he did not need it to get him lots of money and a big expensive car. From an early age he had followed in the criminal footsteps of his two older brothers and his interest in football had waned.

As Buckshot put away his tools and locked up for the night he was still arguing with himself about if he could believe a word Sergeant Boyd had told him. As a matter of policy it was always for the best if cops were never believed, whatever they said. He thought then that he would not go calling to number 67 Franchise House – but he would hang around the car park outside the tower block for an hour before training just to see if there was any sign of her.

Marcia Yuell thought she had been on a journey down some dark pit: everything had seemed to be going wrong from the evening she had accepted a lift from Mervyn Palmer in his brand new Austin Princess. There had been many times when she had thought about why she had ever gone with him, without coming up with any clear answer. But lots of things hadn't been clear to Marcia since the day when as a fifteen-year-old her mother's boyfriend Lynton had come to her bedroom. Nine months later she was having his baby, while her mother cussed both her as a harlot and the "wukless bwoy" she had been seeing at the time. The most Curtis and Marcia had ever got up to was a long snog in the back row of the cinema and she never did get around to telling her mom the real identity of Tania's father. Deep down inside of her she had been feeling worthless at the very moment that Mervyn had pulled up in his car.

But things began to change when Mark had telephoned her the previous evening. He said he had just finished playing football with his brother and wanted to come and see her because he had some important news. As she waited for Mark to turn up she rang Lorna again just to confirm what she should say to him. "Don't sell yourself cheap, those days are over, Marcia," Lorna had said.

There was a strange look on Mark's face as he arrived at her flat, Marcia thought it was like he was excited and afraid all at once. She had been ready to tell him she was finishing with him – on her terms – but before she could say anything he began to tell her of his secret savings plan. He said he had been saving from his first week at work and even Rachel did not know about it. It was linked with some financial index thing, shares or something, but the most important thing was he now had twenty thousand pounds that was soon going to be forty grand. Marcia was silently calculating and increasing her demands when he said he wanted to spend the money on a house for them. "W-What?" she stuttered.

"I want me, you an' Tania to have a nice house, so we can live like a proper family."

"But you have a family, Mark."

"But I don't love Rachel, you know that, an' I never loved

Rachel, all I ever wanted was to live with you . . . But I was too young, too immature to say wha' I really wanted. I got married because I put other people's feelins before mine, an' yours, but I'm not doin that any more, Marcia. I see this money as a gift from God, like He's tellin me He understood that I made a mistake an' now He's givin me a second chance. Once Nestor an' Desmond give me back my money we're goin to look for a house."

Until he mentioned Nestor and Desmond, Marcia had felt her spirit soar but in a strange way what Mark had said about the money was not that important, it was what he had been thinking of doing for her that mattered. Up until then she had made out that besides Tania, it was the things money could buy were all she would love. But now it was different because she felt that Mark *really* loved her – and she would love him back. He had to get home so they kissed and said they would talk some more at the YMCA the following evening. She closed the door behind him trying to think if she'd ever been happier.

The JA City netball team were looking as crisp as usual but only about half the squad of Sabina Park Rangers had turned up to ogle at them through the chain link fence that ran the perimeter of the court. Horace McIntosh turned to his captain Norman Longmore for some answers. He started off by asking about Audley Robinson.

Norman had already been told by another of Audley's brothers that he had decided he could no longer play for Sabina Park Rangers, or to be more precise, no longer play for Horace McIntosh. Norman didn't think it was up to him to tell Horace and said, "Me see im brotha Tyrone an' him seh that Audley busy, someting to do wid Devon. Visitin an' ting."

"Any sign-a Donovan?"

"No, sah. Me 'ear im dealin wid some political ting now. Him busy too."

Horace took a deep breath to try and relieve the feeling of tension within his chest. He took some comfort in that Mark and Ian Beckford had turned up, particularly Ian as he had another trial with Aston Villa the following evening. Surprisingly, Nestor Riley had turned up again with his kit: it was if he sensed that he might be playing in the final yet, albeit under another name.

The final whistle of the netball game had just blown when there was an unexpected appearance in the midst of the netball players. Mervyn Palmer had staggered onto the court. He looked drunk and he looked vexed. "*h*Everbody, *h*everybody, me want all-a unno to listen to wha' me 'ave to seh." He looked at his son Desmond and scraped his tongue on the edges of his false teeth as if just the sight of him had put a bad taste in his mouth. "A blasted teef is amongst unno, someone who teef mi money." He turned to stare at Marcia Yuell and raised a gnarled finger. "See 'er? She went to bed wid me de odda week fe two hundred pound, plus a tenner for 'er taxi fare 'ome. Den she come to mi yard last week lookin fe more. Man, she couldn't wait to see mi new waterbed an' when me went to mi bat'room to ready miself to nice 'er *h*up again she teefed mi money." He stepped towards her and steadied himself before he went on, "You is a damn prostitute an' a damn teef an' me want *h*everyone to know it – an' me want mi money back!"

All Marcia could think of was not that everyone was listening – only that Mark was. As Mervyn pushed his face into hers she stepped back, to make a little space, before she delivered a left uppercut followed by a right cross. Mervyn's dentures flew across the court before his head hit the ground by a thud. She looked around for Mark to shout out that Mervyn had been lying but he had gone. She ran out of the court shouting out his name only to catch sight of his Hillman Hunter speeding away.

24

Nestor and Desmond had asked Steve Patel how the deal was proceeding. At first he kept his answers to a single syllable. "Good," he said. They then asked him when would there be news and he told them "soon." To the question about when he would take delivery of the heroin Steve thought that rather than repeating himself he would respond with two syllables. "Tonight," he said.

Since Nestor and Desmond had handed over the money to the two Scousers there had been a growing suspicion between the three of them. It was because of Nestor and Desmond's dishonesty that Steve had hired them in the first place and he expected them to attempt some sort of double-cross as it was in their nature. But deep-seated prejudice also played its part. Steve's father had often told him that black people, wherever they were from, were a race of lazy thieves. He could make the odd exception – unless they were either from Jamaica or Nigeria, for without doubt, dishonesty was a genetic trait as far as those few million people were concerned. For their part, Nestor and Desmond figured that Steve would try and skank them in some way, because he was a coolie whose family ran a chain of shops. To them and their friends the poor coolie was all right but the coolie with money would bottle the steam from his piss if he thought it would make him money – and then look for some way to overcharge or sneakily reduce the amount of steam in the bottle. According to Nestor and Desmond, Steve was a member of this breed, or, more precisely, this caste of coolie.

The plan Cecil and Bryce had come up with was simple: Nestor and Desmond were to go everywhere with Steve Patel and once they had got their hands on the million they were to ring and let them know they were on their way back to Wolverhampton. Cecil and Bryce would do the rest but it was for their own good if Nestor and Desmond did not know exactly what the 'rest' entailed.

But as it had to do, the thought of one million pounds had put notions into the heads of Nestor and Desmond about double-dealing Cecil and Bryce. The three hundred grand promised as their cut was now not enough: if they were to keep their promises and double people's money they would have to shell out something in the region of one hundred and eighty thousand pounds, or as Nestor had put it "rasclart pounds". That would leave them a "nonsense" sixty grand each. It got them wondering what would happen if they skanked Cecil and Bryce and, by implication, everyone else who had put in money. They could never return to Wolverhampton – but the place was a shit-hole anyway and they would have a half a million each. Half a million or sixty grand: just where *was* the argument in not pulling the biggest skank of their lives?

With business so slack, Horace had spent the morning ringing around to find out what had happened to his players and issue a warning that those who did not turn up for training on Thursday would not be considered for the final. Mostly, he spoke to the same women he had talked to previously. They had told Horace already that the guys he was after were completely wukless.

He rang Audley Robinson at his place of work and was told he was too busy to come to the phone. He called back a little later and said he would wait on the line until Audley was free. It was almost ten minutes before Audley picked up the phone. Horace could hear nothing but a little static.
"Audley?"
"Yeah."
"It Horace. Me was jus wonderin 'ow Devon is gettin on."
More static and then, "Him not good."

"Oh?"

"Him still on dialysis. The 'ospital reckons him will need a transplant."

"Sorry to 'ear dat, man. Look, I've been ringin aroun de guys dem an' threatenin not to pick dem fe de final if dem nah show on Thursday. Jus to let you know me unnerstan why you can't mek it an' jus to say dat it don't apply to you, jus come to YM on Saturday mornin, nine o'clock, okay?"

"Nah, it's not okay."

"You can't mek it Saturday?"

"Nah, Horace, I ain't mekin it Saturday or any other day 'cause I'm finished playin for your team. This Devon situation 'as put me under some heavy-duty pressure an' none-a mi family want me to 'ave anyting to do wid you or your team 'cause you did wrong, man. You was wrong to bring him outta the police station."

"But, look, Audley, it's a disease Devon 'ave, who was to know?"

"The police still beat him an' you got him out before the doctor could get there."

"But there would-a been a riot, a lot more people would-a got 'urt."

"You mean 'urt like Devon? There's a lotta tings I thought about tellin you, Horace, some bad words come to my mind. But because part of me still thinks you were actin outta best intentions, I'm jus goin to leave it at that I'm never playin for Sabina Park, or any team to do wid you, ever again."

Figuring there was nothing more he could say, Horace gently put down the phone.

Unsurprisingly, Mervyn Palmer did not turn up at the barbershop on Wednesday morning. It wasn't just because of the embarrassing beating he had taken from Marcia but he also had an appointment at the magistrates' court on a charge of being drunk and disorderly. Dressed in his most shabby clothes, he gave the bench a humble apology and told them of his unemployed status. They in turn gave him a forty pounds fine to be paid at five pounds per week seeing he was a hardship case. Mervyn complained this would leave him very short and after a deliberation it was reduced to a weekly payment of only two pounds per week.

He left the courts grumbling about the lack of justice but soon he was back to thinking about the missing six grand. Marcia Yuell worked at a checkout of a low-cost supermarket across town and he made up his mind to see her right away, cuss her and let her employers know they were employing a thief. There was no way he was going to let the matter rest, the broken set of dentures that now sat in a glass in his kitchen were a reminder of a shameful defeat that would vex him every time he saw them.

Before going into the supermarket, Mervyn set his (sore) jaw determinedly. He had intended to get a basket and buy a few groceries and then take his turn at Marcia's checkout but as soon as he saw her, his rage overtook him. "Teef! Teef! Dat ooman teef mi money! See 'er, she a damn teef!"

Marcia froze in fear. The security guard, unfortunately for Mervyn, thought that by the way he was dressed that he was a tramp, probably drunk on meths. And even more unfortunately for Mervyn, the security guard was a man of frustrated ambitions. He had wanted to be a policeman but failed the entrance exam, then a bailiff and then just a guy who drove an armoured wages truck. He fantasised that if had been given the opportunity he would one day foil a gang of armed robbers, receive a bravery award and perhaps make the front page of the *Express and Star*. However, his dreams of glory thwarted, he had ended up wrestling with women who had tins of food they hadn't paid for in their shopping bags. He had waited for a chance like this one for seventeen whole months. Mervyn never saw him coming. He had just fixed his dentures so he could give Marcia Yuell the cussing of her young life when an arm came around his neck and squeezed his windpipe. Mervyn felt his feet leave the floor as the blurring images began to spin. He pulled at the arm in a desperate attempt to take in air.

Marcia looked on as a man with a Teddy-boy haircut ran to the assistance of the guard and took hold of Mervyn's feet. His frantic writhing put the man and the guard off balance and the three of them collapsed to the floor in a heap. Except for the grunts of the men doing the restraining, there was no other sound out of them until the guard asked Mervyn to tap his arm if he agreed he was going to be co-operative and do exactly what was asked of him. The tap never came; the guard squeezed a little harder and repeated his question. Marcia was staring into Mervyn's eyes, hating him for how he had destroyed her chance at happiness with Mark. She put down a bag of frozen peas and left her till. She went closer; her eyes fixed on Mervyn's contorted face. The grunts had ceased, the place was completely quiet as Marcia became quite still and shouted out that Mervyn was dead.

Except that he wasn't dead – not yet. The guard and the aged Teddy-boy scrambled to their feet and looked down in disbelief at the still form that was face-down on the ground. A woman pushed her way forward from one of the queues and shouted for someone to ring for an ambulance while she turned Mervyn over and began to give mouth-to-mouth. She kept the resuscitation going until the ambulance arrived. Marcia had looked on in disgust that, once the woman had removed his dentures, she had pressed her lips against Mervyn's; and in awe that she would do such a thing for a perfect stranger. She thought if the woman had known him for the man he was, she would have probably let him die. Marcia would have. The police arrived with the ambulance and took away the Teddy-boy and the security man who was mumbling that the tramp had fought like a madman and had seemed to possess superhuman strength. As a group of cops began to take statements from everyone present one of them shouted out to ask if there was anyone in the shop who knew the man who had been taken to hospital. Marcia thought it would be for the best if she kept her mouth shut. Mervyn Palmer had already caused her enough trouble.

25

Mervyn Ewart Gladstone Palmer shuffled off his battered mortal coil as he was driven away in the ambulance. It was a testament to his actual popularity – rather than the one he'd imagined – that it would be almost two weeks before anyone missed him. This was partly due to the police mishandling of the affair, or, depending on your view, a brilliant strategy. At first they had a problem with identification, even though they had only recently taken his fingerprints. But in a time before computerisation, matching prints was a laborious and time-consuming affair. Secondly, was the fact he was a black man who had been killed by two white men. It was judged that the atmosphere in the town was just too combustible to put out an immediate appeal for his identity by providing a full and frank description of the man they had laid out in the hospital morgue. Those who knew where Marcia worked and knew of the punch-up she'd had with Mervyn immediately put two and two together. Word soon filtered back to the cops who then confronted Marcia with what they had heard. She admitted she had known it was Mervyn Palmer but had been too scared to identify him in case it led to repercussions for her. The police's response was to say that they would handle how the news would be broken and that she should not discuss the incident with anyone.

In an exercise of news management, the police left it until Mervyn was dead for a week before they first put out that a security guard had saved the life of a young black woman at the checkout. Personal safety issues meant the security guard and the customer who had intervened could not be named but a chief superintendent said he had recommended both men for bravery awards. It was only the following day that the woman's assailant was identified as a 'West Indian, probably in his late fifties'. Once his name was finally publicised there followed a brief campaign of character assassination but even those who had known him best admitted that Mervyn had provided the press with most of the bullets. It started off with the story that followed in the tradition of the British press identifying an 'undeserving winner' – a figure who popped up in the media every few years. All of them had obviously made some pact with Satan and would eventually – and rightly – come to no good. The newspapers were almost gleeful in their accounts that only an hour before he died the 'Wolverhampton pools winner' (who would be henceforth known as 'pools man' in subsequent headlines) had duped magistrates in claiming he was close to destitution. More than once it was remarked that it was ironic that the clothes he had worn to court in his attempt to procure leniency would only a short while later lead him to be identified as a deranged vagrant. Any public sympathy that may have been around for Mervyn evaporated after that. More importantly, as far as the cops were concerned, and despite the best attempts of some political activists, there would be no protests, nor riots, over the death of Mervyn Palmer.

Five minutes after Mark Beckford had left work, an hour earlier than usual, the telephone in his office rang. Marcia wanted to tell him that Mervyn had died. In her confused, traumatised, mind it was supposed to make things right between them. Mervyn had lied about her stealing money and even if the bit about spending the night together was true, all she had done for the money was let him have a bit of a fumble but now he was no longer around to go shouting about it. It did not matter any more, did it? But with every unanswered ring Marcia's hope for the future ebbed away a little bit more.

Mark had been wrong about quite a few things lately. He had made a succession of misjudgements, not only about Marcia Yuell but also of his father Clovis. Contrary to what he had said to his brother following their row, the man had not cooled down, nor exhibited any sign that he felt bad for blowing his top, nor had he offered to give Ian a driving lesson as a way of making amends. Mark's mother had rang him just before lunch to ask if he would take Ian to the trials at Bodymoor Heath and he could tell by her voice that she was still deeply affected by what his father had said to her.

It was quiet in the Hillman Hunter as it sped toward Cannock and the A5. Ian finally said, "Are you still feelin bad over Marcia an' that ole guy Mervyn?"

There were a couple of gear changes before a reply came. "Feelin bad? Man, 'bad' doesn't do it justice. Stupid is a better word. You can take it that I'm feelin very bad an' very stupid."

"If you don't mind me sayin, Marcia is good-lookin an' all that but she's messed up in the head. She got friends that go on the same way, her mother is crazy an' you only gotta look at her daughter to know that guy Curtis ain't the father. When I came around to your place Rachel was talkin to me, even though I wasn't talkin back much. She's a good person, you know, Mark, I mean really good in her heart."

"An' you think I've been treatin her in a way she don't deserve?"

"Hey, I might have stopped goin to church but I still

remember that line about not judgin people lest we be judged. I know it ain't right, what's goin on between me an' Ruth, so all I'll say is Rachel might have things you've overlooked, hidden strengths, if you unnerstan." The car was on the A5 heading for Tamworth before Ian struck up the conversation again. "This thing," he said, "about Dad . . . You know it has somethin to do with Rudolph Naylor, don't you? I've heard that before, you know, Mark. Some kids said it to me at school, they said their parents had said it."

"Yeah?"

"You mean you never heard the same thing?"

Mark completed an overtaking manoeuvre and tried to think about how he should respond. This was the dark family secret, except it wasn't really that much of a secret, it was just something that no one in the family had dared to mention. "Once. It caused a bit of a fight."

"When I heard it at school I went an' arksed Mom about it. She didn't say anythin at first but later on she took me to see him, Rudolph I mean, at his house. She said this is your son an' he jus rubbed my head an' said I was a finelookin bwoy. On the way home Mom made me swear that I never said anythin about it."

"So if it's true, about Rudolph, how does it make you feel?"

"Now or when I found out?"

"Well, now."

"Dad is the only father I've ever had an' like I said before, I love him an' I want to tell him but he won't let me. In a way I kind-a love him more 'cause he ain't my biological dad an' I think he's known about it all along but he's never treated me any worse than you or Marianne."

"Sometimes he's treated you better."

"'Cause I was the baby of the family. An' that's why I want to do good at football, so when I'm rich an' famous an' that arsehole Rudolph comes to check me I will cuss him an' say he ain't no father of mine. My name's Beckford 'cause that's the name Clovis gave me an' I want him in the photographs with me after a final at Wembley holdin the cup . . . You can be in one too, if you want. But I know you should be playin too, if there was any justice."

Mark laughed quietly at the thought. "You know," he said, "I was really jealous when Bert Tomlinson made it plain he was interested in you an' not me . . ."

"You didn't hide it too good either."

"Yeah, well I'm sorry about that, Ian, I should've been glad for you but . . ."

"But you had the same dreams as I got, an' everyone thinks you're the better player an' in my first interview that's exactly wha' I'm goin to say."

For the rest of the journey to the training ground they laughed and joked about the prospects of fast cars and lots of money for Ian once he signed a contract with Aston Villa. As they got to the training ground Mark felt another weight fall from his shoulders: he was no longer burdened by jealousy.

Mark watched from a distance as the game started. He was concerned because Ian had been put out on the right wing even though he was a left-footer. But he was playing well enough to draw two short rounds of applause from the few onlookers for a run and a cross and then a swerving shot from the edge of the box that hit the upright. Mark was happier to see Ian spend most of the second half in his favoured position out on the left wing and now he *was* playing great. Mark did not see Bert Tomlinson before he touched him on the shoulder: he was too engrossed in his brother's performance. "The lad's doing fantastic," Bert said, "it must make you feel proud."

"It does, Bert, it really does. I was jus thinkin about when the baby's born, if it's a son, wha' it might feel like as I'm watchin him play."

"What, you're going to be a dad? Congratulations," the scout said as he offered his hand, "let me know when he's having his first game and I'll be there. There'll be football in his genes all right."

Mark took Bert's hand and it was as if in that simple act it had struck him that he was now actually happy that he was going to be a father, happy that Ian was doing so well, and most of all happy that he still had Rachel. Bert eased his fingers out from Mark's grip a little embarrassed – and puzzled – that he had kept hold for so long. Walking away, Bert glanced back at Mark's broad grin and hoped everything was all right. There were so many thoughts running through Mark's mind: in his pursuit of money and a woman he had almost let his greatest prize slip away. It was if he had been gripped by madness and realisation of the truth came like a flash of lightening. He had been so infatuated with Marcia that he had tried to convince himself that he and Rachel were incompatible, that the decision to get married had been nothing to do with him. Ian's words came back to him: there were many good things about Rachel he had (purposefully) overlooked. He looked back to the pitch and watched Ian dribble the ball effortlessly around a hapless defender and thought about the love for their father he had talked about. The first thing he'd do when they got back to Wolverhampton would be to tell their parents the good news and say if it turned out to be a grandson they would be calling him Clovis.

It didn't quite turn out like that. They had been driving along the Dudley Road when they saw Buckshot sitting in his car. Mark pulled alongside and Ian wound down the window. Once Buckshot had lowered his, Mark called out, "Hey, Buckie, this young guy played brilliant tonight. He's an Aston Villa player for sure nex week." Buckshot's expression lightened as he got out to congratulate Ian. Mark couldn't help himself and told Buckshot that he was going to be a father before adding in response to the quizzical frown that it was Rachel (and not Marcia) who was having the baby. "Yeah, nice, man, nice," said Buckshot, "there were rumours that you wasn't up to it so nice to 'ear everyone proved wrong."

"So wha' you doin here, Buckie?" asked Ian.

"Jus waitin fe someone."

"Like a gal?"

"Hey, the yout is outta order arksin about big-man tings," Buckshot said jokingly. "You only get to know them tings when you mek the Villa first team, right. I'll see you guys tomorra at trainin. So easy, yeah?"

The Beckfords had been gone about ten minutes when Buckshot caught his first glimpse of his sister Shannon. She was arm in arm with another woman of about the same age and Buckshot felt his stomach turn. Sergeant Boyd had been wrong when he'd said she looked awful, to Buckshot she looked a lot worse than that.

26

In the shadows of the tower blocks that loomed large over Blakenhall, was a pub where Courtney Wright could be found most nights. He did his business in the car park that acted as a drive-thru ganja dispensing facility. A car would enter, usually from the right as you looked out from the pub, and one of several young men would approach the driver, take the money and palm the herbal matter in what looked like a brief shake of the hands before the car would exit left. The transaction was over in a matter of seconds.

With Carl Hooper on remand in Winson Green prison,

Buckshot thought he would seek out Courtney's assistance. He had made up his mind to get Shannon out of the flat and take her to their mother. It would be an action that would retrieve some family honour; and it would get Shannon out of a great deal of trouble. Problem was, he needed backup. Only an idiot would turn up alone and try and pull a woman out of a place of work. It was stealing a man's means of earning a living – and the man would rarely let her go without a fight. In certain circumstances that Buckshot played with Sabina Park Rangers might have afforded him some protection as it was well-known that team members like Cecil Grant and Bryce McBean might come to the aid of their fellow players should the occasion arise. But such a notion cut no ice with the Rankin family. Danny was the youngest and while he himself was a fairly unimpressive specimen, he had two older brothers whose reputation for violence meant that there were few people about who would interfere with his livelihood – which was exactly what Buckshot was planning to do.

Courtney gently restrained another guy by the arm and explained it was a friend of his who had just pulled up in his car before he ambled over to Buckshot. "So wha' happen, you come fe a lickle medicine?" he asked.

Buckshot shook his head. "Nah, man, I'm here 'cause I need a favour. Shannon is back an' she's holed up in a flat in Franchise House. I need someone to watch my back as I haul 'er ras out."

The muscles around Courtney's mouth tightened; he knew how a lot of women in that block of flats made money and whom they were making it for. His immediate thought was to agree but within an instant he was thinking of the possible repercussions for him, his woman and their kids. "Yeah, but me-a busy tonight," he said. "Is there any other way besides goin to the flat, 'cause it's like strayin onto another man's territory, if you know wha' I'm sayin."

"I've been watchin an' it don't look like she gets out too often. The gal look sick an' I don't think I can afford to wait around."

A car drew up behind Buckshot's. "Look, man, customer-a come," said Courtney. "I'll see you down Aldersley for trainin tomorrow an' we'll work out somethin. You can't jus rush into this kind-a ting, it could be bad for your health. Let me check out a few tings first, yeah?"

Buckshot appreciated Courtney's considered response: it wasn't quite a 'yes' but it definitely wasn't a 'no'.

Like two vultures looking and waiting for some stricken beast to keel over and die, Nestor Riley and Desmond Palmer had sat in Steve Patel's office for most of the evening waiting for him to answer the phone. It had rung once already but Nestor had told him that neither he nor Desmond was going to collect the body, he could send his cousins if he wanted but they were staying put.

"But lads," protested Steve, "this is ridiculous. All I'm doing is collecting the gear from Birmingham, it'll stay here overnight and then I'll . . . then we'll, take it up north tomorrow and sell it to the costumers I've already lined up."

"Yeah," snorted Desmond, "an' you might jus lose your way back. We tell you already, right, you ain't leavin our sight until we 'ave the dunsai in our hands. Which reminds me, how much is our cut again?"

Steve Patel shook his head and pretended he was looking at some paperwork on his desk. "I've told you guys already and if you're not happy I'll sign a cheque right now for one hundred and six thousand pounds and you can take it to the bank first thing in the morning. By the time it clears I'll have the money in the account."

Nestor wriggled on his seat. "Hol' on, hol' on. You said we would treble our money but me an' Des was workin out that after we pay out wha' we promised we's only mekin sixty grand each an' that ain't treble."

A forceful tap on the desk brought the bundle of paperwork together. Steve said, "I told you bring me one hundred grand and I would treble it. I didn't tell either of you to start collecting money from god-knows-who and promising them you would pay back double. I don't call that smart business but I will give you three hundred and eighteen grand, maybe as early as tomorrow night, and what you do with it is up to you. Or, like I said, you can have a cheque now."

"So 'ow much you mekin outta this?" asked Desmond.

"Desmond, my father has a saying that smart business is my own business and I intend that this will be some very smart business. Now are you still in or do you want your money back?"

"We're in," snarled Nestor, "'cause you've already 'ad our money an' used it."

"Well," said Steve, "that's settled then."

As he pushed the papers into a drawer, Nestor and Desmond exchanged glances. It seemed that Cecil, Bryce and Steve were intent on ripping them off and the only way to get their fair share out of this deal was to skank the three of them – as well as a good proportion of Wolverhampton's West Indian population. Steve Patel had been looking at them from under his brow before he closed the drawer and figured they might be up to something. "I'll tell you what," he said, "we've been friends since we were kids and I don't want us falling out over money . . ."

"That's wha' we were thinkin," said Desmond.

". . . And your money also went towards the coffins . . ."

"That's wha' were we thinkin as well," said Nestor.

". . . So I suppose, it's only fair you get a percentage of that deal too."

"So wha' can we expect to mek outta the coffins?" asked Nestor.

"Obviously nothing as much as the heroin but we could

be talking another ten to fifteen grand a piece. I won't know until I've done all the figures."

The two guys tightened their lips and nodded first to Steve and then to one another. "You know wha', Steve," said Desmond, "I was only sayin to Nes that you is the fairest coolie-man we know."

Steve Patel smiled. "And I was only saying to this man in Birmingham that we go way back, to when we were kids, and I would trust my partners with my life."

All three of them knew at this point that some sort of double-cross was more than likely. They kept smiling at each other until their faces began to ache and it was a relief for all of them when the phone rang. The call lasted all of ten seconds. Steve replaced the receiver. "Guys," he said with a hint of excitement, "we're about to make big money."

They clambered aboard the metallic grey Ford Transit van that had smoked windows and '*A .P Funeral Services*' emblazoned on its sides. Steve said he would do the driving as it was simpler than calling out directions. As they pulled out of the premises they saw Nigel and Psycho sitting inside their car. "Wha' the ras is them guys doin here?" asked Desmond.

"You know how you told Nigel that you had hired the two guys in the RS2000 as security, well it gave me the idea that I should keep those guys on for a little longer, like you can't be too careful. And don't worry, I'm paying them out of my cut."

Desmond gritted his teeth as Nestor checked the door mirror and saw that Nigel and Psycho were following. It was that they were still around – and not who was paying them – that was worrying him.

27

The two coffins in the back of the Transit van were so heavy that it took four men to load each one. They were handled with reverence because of the smack worth a million pounds (at wholesale value) inside of them and not because they contained the remains of the recently departed. In less than two hours after the van had left for Birmingham it was back parked up at the funeral home in Whitmore Reans with Nigel and Psycho keeping a watchful eye on the valuable cargo. Their presence was an unsettling one for Nestor and Desmond and it also threatened to scupper their very simple plan. Once they had collected the money they intended that one of them would push Steve out of the van on their way back home from Liverpool, preferably while they were going at 70mph in the fast lane of the M6.

They were all going to sleep at the funeral parlour, with Nigel and Psycho taking turns to keep watch. Psycho went in search of an empty casket to sleep in while Steve, Desmond and Nestor went to the office and Nigel sat into the van.

"'Ow do we know these guys won't jus drive off while we're sleepin?" asked Desmond.

Steve Patel held up a bunch of keys. "The van goes nowhere without these. You're getting very distrustful in your old age, my friend. Get your head down and relax. I won't bother to say to try and get some sleep as in another five hours we'll be heading north and very soon we will be collecting a lot of money."

With their excitement barely suppressed, the three men sat back in their chairs and rested their feet on the desk. At about three in the morning Steve got up and the other two immediately opened their eyes. "I'm only going to the toilet," he said, "we have another couple of hours before we move."

"Then leave the keys on the desk," growled Nestor.

Steve shrugged his shoulders. "You guys are starting to hurt my feelings," he said with a shake of his head.

Once he was out of the office Desmond hissed, "So wha' the hell are we gonna do now that he has Nigel an' that crazy Psycho?"

"Cha, man, all me know is wid them two guys Steve can tek serious liberties with we."

"That's *h*exactly wha' me was thinkin. Them could shoot our clart an' him save himself three hundred an' eighteen grand, to ras."

"To ras."

"So wha' me think is we go back to plan 'A', right. When we collec the dunsai one of us rings Cecil an' let him know where we are. Let him an' Bryce earn them money an' tek care of the two crazy guys. At least that way we come outta this ting with somethin, seen?"

Back to thinking that three hundred grand wasn't so bad after all, Nestor said, "Seen . . . When we come back, as long as no one has shot our clarts, we get Steve to stop at a service station an' then we mek the call to Cecil."

"Do you think Steve would really 'ave them guys shoot we?" asked Desmond.

Nestor deliberated for a second or two. "Nah, the man sarf but the way the guy go on 'as truly hurt me, it like him don't trust we, like we would skank him."

Nestor lied so habitually and sounded so sincere that Desmond was confused. "But we was gonna skank him, right?"

"Yeah, man, but that ain't no reason fe Steve to go on in such a way. I mean, me an' you 'ave been friends with this man long time."

"It's true, you know," said Desmond, readily convinced

by Nestor's argument. "The man too feisty, we deserve better. Cha, we ring Cecil fe definite. An' you know wha? Me nah believe he was ever gonna give us any money outta the coffin deal."

"The man a deceiver, to ras."

"Deceiver, yes," said Desmond, "but don't say anymore 'cause me is jus gettin vexed wid the guy an' im damn coolie carry-on."

Steve Patel, who had been listening on the office intercom he had rigged up and redirected to the washroom, did not quite make out everything Nestor and Desmond had said in their hushed, but rising, tones. But he had heard enough to confirm what he had thought all along about what the two might get up to. He put away the intercom speaker and returned to the office and put his feet back onto the desk. As he closed his eyes he still had a broad grin on his face as he thought of Bryce McBean and Cecil Grant being tethered to a bed. Psycho had wanted to shoot them but Steve said that gagging and binding them would do. Steve opened his eyes slowly again to see Nestor and Desmond frowning at him distrustfully. "Just thinking about my share of the money, lads," said Steve, "that's all."

At precisely 5.00 am, Steve Patel got up from his chair and made everyone some coffee. Once Nigel and Psycho had gone to their car the other three got on board the van. Steve told Desmond to drive. "Where we goin?" he asked.

"I really don't know," said Steve. "We follow Nigel and as far as I know we're going to Liverpool. Once we get to the outskirts he has to ring someone for further directions."

Nestor and Desmond exchanged anxious glances. They always felt apprehensive about going somewhere new (as they were fervent believers in safety in numbers – especially when up to no good) in case it turned out that they would be the only black people in the place. They had only found out there were any black people in Liverpool after seeing

TV pictures of the riots during the previous year. "Maybe we're headin to Toxteth," Desmond said hopefully.

"Who knows," said Steve.

The journey along the M6 and then the M62 was uneventful. It wasn't until they left the motorway did they see Nigel leave his car to make a call from a public telephone. He left the kiosk glum-faced and approached the van. "Right, lads, we're heading into bandit country and going through the tunnel to Birkenhead. I hope you fellas have brought your passports and got yourselves inoculated."

Nestor and Desmond did not get the joke and started to cuss that no one had said anything about leaving the country. "Pulling your pissers, boys," laughed Nigel, "just pulling your pissers. We're heading across the river, the way the traffic is I'd say we'll be another twenty, twenty-five minutes. Try not to lose us, okay?"

Desmond did not like the tunnel one bit, as the thought of so much water overhead disturbed him and he wondered out loud why Steve did not arrange to have the transaction take place in Wolverhampton. "The money in drugs," Steve explained, "is in the transportation. The people who grow it get a small amount; the ones who collect it and take it to Pakistan get more. The people who do the processing and bring it from Pakistan to England get a lot more and now that we have taken delivery and are bringing it to the number one wholesaler in this part of the country we get more still. He in turn will make a lot more money than us because the further it goes up the line the bigger the risk, so the bigger the reward."

It wasn't until they were pulling into a large and empty warehouse that Steve asked them if they were scared. Of course Nestor and Desmond were and, of course, they denied it. "Good," said Steve, "because I am. But my business associate in Birmingham assures me that these are strictly businessmen. He said that the only time there is violence in this trade is when someone tries to pull a double-cross." He paused for dramatic emphasis and then added, "Double-crosses make bullets he said."

"Then everythin cool," said Nestor, indignant, "'cause we ain't double-dealin no one."

"That's exactly what I told him," said Steve.

They pulled up behind Nigel's car. After a brief talk with a burly man in a donkey jacket, Nigel beckoned for the three to get out of the van. "This is my mate Snotser," he said by way of introduction. Snotser's line of patter was similar to that of Psycho's: barely existent. He crinkled his lips in the direction of the three men as though they had just emitted a foul odour. "He'll be taking the van for a short drive," Nigel went on.

"Hey, man, wha' the bloodclart?" Desmond called out. "Where's the money?"

Nigel and Psycho shared a short, derisive, laugh. "Amateurs," growled Psycho.

"I'll be gone for a little while," said Snotser, "so my associates can make sure everything in the boxes is how it should be." He nodded in the direction of a dilapidated office and the badly worn sofa inside it. "Make yourself comfortable and Nigel will fetch you something nice for lunch from the chipper later on."

The three Wolverhampton men looked at the trail of blue smoke left by the van as it sped from the warehouse and hoped that was not the last they had seen of it.

28

"I don't unnerstan it," Horace McIntosh said to Frank Grant.

He had just read the *Wolverhampton Chronicle's* preview of the upcoming Watney's Red Barrel Challenge Cup final. The photograph that accompanied the piece was of the rival Afro Football Club. Frank said, "At least dem de same colour. I mean, dem could-a put a picture of a white team an' den black people get no credit at all."

This was of little compensation to Horace. "Would Manchester United feel de same way if dem had been confused with City; or Arsenal with Spurs? Dem nah turn aroun' an' say at least dem got de right colour team. No, sah."

"Well, true, true," conceded Frank, as Horace was already ringing the newspaper to vent his frustration. The reporter on the *Chronicle's* sports' desk could not apologise enough and promised to put things right the following week when they printed a full report of the final. "And hopefully, Horace, we'll have one of you holding the cup."

Horace was not as confident. "Well, we've 'ad a few mishaps dis week, injuries an' ting, but we 'ope to put on a good show."

"Oh? How many of your players are injured?"

"Three an' one banned so we 'ave four first-team regulars missin at de moment but we 'ave our last trainin session tonight so I'll know more den."

"We're hoping for more than a good show, Horace, your side will be defending the town's honour and I know you won't let us down. I'll see you there Saturday and wish all your players good luck from me when you see them tonight."

The apology and good wishes took the edge off Horace's

annoyance and he put down the phone doubting if he would see all his players that evening. Gazing at the press cuttings of past glories festooned around his mirror, he thought he had better stop the wishful thinking and start facing up to the reality of who would be available for the final. He had to face up to a worse case scenario and begin making contingency plans.

The turnout for the last training session before the final had been little short of a catastrophe. The list of the missing now included Desmond Palmer, Nestor Riley (who Horace was now reluctantly considering playing under another name), Cecil Grant and Bryce McBean as well as Carl Hooper, Audley Robinson and Donovan Brown. Out of usual first team squad only the Beckford brothers, Buckshot Pinnock, Courtney Wright and Norman Longmore were present. Even a lot of those players who only got the occasional game, but rarely missed training, had not bothered to turn up. "Shall I warm them up?" asked Norman.

Although his disappointment tempted him to send everyone home again, Horace told his team captain to go through the usual routine. As they finished the exercises three players (who in reality usually just helped to make up the numbers) arrived. "So where's everybody?" asked one. When all he got in response was a shrug of the shoulders he said, "Rahteed, these guys too slack. It's the final Saturday, isn't it? If we didn't 'ave a weddin to go to, Horace, you might've ended up even givin us a game."

Bad-tempered, Horace told him to keep quiet and join in with the workout, if that's what he had come for. The training finished a little earlier than usual and Horace had intended to use the time for a pep talk, a talk he had rehearsed over in his head since the victory in the semifinal. There had been so many little daydreams in which he told his players that this final was supposed to be giving a message out to all those who had jeered, made monkey noises and stoned the minibus; and likewise to those who wanted to retreat into a little black league. Perseverance had won out – a black team had triumphed over all that had been thrown at it. He asked his players to line up in front of him. There was a long pause, a deep breath and then he held his arms out, with his palms turned up, as if he were inviting them to say something. When nothing came, Horace let his arms down and slapped the side of his thighs. "So wha' happen? Only two weeks ago *h*everyone was turnin up fe trainin, we went over Nottingham an' *h*everybody was deh, now two days before de final, de biggest match in de history of de club, me nah know if me could *h*enter a five-a-side team. So wha' happen, can somebody tell me wha' happen?"

After a long and awkward silence Norman Longmore spoke. "Tings change, coach. It nah to do wid football, it's wha' happenin in dis town."

Horace shook his head. "Don't you tink me don't know wha'-a go on, dat me don't 'ear stuff in my shop *h*every day? There's someting else, is it about Devon an' me pullin him outta de police station?"

Courtney Wright took his turn. "Don't beat yourself up over that, H," he said. "I got two brothers, vexed like hell an' now them got a filter in them brain that only allows them to hear or see wha' adds to them vexation. The yout is bullin for a fight an' everyone who don't is somehow sidin with the enemy. The whole place is goin to hell an' them wanna mash up the government but 'cause them can't reach it them gonna mash up someting, even if it them own yard. We're down a few more players tonight but I say we turn up Saturday at the YM like we planned an' if enough don't turn up we go aroun to them yards an' haul them ras out."

The rest of the players nodded and it seemed to Horace that Courtney had talked some sense and he felt a little less stressed. "A'right," he said, "Courtney is right, fe once. We turn up at de YM at nine o'clock an' we go get some breakfast. So before unno go, all me arks you guys is dat unno turn up on time 'cause me 'ave a feelin dat we's gonna 'ave to go knock on a few doors on Saturday mornin."

In the changing room Buckshot told Courtney he liked what he had said to Horace, particularly the bit about hauling "them ras out". "So I'm gonna go get Shannon an' haul her ras outta that flat right now." He was really asking if Courtney was coming with him.

Courtney understood. He nodded and opened up his sports bag to show Buckshot the cosh made from a piece of lead pipe in a soft leather casing. "Ready if you are," he said. Two minutes later they were in Buckshot's car and heading for Blakenhall.

On the way, Buckshot asked Courtney if he had ever used the thing in his bag. Courtney answered he had and left it at that. He had obtained the cosh from a white guy he had gone to school with after Dermot O'Gorman had visited him in hospital as he recovered. Although Dermot didn't know all the identities of the ten or more who had laid into Courtney as he was on the ground outside of the Molinuex, he knew who the leaders of the gang were. The gang was made up of the shit-for-brains sort who ambushed away supporters as long as it was at least four-to-one in their favour. They were the sort who as individuals would go to work on a Monday and boast about beating up a coon, while omitting the fact there had been another nine who had assisted in him. The supposed hardest of the hard was the so-called leader of the North Bank crew named Dave Rattigan. His chief claim to fame was that on several occasions he had worn the scarf of the opposing team and milled around with its supporters before choosing his moment (when they weren't looking directly at him) and then laying into a hapless and unprepared fan. According to Dermot, before a home match Rattigan drank at a pub on the Waterloo Road across from the Molinuex ground and it was there Courtney had put the cosh to use. Dermot had given the signal and Courtney had brushed past two guys giving out National Front pamphlets as he strode into the pub and followed Rattigan and his mate into the toilets before leaving them unconscious in a pool of blood. On the way out he gave the two Fronters a smack of the cosh too.

As they pulled up outside Franchise House Courtney asked Buckshot what he had in mind. "Knock the door an' pull her out," replied Buckshot. "If anyone else is in there I'll jus tell them back off."

"An' if that someone is Danny?"

"Tell him the same ting. I know the Rankins from school an' them bad for true but as my ole man says, 'duppy know who to frighten.'"

With the cosh pushed into his waistband, Courtney followed Buckshot up the concrete stairs to the sixth floor, once they found the lift was out of order. Buckshot knocked on the door of flat 67 . . . and then again . . . and again. Courtney was about to suggest that they come back another time when a chalk-white girl opened the door. She seemed untroubled by their arrival. "Wha' happen," she said in a passable attempt at a Jamaican accent.

Buckshot said, "Is Shannon 'ere?" As soon as her mouth started to form the 'y' in yes, he pushed past her. He found Shannon sitting on a stained beige sofa that was surrounded by greasy cardboard cartons. Her glazed eyes looked up at him as he called out her name.

"Vince," she said in a sleepy voice, "how did you know I was here?" He was too busy studying her mottled complexion and her painfully thin arms to answer. "An' who's your friend?"

Buckshot ignored her question and said, "Shannon, you're comin home with me!"

She started to giggle as he pulled her up but once she was on her feet the laughter changed to whimpers as she struggled to free herself from his grasp. The white girl started screaming and a door to a bedroom opened. Danny Rankin stepped out scratching his head and yawning. "Wha' the bloodclart-a go on?"

His eyes moved to the cosh that smacked into the palm of Courtney's hand. He scratched his head some more, "But wait," said Rankin, "It's Shannon's brotha, isn't it? An' Courtney the man who deal wid im lickle weed runnins. Man, me know unno from Sabina Park Rangers, remember? So wha' happen, man?"

"I'm 'ere to tek Shannon home," said Buckshot. "I ain't tekin no fe an answer, right?"

"Hey, ole man," said Rankin now looking at Courtney again, "you can put that ting away before tings get outta hand 'cause me jus want her gone. Long time me tell her to go back to her family but she nah leave. Please, man, do we all a favour an' tek her clart back to her yard."

It wasn't the response neither Buckshot nor Courtney had expected, neither were they prepared to believe everything that Danny Rankin told them about how Shannon had ended up in the flat in Blakenhall. According to him, he had been in Hamburg when he'd heard about a Wolverhampton girl who was in trouble and had decided to check her out. "Look, man," he said to Buckshot, "'cause you're her brotha, outta respec, me nah go into detail, but me find the gal in real narsty shit. Anyway, Shannon an' Cilla here are good friends an' because me play football wid you me bring her back. Seriously, she nah work fe me. A smack-head ain't no use to me, if you unnerstan, them burn up too much profit. So go on, man, tek her an' try an' get her off that shit she usin."

Shannon was crying by this point and screaming at Danny Rankin. Courtney sucked his teeth regretfully before taking hold of one her puny arms and leading her out with Buckshot. On their way down the stairs Danny shouted out that he hoped they'd win the cup on Saturday and that he might come along to give some support. Neither man was thinking about the cup: Courtney was feeling bad for Buckshot but he was also feeling ashamed of himself that he had not listened to his better instincts and had stayed away from the deal Nestor Riley and Desmond Palmer had offered. They had asked him what black person did he know who used nasty shit like heroin. He hadn't known one then but he did now. As they put Shannon into the car, part of him was hoping that something would go wrong with the deal: he couldn't afford to lose the money – and he would like to see it back – but now he wasn't sure if he wanted to see a profit. It was tainted money now.

Buckshot sat in the back of his car with Shannon and asked Courtney to drive to their mother's place. And as if he had been reading Courtney's thoughts, he said, "Bwoy, when we was comin down the stairs I kept thinkin 'bout Nestor an' Desmond . . ."

"I know, man, I know," said Courtney. "I feel exactly the same way. Seriously, I hope they don't get that stuff an' we'll jus end up with our money back."

29

Although Buckshot and Courtney were having second thoughts about their involvement, the deal Nestor and Desmond had offered them had finally come to fruition. The Transit van had been away for more than five hours and despite several invitations, none of the guys from

Wolverhampton felt like eating pie and chips, or anything else for that matter. The most they had was a few sips of warm *Lilt* just to keep their mouths from drying out completely. The sun was high and shining through the skylights in the corrugated roof when the burble from the van's exhaust got the three guys to their feet. Their legs weak and tingling, they walked from the tumbledown office and watched Snotser as he got out and went to the back of the van. He opened the rear doors and gestured for them to join him. Inside were the two coffins and Nestor's guts twisted a little more. Perhaps the stuff they had brought from Birmingham was no good and they had been ripped off. Perhaps there had been a double-cross and they would be the ones to pay for it.

Stone-faced, Snotser said, "The gaffer said the gear is, erm, excellent. He's very pleased. He said count the money before you leave, he won't be offended." For the first time, there was a hint of a smile on his face. "Don't just stand there, lads, like, start counting."

Within seconds, the coffin lids were off and Steve, Nestor and Desmond were in the back of the van passing around bundles of money to one another as if they were Christmas crackers. The three of them giggled excitedly. Steve Patel now seemed unconcerned that Nestor and Desmond were now actually seeing and touching what he was making out of the deal. He brought about some cooling of their excitation when he cautioned that they should check the money by pulling a note out at random to make certain it was genuine and then count the bundles. "Otherwise we will be counting all night," he said, "and personally I'd like to head for home as soon as I can. I don't feel safe in a strange place with all this money around."

The money was mostly in five and ten pound denominations with a smaller amount of twenties in bundles of ten thousand pounds. Once the last of them had been checked the lids were replaced. "Happy you came?" asked Steve.

"'Appier when we 'ome," said Desmond.

"You're right. I'll just make sure everything's okay with Nigel and his friend and then we'll head back to base."

Nestor and Desmond each knew what was on the other's mind. Before they had set out they thought they had finally agreed to let Cecil and Bryce take care of the Scousers and earn their cut but now they had actually touched and smelled the money they were back to skanking and having it all for themselves. "You know wha'," said Desmond, "me was thinkin about when we pull into the service station . . ."

"About not botherin to ring Cecil?"

"Yeah, man. Look, we'll tell Steve go into a service station on the way back an' then you tell him you wanna drive the rest-a the way. I'll sit nex to you so Steve is by the door, right. Once we get to seventy I'll lick him in im face, open the door an' push him out."

"Wha' about the two crazy bastards?" asked Nestor.

"Well, if them behind, them'll pull up, or run him over. If them in front we jus carry on till the nex exit an' let them go past it before we turn off."

"Yeah, man," whispered Nestor as he watched Steve Patel approach, "it sound good."

Steve got behind the wheel and said, "I told the guys I would pay them at Chorley service station, I think it'll be safer for us if it was somewhere with a lot of people around. And then maybe one of you guys can do the driving because I'm feeling bloody knackered."

Nestor gave Desmond a sly smile, the only outward sign of his growing excitement: it was if Steve was playing into their hands.

After a few miles of careful driving they pulled into the service station with Nigel and Psycho behind them. Steve drove around for a few minutes looking for a spot so they could keep a watch on the van as they got themselves something to eat. The two Scousers would stay in their car and keep guard. Desmond didn't like the way Psycho looked at him as he walked past the car and for a moment (and only a moment) thought it would be worth the money to have Cecil and Bryce take care of him.

The food was of the usual standard for service station fare: total crap but all three were starving as none of them had eaten a thing all day. Steve Patel had managed three barely warm chips and one bite of a sausage, which tasted more of sawdust than meat, when he told the other two he'd had enough. "I'm off to the toilet, okay, guys?"

Nestor sent crumbs of a burger bun over the small square table as he snarled at Steve to leave the keys. Steve Patel sighed and shook his head as he pulled the keys from his jacket pocket and slammed them onto the red laminate tabletop. In his frustration he had also pulled out a white envelope with the keys and did not notice that it had fallen to the floor. "Your bloody suspicious mind is really starting to piss me off. As far as I'm concerned this is the last time we do business," he hissed before storming off.

"Him never spoke a truer word, to ras," snorted Desmond.

"To ras. Hey, wha' you think is in the envelope?" asked Nestor, as he lifted it from the floor.

"Cha, man, jus open it an' see. Him didn't even notice it came out of im pocket."

After looking over his shoulder to check that Steve was out of sight, Nestor ripped it open. For several seconds he turned the contents through 180 degrees and back again as he tried to make sense of the black and white Polaroid. "Wha' is it, guy?" Desmond asked impatiently. When the moment of realisation came, Nestor dropped the photograph as if it had given him an electric shock. "Man, oh man," he mumbled, "it's like Cecil is doin a ting with Beanie."

Not understanding what he had heard, Desmond asked

to have a look for himself. He too turned the photograph through 180 degrees and back again. "Bwoy," he muttered, "it Cecil alright an' him looked vexed . . . Mi rahteed, it does look like dem doin a ting . . . But wait, it look like him tied up too . . ." He put down the photograph and looked at Nestor as the truth dawned on him. "Blues-beat, dem both tied up."

But Nestor wasn't paying attention: he was too busy looking over Desmond's shoulder and through the window as a smiling Steve Patel held up what looked like an ignition key before he climbed inside the Transit van. Desmond was asking what was wrong as Nestor got to his feet but he had temporarily lost the power of speech and it was all he could do to raise a hand and point as the van reversed. Desmond looked; slowly hauling himself upright, along with Nestor, he watched as the Transit van disappeared behind the petrol pumps as it headed for the southbound lanes of the M6. Desmond instantly knew that was the last they would ever see of Steve Patel and became overwhelmed by the visions of the terrible vengeance that would now await them in Wolverhampton. He reacted in the only way he could in the circumstances – and fainted.

He woke up with Nestor bending over him and attempting to haul him upright by his lapels. "Bwoy, wha' a dream," he said, "me jus dreamt Steve drove away wid all the money."

As their faces became level, Nestor snarled it had been no dream and Desmond's knees gave way again but Nestor kept hold of his lapels and said, "Hey, you can quit this faintin shit 'cause it ain't savin our ras!"

"Blouse and skirt, man, wha' we do now?" whined Desmond. "Dem will kill our clarts if we step back in Wolves now an' nah forward the money."

"Think straight, man," Nestor replied while giving Desmond a little shake. "We have to go back. We have to collec your cars, sell them an' anyting else real quick an' then we go. We have a few days, right? No one knows wha' go on today an' them don't need to know."

"But wha' if anyone find out?"

"Them find out nothin, man. I mean, Steve ain't gonna go around tellin anyone, is he? The bastard will never even step foot in the place again."

"Man, if me *h*ever get mi hands on that double-dealin coolie, me-a cut off im bloodseed. Me tell you he was a deceiver!"

"Cha, the only ting me lay on Steve is mi ole man's mash-ate," snarled Nestor, "but right now we's gotta think survival. You get me? Sur-vi-val an' get back to Wolves. You have money?"

"A pound. The rest of mi money is in the back of that van, to rasclart."

"Look, Des, we ain't countin no money in the van, otherwise me would suggest hirin a 'elicopter. Well, all me got is four quid so it looks like we's hitchin a lift."

"Wha' about ringin Cecil an' tell him come pick us up? Tell him we 'ave a photo he needs to come an' collec."

Nestor pondered over Desmond's suggestion for a few moments. It was a good idea, if Cecil and Bryce had untied themselves and were in a position to even answer the phone. He thought it was worth a try but reckoned he would only mention the photo as a last resort, after all both Cecil and Beanie had access to firearms and might just shoot them rather than risk word getting out about the photograph. Four hours and thirty-three attempted calls later they decided they had better get to the slip road and try thumbing it.

30

It was in the early hours of Friday morning that Nestor and Desmond arrived back in Wolverhampton. After several hours of fruitless thumbing, a *Goodyears* lorry had finally stopped. The driver was a Jamaican who said two black guys standing together looking for a lift must be born-optimists. He said he was heading for the tyre plant on the Stafford Road if that was any good to them. "Good?" laughed Desmond, "it only a mile from where we-a go. Any chance you can tek a route that can drop we on the Newhampton Road?"

Such brazenness had the driver angrily reaching for his door but Desmond prevented it closing and assured him he had only been joking. "Cha, man," said the driver, "me can see you too feisty. Typical, man, typical. Me see two black men an' stop to 'elp dem out an' unno start tryna tek a liberty before unno *h*even get into mi cab." He drew a machete from underneath his seat and started to threaten. "Let go-a mi door or me chop up your blood . . ." Desmond jumped back as Nestor protested that *he* hadn't opened his mouth but the door slammed shut and the truck drove away. Nestor was contemplating finding a rock and hitting Desmond on the back of his head with it just as another truck stopped. The driver was a white man this time but they were unusually comforted to hear a Black Country accent when he asked to where they were heading. "Wolverhampton," answered Nestor, "but we'd be happy with anywhere close so we can get a taxi." The truck was heading to Willenhall and Nestor shot a threatening look at Desmond before he said that would be just fine. They spent most of the journey talking about the Wolves' lousy season. It confirmed in Nestor's mind that most Wolves' supporters would talk happily for hours about all that was wrong with the side, such as its perilous flirtation with relegation, and only a few begrudging moments on what had gone right, reaching the semifinal of the FA Cup for example. "Wolves would do all right," the driver told them, "if it wasn't for the shit players and the shit manager."

"At least them doin someting 'bout the shit ground though, with that new stand, ain't they?" ventured Desmond.

The driver looked across at him as if he were considering stopping the truck and putting them out. "It's the one thing about the Wolves that the true supporters like," he said. "It's part of the history, that ground, and it also gives us something to complain about when the twats are playing well. That's what we pay our money for, a good excuse to be bloody miserable without having anyone around to tell us to snap out of it."

Nestor and Desmond nodded as if they understood but white people and how they enjoyed themselves had just become an even deeper mystery to them.

After a few hours of rest at Desmond's place and a breakfast made by Jas (who was in a dressing gown Nestor thought was a suspiciously feminine shade of pink), they headed to the funeral home only to find Cecil and Bryce had got there ahead of them. Nestor's first instinct was to ask how they had got free and his second was to lie to Cecil and pretend that the hand-over had yet to take place but both were successfully suppressed when he saw Cecil's vexed expression and that he had a gun in his hand. "So wha' happen?" snapped Cecil.

"The coolie skank us!" replied Nestor without hesitation. "Him tek all the money, the whole million an' left us at Chorley service station with a fiver between us! He had them two guys with him . . ."

". . . The guys who tie you up, like you an' Beanie go on like batty-men," Desmond interjected.

"An' 'ow you know about that?" bristled Cecil.

"'Cause we see the photo, to rasclart," Desmond chuckled.

"Where is it?" Cecil demanded as he put his gun to Desmond's head.

"Mi yard," Desmond answered. "Steve left it on the table in a *h*envelope to distract us while him teef the money. An' it definitely distracted us, seein you an' Beanie go on so..."

Nestor looked at Desmond and wondered if the shock of losing so much money had turned him daft. It was bad enough that he had rubbed up the Jamaican truck driver the wrong way but at least that had only left them stranded for a little longer. However, riling a man who has a gun at your head was to risk losing something worth a lot more than money, a piece of brain for instance. Nestor thought he'd better say something before Cecil pulled the trigger. "Ole man, we'll give you the photo as soon as we done here. An' *h*everyting cool, man, me an' Des ain't gonna say a ting about it, are we, Des?"

"We ain't worryin about that," Beanie said through tight lips, "because you guys is dead once the people hear them money-a garn. Mi rahteed, me wouldn't wanna be unno when them find out them 'ave been skanked."

Suddenly back in the real world and aware of his predicament, Desmond gave a nervous nod of his head. "We give you the photo as soon as we done 'ere," he said. "But *wha' are* we gonna do 'ere?"

Cecil lowered his gun and Bryce said, "We's gonna wait for Steve's cousins to turn up for work an' do everyting an' anyting to find out where him gone."

Twenty minutes later two men came into the premises but they weren't Steve Patel's cousins. The two white men gave the four black men a curious look and asked what they were doing there. "We work here," said Nestor, "well two of us do, anyway."

The older white man scratched the back of his neck. "I don't know how that can be, we told Mr Patel that we would be using our own staff."

"Own staff? Sorry, man, but I don't unnerstan."

"When we bought the company, we told Mr Patel that . . ."

"Hol' on, man, hol' on. Wha' you mean when you bought the company?"

"I mean my partner and I bought this company more than a month ago. Didn't Mr Patel say?"

Nestor, Desmond, Cecil and Beanie simultaneously muttered curses through their clenched teeth in a moment of shared fury before they brushed past the two white men and went outside. It would, over the years, become part of the local folklore that Steve Patel (probably aided by his two cousins) had pulled one of the greatest skanks *ever* perpetrated on the town's black people – with the possible exception of the African slave trade. But right then Cecil Grant and Bryce McBean were counting their own losses while Nestor Riley and Desmond Palmer were only thinking they had less time than they thought to raise what money they could before getting out of town.

"Right," said Cecil. "Me an' Beanie give you three grand so me reckon that means you owe us six."

"But . . ." Desmond began to protest.

"But nutten, that the deal we mek an' you're gonna go sell them cars of yours an' bring we the money by Monday or we mek sure everyone knows wha' go on an' let them kill unno."

Desmond drew breath to say something that would appeal to Cecil's better nature but he could tell Cecil was having none of it and then, in a moment of insanity, he almost said that the Polaroid would cost them the six grand. Cecil sensed what was going on in Desmond's mind and said, "But before all that, the first ting we do is go back to your yard an' get that photo."

When the four arrived at Desmond's place they discovered that Jas had slipped into something more comfortable, namely a miniskirt and blouse. Nestor began to curse profusely as he laid eyes on the freshly shaven legs and then protested to Cecil and Beanie that he found this sort of behaviour totally out of order. "Nah, man," he said to Desmond, "this is me an' you finished, guy. If you wanna carry on with this foolishness then carry on but I ain't lettin no one accuse me of bein no batty-man because of you an' the girly-man."

Desmond only laughed and handed Cecil the photograph as though he couldn't see why Nestor was getting all upset. He said, "I was tellin Nes when we were comin back from the Star an' Moon after it got mashed up, that people around 'ere have to mature themselves. Puttin on a dress don't mek a man a batty-man, right, Cecil? I mean, you can't judge by appearances, or photos, right?"

Cecil rubbed his chin and shot a glance at Beanie. "Bwoy, I ain't sure, you know. Look, man, I never said this before but mi Uncle Frank was sayin that your ole man told him that them people in Jamaica used to put you in your dead grandmother's dress an' then lock you in a cupboard when you misbehave 'cause the beatins had no affect. Now I reckon that must have had some affect on your brain if you don't see that wha' this coolie-bwoy you live wid is doin is weird, to ras."

"To ras!" howled Nestor. "That's it, now me see it! Des, them people in JA have messed up your head good an' proper. An' mek this clear in your mind, if nutten else clear, no rahteed friend of mine lives with a man wearin a rahteed dress. Seen?"

Desmond was still laughing as he opened the front door and gestured with a sweep of his hand for the three guys to leave. "Bwoy, all-a unno wanna grow up," he called out after them. "Jas wants to go home an' thinks this is the way he can get me to let him go 'cause he knows me deal with a heap-a immature guys but all he's done is get himself another beatin." He closed the door and, still laughing, shouted to Jas to fetch him the rubber hose and prepare himself for a whipping.

31

Mark Beckford thanked God it was Friday and that he had finished work for another week. There had been a lot of activity in and around George Rowley's office as groups of auditors went in and out. He still felt a twinge of remorse about his part in George's downfall but it lessened with every passing day and as it did, ideas about what he could do with the money (once Nestor and Desmond returned it with interest) began to increasingly play on his mind.

As he left for home the few colleagues who knew of the upcoming final, mostly those who attended the prayer meetings, wished him good luck. They noticed how his response seemed less than enthusiastic, even a little sullen. The truth was that all the emotional trauma of the past week had left him drained and the poor turnout for the training session of the previous night had undermined his confidence in his team's chances of winning the cup. But more than anything else, he was still brooding over Marcia Yuell and the way he had treated Rachel. A week before, he was convinced that all he was doing was so right but now it seemed so wrong, so terribly wrong. He wanted to make a fresh start with his wife but did not know how to without telling her everything – and while confession might be good for his soul he was scared about what damage it might inflict on Rachel and their unborn child.

The one good thing that had come about recently was his renewed relationship with his brother. Ian had suggested that they spend an hour over the park kicking a ball just to keep loose and while Mark wasn't particularly keen he felt obliged to make the effort. He had told Ian they would meet up on his way home from work, as he wanted to spend the evening in with Rachel. They got changed in their parents' home and jogged over to the West Park.

"I was thinkin of havin a talk with Rachel," Mark said as they ran.

"About Marcia?"

"That's wha' I was thinkin. Honesty bein the best policy."

"Sometimes it ain't. I mean, I'm thinkin of tellin Ruth tonight that I ain't seein her no more but I ain't gonna say it's 'cause she's pushin forty an' startin to look like it. I'm gonna make an excuse, you know, make out that I gotta concentrate on football an' tell her how much I really think of her an' say I'm sorry that it's endin. See, the action is gonna be the same but tellin the truth about what's happenin is only gonna add to the hurt . . . Wha' I mean is, you've finished with Marcia, that's the action that's gonna be good for your marriage but tellin Rachel about it has to hurt her, might even hurt your marriage. I mean, is it wha' you do or wha' you tell her that's gonna help make things right? I don't know the answer, Mark, I'm jus arksin the question."

Mark didn't have the answer either and they ran the rest of the way to the park in silence. They kicked their ball for a while and then joined in a game with a group of kids before they decided that they had better not overdo it and headed back. They were running on the grass verge outside of the park's perimeter fence and speculating about how many players Horace McIntosh would have for the team when a police van pulled up just ahead of them. Two cops got out, one of them pulling on a pair of leather gloves as he did. The first cop put out a hand and gestured for Mark and Ian to stop. "Okay lads," he said, "what exactly are you running from?"

Ian laughed briefly at the question. "We ain't runnin from anythin."

"We're comin from the park," said Mark, as he held up the ball he was carrying.

The cop turned to the one with the gloves. "Didn't we just have a report of someone stealing a football from some kids in the park?" he asked, as three more cops came out of the back of the van.

Mark could see the anger rising in his younger brother and thought he'd better do the talking. "If you did, officer," he said, "this isn't the ball you're lookin for. We jus went over to the park for a bit of practise. We got a big match tomorrow."

"What, is it that you boys are making out that you're playing in the FA Cup?" To his colleagues he said, "Which one of these do you reckon is Garth Crooks?"

Mark forced a nervous smile and said, "No, it's the Watney's Red Barrel Challenge Cup final."

The cop's mouth twisted sardonically. "Ooh, the Watney's Red Barrel Challenge Cup?" he said. "Somehow I don't think you'll be playing anywhere tomorrow. Right, put your hands on the van and let's see what else you two thieving monkeys might have nicked."

The policemen closed in as Mark was about to protest and he didn't see the half a house brick that felled the first cop. Suddenly the air was full of missiles raining down on them and the police van. Amid the howls of pain and curses Ian took hold of Mark's arm and screamed at him to run. They hadn't got more than a few strides when a cop grabbed Ian. Almost immediately the cop let go as he got a brick in his face. A natty-haired youth who, along with a score of others, had run from the park on seeing the police van come to a stop and had guessed what was about to happen – even if Mark and Ian hadn't. More missiles poured down and the road was already filling with rubble and looking like a demolition site as the Beckford brothers sprinted away. They only stopped to catch their breath once they were in their parents' driveway.

"Shit," gasped Ian, "I don't think Horace could afford to be another two players down. But you never know, he might've come an' pulled us out like he did with Devon."

"Yeah," laughed Mark, "but we better not say anythin about wha' has jus gone on when we go in. You know how Dad reckons that anyone stopped by the cops must've done somethin."

"Hey, the last person I hear sayin that was you," said Ian.

"You sure? Well, if I did I've just changed my mind."

Nestor Riley had got Cecil Grant to give him a lift home after they had left Desmond's place. Cecil was still laughing at Jas being dressed in a blouse and skirt and Desmond's attitude. "It's like the guy don't give a damn that we see wha' go on. But, you know, the man ain't righted."

"To ras," murmured Nestor. "Any man who kidnap someone jus so them can fix im cars ain't right. Nah, man, Desmond is well mad but it only now me see it."

Cecil carried on laughing until just before he let Nestor out. He was back to his usual nasty self as he warned Nestor that he and Beanie had better get the money owed to them by Monday. "Don't waste no time," he warned, "you go with Des an' mek sure you raise the dunsai."

Nestor thought an appeal for more time would be a waste of breath and went into his mother's house. No one was home as he tried to figure out if there was any advantage for him staying in Wolverhampton any longer. He could certainly see the disadvantages in hanging around; they were mostly in the shapes of a machete-waving mob or Cecil and

Beanie. They would get their money from the sale of Desmond's BMWs and if other people wanted to kill someone they could always find Desmond and vent their anger on him – and Jas. The cross-dressing Jas was indulging in was another good reason for Nestor to leave town quickly, before anyone else found out about it and damaged his good name as a strictly heterosexual lover-man.

He was already packing a suitcase when the telephone rang. It was his mother; she was crying and saying something about baby Peter and a life-support machine. It took three times of asking but Nestor finally agreed to go to the Royal Hospital and find out what all the bawling was about.

32

Like Nestor Riley, Mark Beckford had also returned to an empty home. When he had called out Rachel's name and there had been no reply he became anxious and went from room to room to look for her. The scene he had feared most was in their bedroom: she had emptied the wardrobes of her clothes and her suitcases had gone. He had thought about telephoning her parents but after picking up the receiver he put it down again without dialling and thought it best if he went there straight away; she couldn't have gone anywhere else – and he thought he knew why.

Rachel's father, Edward Facey, opened his door and confirmed she was there when he greeted Mark by saying that she did not want to see him – before the question was even asked. He also communicated that Mark was not welcome inside by the way he stood in the doorway with his arms crossed over his broad chest. "But I jus need to talk to her," Mark said, "there's stuff I gotta explain."

Edward Facey said, "Come back tomorrow, Mark, she's too upset to talk right now."

"What's got her so upset?"

"I think you would know more about that than me."

"Well, would you jus arks her if she'll see me for a minute, please?"

After a moment's hesitation Edward went inside and seemed to be away for an age. When he reappeared he was shaking his head as if bemused. "Come into the front room," he said, "she jus dryin 'er eyes an' says she'll talk to you there."

As it was in his own parents' home, the front room of the Facey household was a place of many ornaments and rarely used furniture. It was only the second time Mark had been permitted in there, the first was – accompanied by his mom and dad – to discuss his marriage to Rachel. As a clock ticked loudly on the mantelpiece, Mark strained his ears for sounds to warn him of Rachel's approach. He heard nothing until the click of the latch. She came in with watery eyes that made him drop his head in shame. He waited for the click that told him that she had closed the door before he looked up again. She stood biting her quivering lip. "Why are you here?" she asked.

He tried to bring a little saliva into his dry mouth before he spoke. "To talk, to explain."

"Explain about what, about your secret savings plan worth twenty thousand pounds and how you gave it to two crooks so they could double it in some nasty, underhand way so you could then buy a nice house for you and Marcia Yuell?" He questioned her about how she had found out with a look and Rachel went on, "Yes, she came around this afternoon and told me. Thing was, I had known all about her from before we were married. But I loved you, Mark, and I prayed, I prayed every day that God would at least let you see what I was trying to give to you. Love, it was real love I wanted to share with you."

"If you knew before, then why did you marry me, or why didn't you give me an ultimatum, you know, 'it's me or her' type of thing? Why didn't you help me stop it goin this far?"

"Don't you dare even try and make out that somehow I'm responsible for this because I didn't say out loud what my heart was telling you. I let every action I made show you that choice but you were too blind to see."

"But I don't understand, Rachel, I don't know how, if you knew about Marcia, how you could've married me."

"Because love is the closest thing to insanity, because it makes no sense and I must have been crazy to think you would see my love while she was still available."

Her silence combined with the loud ticking of the clock to put pressure on Mark to come up with a response. It was almost as if there was too much to say and as the words lined up on his tongue they had become all jumbled up. "I-I was confused," he said softly, "I was mixed up. I've been doin some things that don't make a lot of sense, even to me. An' I've prayed too, Rachel, I really have but I can't say which was God's voice an' which was my own. The stuff I was sayin to Marcia, about the savins plan, that wasn't true. I . . . I stole it, from work. I was tempted, I couldn't help myself an' as soon as I did it I wanted to give it back but it was too late. Anyway, it turns out that George Rowley, the guy who held the prayer meetins in his office, he had been stealin money from the company for years, they reckon over three hundred thousand an' still countin. The police jus put the money I took down to George an' so I got away with it. But because I wanted to get rid of it I gave it to some guys who are bringin in cheap coffins from India, they said they would double it but I mean it when I say I don't care now if I never see it again."

Rachel put a hand to her mouth and began to look at

Mark in a way she had never done before. Now she was ready to ask the question that had ran through her mind so many times but thought she would never have the courage to utter. "Why did you marry me, Mark?" The clocked ticked and when it looked like he was not about to give her an answer, she asked, "Did you ever love me?"

He silently repeated her question to himself. "I never loved Marcia," he said, "I was infatuated but I didn't love her. An' why did I marry you, do you want the truth?"

Rachel held her breath and in her mind she was saying 'no' as her mouth said, "Yes, yes, I do."

In his mind he was saying: 'Because of my parents; because I once had a passion. Because of somethin that was gradually taken away from me an' I thought I could replace it with another sort of love. The love I lost had preoccupied me every day since I was seven years of age, an' that's why I got married, it was somethin to take my mind off all those never-to-be-fulfilled dreams.' But out loud Mark said, "Because I loved you."

"I wish I could believe you," Rachel said. "I told Marcia that there was something that I thought you loved more than either of us. When I was talking with Ian about his trials with Aston Villa I was thinking how much of it must have been hurting you. While I was packing I came across all those scrapbooks you've kept, all those football annuals, and I remembered how you used to tell me about your dreams about being a professional since you were a little boy and how you used to go to bed in a football strip. And that's your problem, Mark, in many ways you're still that little, disappointed boy and until you grow up, and out of it, there will be nothing about life that you think will make up for it. Look at all these grown men, these ex-footballers in the newspapers, who have invested so much of themselves in what's only a game. And when they can't play anymore they do drink or drugs because no matter what car they drive, or big house they live in, no matter what family they have, nothing can replace playing football. And you know what, Mark, it's so sad, so pathetic that this big wonderful world isn't much bigger than a football pitch to them, or you."

"That's where you're wrong about me, Rachel, but even a couple of days ago you would've been right. I was sick with jealousy over Ian but we had a talk an' then I realised how much I had to be glad about, you an' the baby, an' more importantly in some ways, I was glad for Ian. Now I'm a man I've put away childish things. I've gotten over football."

"But I bet you're hoping for a boy, right? I bet when you see what Ian is doing, there's a part of you that's thinking a son of yours will do that, or maybe more, too." The way Mark dropped his head told her she was right. "Well, I tell you now," she went on, "the way I'm feeling, no son of mine will ever play football, I'd want him doing way more with his life than playing a game. I'd want him to grow into a proper man, and not be a boy in a man's body."

Mark thought about what Ian had said about Rachel's hidden depths; mostly they were hidden only to him. "Where do we go from here?" he asked.

"I don't know Mark. I'm not sure if I want to go anywhere from here with you. You've made a fool out of me, Mark, and I'm not sure if I can take the chance to let you do that to me again. Give me a few days and I'll be in touch."

Mark nodded and as he went to the front door he tried to kiss her lips but she turned her face and it landed on her cheek. "I will call you," she said. As he walked out along the driveway to his car she shouted, "Good luck for tomorrow." She thought it was a good sign when he stopped and asked her what was happening tomorrow. "The match," she replied.

"Oh, yeah," he said, "the match." He went on a few paces before he stopped to ask her if it would change anything if he didn't go to the match, if he came and talked with her instead. But by the time he had turned around she had closed the door.

As Mark was heading home his brother Ian was being taken to hospital in the back of a car. Ruth Martell had been playing music in her bedroom and there was so much noise that he hadn't heard the three pairs of feet thundering up the stairs.

Ian had gone to her house to tell her that he was not going to see her again. He gave her the line about concentrating on football but it didn't come out as well as he had rehearsed. Ruth said that she understood but then, to his surprise, she began to cry and said she would miss him. Ian was ready to go at that point but Ruth insisted, for old time's sake, that they go upstairs just one more time. He didn't feel like it but he hated the way she was crying and he let her lead him by the hand the way she had that very first time. Unlike that first time, he needed some coaxing into bed but it didn't take him long to forget his regrets about coming to her house instead of telephoning – that was until the bedroom door crashed open. He was out of her bed with one of his legs already in his trousers before Ruth was shouting, "Harry! It's all my fault!" It was enough to distract the three men while he got his trousers on, if not properly fastened.

Ian looked at the three men wondering which one was Ruth's husband, as none of them looked like the guy in the wedding photos. "Tell them, Ruth, tell them you told me you were divorced!" he said while a hand reached down to find his shirt.

But Ruth hadn't heard Ian and then said something that would echo in his mind for years to come. She said, "If you have to hurt him, don't touch his legs, he's going to be signed by Aston Villa next week. Please don't touch his legs."

The barrel-chested man with the crew cut gave her an evil smirk. "Get your shoes on, sambo, we ain't going to hurt you. But I want you out and I want you to promise me that you're never coming back here."

Ian didn't bother with his socks and pushed his feet into his shoes. "Right, right, anythin you say, man," he said, as every fibre of him trembled. "I didn't know she was married, I swear."

Ruth stayed in bed with the duvet pulled up under her chin. As they went downstairs Ian could hear her crying while shouting out to the men not to hurt his legs. But of course that's exactly what they did, once they had him outside and after they had punched him to the ground. While one man knelt on his chest and another pinned his feet, the guy with the crew cut produced a hammer from the back of his car and brought it crashing down onto Ian's kneecaps and shins. Ian screamed out in agony before the pain had him blacking out. He came to as they pushed him onto the backseat of the car. He had never felt so cold; his teeth could not stop chattering as his muscles went into continual painful spasms. He remembered seeing a stream of blurry orange streetlights and then nothing else until he woke up on a trolley as it was being pushed to a ward from the A&E department of the Royal Hospital.

Three hours later his parents and Mark were at his bedside once the police had finished questioning him. He had told them he had been walking along the Tettenhall Road when a car stopped and three white men got out, racially abused him and attacked him with a hammer. It wasn't dissimilar to an attack that had taken place a month before in which a young black guy was stabbed. His mother wept, and so did Clovis as he took Ian's hand. Despite the pain, Ian felt happy right then. "I love you, Dad," he said and Clovis did not pull away his hand.

Once he was alone with Ian, Mark asked him for the truth. "You went to Ruth's?" Ian made a slow nod and Mark continued, "an' the husband came back."

"Somethin like that," Ian said with a painful swallow. "But that's between me an' you, okay? It ain't goin to do nothin but add to the hurt if mom an' dad found out wha' really happened." He looked down to his legs that were encased in plaster. "I want you to go now an' get some sleep, Mark. There's a big game to play an' I want you an' the rest of the guys to go an' win it for me. Tell Horace you have to bring me that cup to see."

Mark squeezed his brother's hand and said he would do his best. As he left he heard Ian begin to cry. He knew Ian's tears were flowing not just because of the pain in his legs but also over his shattered dreams of becoming a professional footballer. In the corridor Mark pushed his back against a wall before going outside. He had thought about not turning up for the match but as he wiped away a tear of his own, he silently promised his young brother that he would do his best to bring him that cup.

33

Horace McIntosh hadn't slept well, there had been too much going on in his head about the final; he'd long stopped thinking about tactics, he was mostly preoccupied with thoughts of if he would even have a team to field. In hindsight, too much had been made of Sabina Park Rangers being the first black team to reach the final of the Watney's Red Barrel Challenge Cup, which teams throughout the West Midlands had competed for since the 1960s. The little bit of hullabaloo it had caused had given his players the idea they had already achieved something but Horace knew that history rarely remembered losing finalists. He so badly wanted to go into the record books by winning this match but now he would simply settle for avoiding the ignominy of being the first team in the history of the cup that was unable to put out a full side for the final. In desperation, he had taken the precaution of registering himself and Frank Grant as players. He knew that not to turn up with a full team would further entrench the stereotype of black players being ill-disciplined and undependable and he was determined that was not going to happen – even if a good proportion of his players just so happened to be ill-disciplined and undependable.

When he set off for the YMCA there was no room in his troubled mind for the fact it was his wife's birthday, or that he had not seen Mervyn Palmer for a few days, or even any worries about the money that he had given to Nestor. All he could do was to cling to the remote hope that, against almost impossible odds, he and his team might be making history very shortly.

Frank Grant turned up with the hired minibus but the only players to have arrived by nine o'clock were Norman Longmore, Courtney Wright and Buckshot Pinnock. Out of the three, it was only Norman who had got there without any trauma. Courtney had had another violent argument with his two brothers over the right and wrongs of playing for Sabina Park Rangers because of the supposed treachery of Horace McIntosh and he had ended up giving Patrick a smack in the mouth. Buckshot still had to cope with the aftershocks of bringing his sister back to their mother's home. He had also brought his father there the following night, which turned out to be a big mistake, and amid all the recriminations Shannon had screamed that she hated her family and wanted to kill herself. In short, it wasn't the best preparation for a match that Buckshot had ever had.

"Right," said Horace, "we give it five minutes an' den we go haul ras."

"Scarab beetles, to rasclart," grumbled Frank when the five minutes had elapsed. "Me an' Horace are like dem scarab beetles lookin fe lickle balls-a dung to push aroun de place."

No one had a clue what he was talking about as they headed off to begin their search. They started by calling to the houses that were closest to the YMCA and tried for Bryce McBean first. A puffy-eyed woman with a stocking on her head called out from a bedroom window that he wasn't there. The next to be visited was Desmond Palmer's place. Jas's appearance at the door brought about a bit of head scratching inside the bus before Desmond climbed on board. It wasn't just the dressing gown and furry pink slippers but from the minibus it looked like Jas had lipstick smudged across his mouth. Someone said it was probably strawberry jam. "Mi rahteed," gasped Norman Longmore, "me tell you guys straight, if dat was happenin back-a-yard, people would jus come an' burn him out. No, sah, dem nah tolerate dat sort-a carry on in Jamaica, to ras." It was on all their minds that if Jas was of a different sexual persuasion, then a question arose of what was Desmond's real reason for bringing him into his home. In the mind of the 'super-macho' Jamaican male there was no room for any sort of conduct that could call into question his masculinity. Crying in public, or holding hands with a woman while out shopping, tenderness toward a boy child (in case he grew up to be chi-chi), wearing ankle socks while playing a racquet sport (hence the real reason for the dearth of black male tennis players) were all deemed unacceptable. But what Desmond was doing was going way beyond this sort of highly suspect behaviour. Up until then, he had conformed perfectly to the archetypal black man (although many people would call it playing up to the stereotype). In the rankings of what a black man 'should be' he was a 'five star-rahteed-general'. He had possession of several highly-polished and expensive cars, which could screech to a halt on seeing a crisp-looking girl walking along the pavement; the ability to chat up the crisp-looking girl no matter how much traffic was building up behind; an uncaring attitude toward the women who had bore him children; and the natural inclination to drink barley wine straight from the bottle. Yet, Desmond seemed to be willing to fritter away his status and not just get busted down to private but maybe even dishonourably discharged from the ranks because of a hitherto unheard of tolerance of an alternative lifestyle. As the guys on the minibus saw him leave the house with a broad grin on his face they muttered that the guy must be mentally ill – he just didn't seem to care what it looked like.

But Desmond did not like the way his team-mates were looking at him as he took his seat and immediately surmised what had brought about their wary expressions. "Look, man," he explained, "Jas does im own ting, right. Me beat im sorry ras last night but him say it nah change him. So I tell him me nah give a bloodclart 'ow him dress as long as him look after mi cars dem." As a few sniggers went up he said, "It about time some-a you guys matured yuhselves. Jas wearin a dress don't change him bein the best mechanic me know . . . no disrespec, Buckie, but me talkin about a BMW specialist."

Buckshot bristled at this. "Tell you wha', Des, come check me Monday an' me put on a nice red halter back while me change this clutch an' then let me know wha' you think."

Amid the laughter and Desmond's muttering for the need for more understanding, Courtney directed Frank to another house where, this time, they did find Bryce McBean. After shooting a warning glare at Desmond, Bryce in turn gave directions to where Cecil would be. Cecil was not being very co-operative until his Uncle Frank kicked the door and using several dozen Jamaican profanities told him he had one minute to get on the bus or he was coming in. Frank Grant was still cussing, even though Cecil was on board, as Horace told him to go to Mark Beckford's house. The absence of the Beckford brothers had troubled Horace the most as they were not only his best players but also amongst the most dependable. Mark trotted out, his eyes looking bloodshot, to break the news that Ian had been injured and was in hospital.

"How bad is he?" asked Horace.

"Very bad, H. He's got to fractures in both legs an' there's talk about him havin pins put in."

"So wha' happened to the guy?" asked Buckshot.

Mark hesitated. He was torn between telling them that his brother was a victim of a racist attack (as the cops had been told) and the truth about how he had come by his injuries (which would have to include some embarrassing and salacious details). What Ian had told his parents and the cops was partly true, even if it certainly wasn't quite in the proper context. "So wha' happen?" asked Norman Longmore.

Mark made a snap decision to go for his own version of the truth. "As far as I know it was an argument over some woman."

Everyone in the bus sucked at their teeth and shook their heads in a knowing way. Women, or more precisely men's pursuit of women, had led to many a downfall, especially in football. Horace surveyed the bus, so far he had only seven players and if even he and Frank donned the strip, he would still be two short. "Let's head to Nestor's," he said.

As they drew up Nestor was piling luggage into the back of his Ford Capri. He looked momentarily startled and then very worried when he saw who was inside the bus. Horace was not taking no for an answer, even when Nestor said he wasn't eligible to play because of his sending off in the semi-final. "You can be Audley," Horace responded. With great reluctance, Nestor clambered onto the minibus to be met with hostile stares from Cecil, Beanie and Desmond – who asked if he had been going somewhere. Nestor wanted to make clear he was no longer associated with Desmond (in case it was rumoured they were involved in some bizarre threesome with Jas) and so he directed his reply to Cecil. "My ole lady, she wants me to tek some stuff to a jumble sale." A disbelieving Cecil was about to issue a threat when Horace called out from the front passenger seat to ask if there were any suggestions about where they should head to next to find someone to play for them. "Blouse an' skirt," muttered Norman Longmore, "dis is a disgrace, man. Dis look bad fe black people if we nah turn up with a whole team. Wha' about if we go around to Audley an' I talk to de guy?" Horace immediately said that Audley had made it plain that he was not going to play for Sabina Park Rangers ever again and Horace was not going to let anyone beg Audley. Buckshot and Courtney offered a few names but at so early in the morning (almost ten o'clock) it was doubtful if any of them would be awake. "This is a waste-a time," said Nestor. "I might as well go an' help mi ole lady with the jumble sale if we nah have a whole team. Cha, man, jus let me out 'cause me have better tings to do back at mi yard."

Beanie leaned over and prodded a finger into Nestor's chest. "Me nah think so," he said, "you an' Des ain't goin nowhere today unless me an' Cecil go wid you. We 'ave some cars to sell later."

Norman Longmore picked something up in Beanie's tone and words. "Wha' happen?" he asked. "Is mi money a'right?"

Beanie said, "Your money garn, my money garn, *h*every-body's money garn. The coolie teef it an' garn."

"Jee-sas!" howled Norman. "Me knew it too good to be true, to rahteed! From the first time me heard about it at Aldersley me knew it was a skank. Me say coolies would not let a black man in on a deal dat was any good! Dem coolies are damn teefs me-a tell unno. No, offence, Bucks."

For the second time that morning Buckshot was bristling. It was bad enough to be relegated behind the cross-dressing Jas as a mechanic but Norman Longmore had hit his most sensitive button. Throughout his childhood he had listened to derogatory comments about people who originated from the Indian subcontinent only for someone to turn around and say they weren't referring to him. Until they had mentioned it, he hadn't thought they were. His mother, her parents and grandparents – and maybe her great-grandparents – had been born in Jamaica but he was sick and tired of the prejudice of people like Norman Longmore who made out they were all less Jamaican than he was. It was the same with Bob Marley, who was then lying on his deathbed. Norman, the self-appointed spokesman on all Jamaican cultural affairs had said that Marley's music was a sell-out version of reggae. "An' you know why dat is?" he'd said, "'cause im daddy a white man. It de white man in him dat is sellin out black people's music, to ras."

"You know wha', Norman," Buckshot snarled, "Me sick an' tired of the racism comin outta your big mout' an' I do tek offence."

"Racism," huffed Norman, "ras, bwoy, black people can't be racist."

"It's true," said Nestor in an attempt to create a diversion, "Norman, me hear more sense come outta your battyhole, 'cause most-a the time it-a pure bullshit that come outta your mouth. Man, me don't know wha' you teach but the pickney mus come out more stup-pid than when them go into your class. Buckie right, man, you too racist the way you go on 'bout coolies." Within seconds the inside of the bus was a mass of heaving bodies as Norman tried to grab hold of Nestor (as he thought of his lost money) as Buckshot jumped over a seat at Norman. It took Horace and Frank to restore order by opening the rear doors and pulling people out and separating them. "Hol' on a minute, hol' on," said Horace, "dis nah de time an' place to sort dis out."

The rest of the guys came out of the minibus while Norman squeezed his head with his two hands as if he were trying to stop it exploding. "Me want mi money back!" he yelled at the top of his voice. "When me tried to give five hundred him insist on a t'ousand, dat's what's vexin me!" He turned to Courtney and Buckshot. "Wha' about you guys, don't you feel the same way?" Truth was, they didn't – but they knew what the money was really used for and the consequences for people like Shannon were too fresh in their minds for them to get as agitated as Norman. And besides, there was no way Buckshot was going to agree with whatever Norman was saying from now on. Courtney said, "Put it down to experience, man. No one forced we."

"No, sah," said Norman, "me nah put it down to nutten but a skank an' me want mi money back." To Horace he said, "Sorry, coach, but me nah play wid teefs. Me go home."

It was then Mark Beckford spoke up. "Hey, Norman," he said, "you said a minute ago that it would be bad for black people if we don't turn up with a whole team; so is it all changed now 'cause you lose some money?"

"Me nah call a t'ousand pound 'some money'"

"Tell him how much I put in," Mark said to Nestor.

"Twenty grand, to ras, him put in the most," he replied.

It was enough to stun everyone into silence. "Life savins," explained Mark. "But you know wha', my kid brother is lyin in hospital with his two legs broke an' he arksed me to go win this cup for him. He knows he might never play football again, a young guy, jus seventeen an' about to sign for Villa, the First Division champions; can any-a you guys imagine how that mus feel? Jus think about if it happened to you when you were his age. I tell you wha', in comparison, twenty grand is nothin. All I arks you guys is to stop arguin for the nex couple-a hours, an' that we go win this cup for Ian."

For a few moments the players of Sabina Park Rangers stood in the street with their heads bowed in shameful contemplation – until a car pulled up. It was Donovan Brown with his brother Elroy and Danny Rankin coming home from a blues party. "Hey," Donovan called out. "You guys are hard to find. We's lookin to come give you some support."

Horace McIntosh filled his chest with air and as he exhaled he gave a silent prayer of thanks. "Support? Heh, you t'ree guys are playin. Right let's get back in de bus, we 'ave breakfast to get an' den we go mek 'istory!"

He and Frank Grant exchanged proud smiles, against all odds Sabina Park Rangers would field a full team for the final – and they would indeed make history.

Epilogue

It's a pity that I cannot end this story with the line that Sabina Park Rangers made history and leave it at that – but I did promise to tell the whole, never-told-before truth. Those of you who like happy endings I would advise to stop reading now. But for those who are a little more hardened to life's adversities, or just curious, here is what happened in the final and what befell the members of Sabina Park Rangers Football Club following that historic match.

Once everyone had got on board the minibus they headed for a Caribbean restaurant just off the Soho Road in Handsworth, Birmingham, after ensuring the three new members of the team had boots to play in. Because of his undoubted ability, the presence of Danny Rankin heartened some members of the team, vexed others – especially Buckshot when he asked about his sister – and, unfortunately, emboldened Nestor Riley. Danny and Nestor had gone to the same school and Nestor immediately felt they had rekindled their friendship when Danny sat down next to him. The idea that somehow he now had the protection of the Rankin brothers led him to start passing comments over breakfast about secret photographs, suppressed sexuality and the like. Most of those who were listening thought he was making assertions about Desmond and Jas and took Desmond's laughter as more evidence that he was off his head. But like Desmond, Cecil Grant and Bryce McBean knew to what Nestor was actually referring and were silently fuming. They decided then Nestor would be taught a hard lesson the first opportunity they got and in doing so also prevent him from leaving town too soon.

That opportunity came within the dying minutes of the first half of the final. It was one-all, thanks to a brilliant individual effort by Mark Beckford and Sabina Park Rangers were holding their own against the team from Oldbury's Rubery Owen engineering works. That was until Cecil Grant slid in, with all studs showing, and committed a hideous foul that had the guy he'd tackled heading for hospital with a suspected broken ankle. Cecil only stayed on the pitch because the player he'd taken out of the game was Nestor Riley. The baffled referee was convinced by his argument that it was an accident – as he was hardly going to do that to one of his own side, in the cup final, on a purpose, now was he? With the clock running down to halftime, Horace McIntosh came on as substitute – as it was a choice between him and Frank Grant – and with his first touch he gifted a ball to an opposing striker who then slotted it past Courtney Wright in goal. It got much worse in the second half. Danny Rankin was proving to be a liability as his play on the pitch reflected the way he lived his life: selfish and undisciplined. Out of sympathy, when Buckshot got the ball he would not pass it to Horace and out of principle he wouldn't pass it to neither Norman Longmore nor Danny Rankin. Consequently he was trying to make a lot of difficult cross-field passes that were intercepted by the opposition more times than not. In a public show of his disapproval of Desmond's domestic arrangements, Norman would neither make a pass to him, nor even call for the ball when it was in Desmond's possession. The Brown brothers, who had been magnificent in defence, began to flag. They had been without sleep for over thirty hours and while future generations of ravers had the use of amphetamines, all these guys had to keep them going were almost unnatural levels of stamina and the coffee they had drank with their breakfast.

At four-one down his side's team spirit gradually evaporated, as Horace McIntosh pushed his fifty-six-year-old body well past its limit of endurance. With twelve minutes to the final whistle his body decided to disobey any further command his brain was giving it – even to stay upright. Horace had been trying to chase a man at least thirty years his junior when he suddenly fell face-first to the ground. The referee blew his whistle immediately. At first it was feared that he'd had a heart attack, or a stroke, but thankfully it turned out that Horace's collapse was due to exhaustion – of both body and mind.

Horace McIntosh was taken off by stretcher and, along with Nestor Riley, was to spend the best part of the next forty-eight hours in Selly Oak hospital. Perhaps it was only right that Horace was not there at the game's end. His team had indeed made history – by losing 8 – 1, which was by far the biggest margin of defeat in the history of the cup.

On their way back to Wolverhampton, the team called into the hospital and though they were not allowed to see Horace they were assured that he was not in danger. The only team members who bothered to check on Nestor were Cecil and Bryce – and that was only to threaten him again. It was as they tramped back out to the minibus that the recriminations began. Over the years the personal differences within Sabina Park Rangers had been put aside for the good of the club but now it was if every player sensed there was no longer a team. It was Norman Longmore who started it off by castigating every performance but his own and telling everyone they had let down the entire black population. "Is that jus of Wolverhampton or of the whole world?" asked Courtney Wright. This only prompted Norman to launch into a diatribe about what was wrong with black people in "Hinglan" before he fixed his stare onto Desmond and returned to his rant about the money he wanted back. "Cha," said Buckshot, "I ain't listenin to this all the way back to Wolves. I'll see you guys later, 'cause I'm catchin the train." Courtney pulled his bag from the bus and said he was going with Buckshot.

Later that evening, Agnes McIntosh found her husband was inconsolable as he lay in bed amongst the tubes and wires to the monitoring equipment. He had once hoped that this game would be a shining beacon of achievement for local amateur black football but now he could only hope that the press would repeat the mistake of publishing the wrong photograph alongside the match report. Or failing that, he wished some catastrophe would occur before he returned to Wolverhampton in order to divert people's attention away from the result, for he knew that his fellow Jamaicans, in particular, were not averse to revelling in another person's misfortune.

Horace would have done well to remember that his mother in Jamaica had used to warn him to be careful what he wished for in case he'd get it, for catastrophe was awaiting back in Wolverhampton. By Saturday afternoon, around the time Sabina Park Rangers had conceded their sixth goal, a mob had turned up at the door of Desmond Palmer's home. Word was going around that Steve Patel had left town and they wanted to hear Desmond tell them that their money was safe. When they saw Desmond's smashed up BMW they thought the rumours had to be true and that another mob had beaten them to it. Jas was back in his blouse and skirt and had the presence of mind to wrap a towel around his head as he heard the pounding on the front door before it crashed open. Luckily for him, the horde in the hallway believed he was a woman and after a few gropes of his batty permitted him to flee before they wrecked the place.

Now the mob's blood was well and truly up, some of them were even willing to take on ghosts as they headed for Steve Patel's funeral home. In a strange twist of fate it was at that same time a carload of skinheads had made the mistake of coming into Whitmore Reans looking for a black or Asian person to attack. They were just about to set upon a twelve-year old black boy when the group of well-vexed West Indians rounded the corner. There then followed a lot cuss words and quite a bit of bawling as a few swipes of a 'mash-ate' slashed the tyres of the skinheads' car to make sure they weren't going anywhere very quickly. A big guy named Rodney (a cousin of Carl the goalkeeper) had forced one skinhead onto his knees who, rather touchingly, cried for his mother – just as a police van rounded a corner. With its siren blaring and lights flashing, the van screeched to a halt and the cops spilled out – only to, just as rapidly, retreat back into the van under a barrage of missiles. The skinheads took full advantage of this diversion and piled into their car and left the scene amid the rumble of bare metal rims moving rapidly over the tarmac. The cops' appearance on the scene had added only hatred to the rage prompted by the skinheads' arrival, which in turn had amplified the vexation of those who thought that they had all been skanked by Nestor, Desmond and Steve Patel.

Steve's father still had a shop on the Newhampton Road and it didn't take long for the minds of the well-vexed to collectively figure out that most of the stock rightfully belonged to all those innocent people his son had defrauded. The shop was completely ransacked before the police got there (as they had been implementing their plan to completely seal off the roads into Whitmore Reans in order to contain the long-expected uprising). But as night fell the rioters returned to burn it to the ground, along with several other business premises.

The cops weren't the only ones to have planned for this eventuality and when the minibus carrying the players of Sabina Park Rangers were prevented by a roadblock from returning to the YMCA, Cecil and Bryce told Desmond they would postpone their business with him until Monday. They had plans of their own which involved electrical goods stores and empty lockup garages.

With so much going on in the town, Horace McIntosh did not have to worry about his team's defeat attracting any sort of widespread ridicule. When the match reports were published they were, in the main, generous enough to use phrases like 'unfortunate' and 'brave' about Sabina Park Rangers' performance. But in truth, the reporters were describing Horace and paying tribute to his efforts rather than those of his team.

Desmond Palmer returned home to find Jas had gone and as he surveyed all the damage the police turned up to tell him what had happened and, almost as an afterthought, that his father Mervyn was dead. He tried to hide his excitement when in answer to his question, the cop told him he was the first next of kin to have been informed: he knew that somewhere in his father's house the old bastard had hidden thirty-five thousand pounds. With the exception of Norman Longmore, Audley Robinson and Mark Beckford, Desmond returned the money to his team-mates – and because of the damage done to his home he also reimbursed the handful of vengeful types who he thought he would not be able handle on his own. As a matter of policy he would not consider refunding Christians, females, the old or anyone he figured did not pose a physical threat. He was still left with seven grand from the money he had found behind the skirting board and reckoned what he had given back was a good investment as he needed to move around freely and without fear of attack if he was going to conduct any sort of business. He did find Jas a few months later and discovered he had an arranged marriage lined up. But as the years went by their previous master/slave relationship became a friendship; Jas would come and service Desmond's cars and walk around in a dress for a few hours, which was something he was unable to do in front of his family. Jas often talked about stuff he could not share with anyone else – and Desmond not only liked that, perhaps he also understood.

That Desmond had given back any money at all, also gave the impression that he was a totally innocent party – unlike Nestor who had discharged himself early from hospital. Nestor ignored the pleas of his mother to stay for the sake of his dying child, and fled to London – which was also, by coincidence, the place to where Steve Patel had gone. But London is a vast city and they never did meet up again although the two of them did go to prison around the same time twelve years later. Nestor was sentenced for savagely beating a Jamaican woman who was smuggling cocaine in her body's cavities for him; and Steve was sent down for his conspiracy to import cocaine but in fact it was a Customs and Excise 'sting' that had taken him in.

In order to pacify his uncharacteristically angry flock, (they had wanted to expel him until it was revealed that he owned the building that housed the church) Rudolph Naylor had to sell up some of his other properties, including the workshop Buckshot rented from him. Buckshot was relieved to have the excuse to leave Wolverhampton and set up a garage business in Stafford. Shannon's return had complicated a lot of things. Buckshot thought if he didn't get himself far away he would be dragged into the maelstrom that had engulfed his sister – and anyone else who got too close to her. To his great pleasure, some years later he was to read about Norman Longmore's suspension from his teaching post for allegedly racially abusing his Asian pupils. It was reported with unalloyed glee by some sections of the press that a black teacher had been suspended for racist behaviour and it served as the pretext to attack "the politically correct thought-police". Norman eventually returned to work more than nine months later when it was accepted by his local education authority that 'coolie', like 'cha-cha man', was a Jamaican term of endearment for people whose origins lay in the Indian subcontinent and 'damn coolie' was even more so. The experience unsettled Norman and he returned to Jamaica with Euphemia and their daughter in 1990 but discontented with what they found there they came back to England. A few years later Norman got involved in local politics and was eventually elected as a councillor.

Courtney Wright remained affected by Shannon's addiction and once heroin started to be sold in the same pub from where he conducted his ganja dealings he decided to leave that life behind. With the support of Lynette, he eventually became a qualified youth worker and it was only when he set up a football team of his own did he then fully understand the frustrations that Horace McIntosh must have experienced.

The police's containment of the riot in Whitmore Reans had thwarted the plans of Cecil and Bryce to get into the wholesale supply of stolen electrical goods but another opportunity came along two months later when a more widespread insurrection erupted in the town; as it did in Handsworth, Southall, Bradford, Toxteth and Mosside to name just a few other places. But even then Sabina Park Rangers still managed to get a mention in local headlines when Audley Robinson was charged with going equipped to steal petrol and was remanded to HMP Winson Green. Audley was eventually found not guilty and Cecil and Bryce were never even charged for all they had got up to at that time. For the next few years they periodically carried on with their careers of armed robbery and big Carl Hooper continued to steal cars for them but after his mother and his dog Eastwood died, Carl seemed to be in prison more times than out. His last arrest was while driving a stolen car to Stafford to show Buckshot his new puppy. As time went by, and testosterone levels dropped, Bryce left all criminal activities behind after finding himself a good woman to settle down with. Cecil, on the other hand, found God after a car crash that left him in a coma for several weeks. As he came to, the face of Jesus appeared in some mashed potato he was about to eat and so began a journey which culminated in him becoming a minister. The hospital refused on hygiene grounds to preserve for him that sacred helping of mashed potato.

But while Cecil was undergoing one of the greatest conversions since Saul on the road to Damascus, Mark Beckford was gradually losing his faith but after all his own mistakes he did try to keep true to the bit about 'not judging unless ye be judged' and became less of a sanctimonious pain in the backside. Understandably, Rachel did make him crawl for a period but took him back before the first of their three sons were born – and true to her word, none of them played football except at school. They moved house shortly after their first addition to the family and their marriage thrived despite Mark being made redundant and even after Marcia Yuell threw herself from a window of her seventh-storey flat with her young daughter in her arms. She did not leave a note to say why she had committed suicide and took Tania with her but the more people found out about her life the more reasons were put forward for why she had killed herself and her daughter.

Ian Beckford never got to sign for Aston Villa, or any other professional club. He took his A-levels, went onto college and eventually became a physiotherapist. He was around twenty-three and living in Leicester when he received a letter that had come via his parents' address. It was from Ruth Martell. She wrote that over the ensuing years she had been driven almost insane by the guilt of what had happened to him and confessed that she had been divorced and very lonely from that very first time she had seduced him. She had made it up about her husband being away weekends because she did not want to come across as so desperate. Somehow she'd fallen hopelessly in love with Ian, so much so that she could not bear the thought of him leaving. Ruth had never been married to any of the men who had burst into her bedroom, she had hired them as part of a crazy scheme to prevent Ian from having a football career and leaving her all alone. Ian often thought about writing back to Ruth to say he had forgiven her but, unsure if that were true, he never got around to it.

Following his first complete rest for over a decade, Horace returned to his barbershop a week after the final. He found that Frank Grant had painted the place and removed the press cuttings that had surrounded his mirror for years and put them into a scrapbook he'd bought. Frank reckoned that after witnessing the fight in the minibus before the final, Cecil's assault on Nestor during the game and then the post-match arguments, that there was too much bad feeling running through the team for them ever to play together again. He handed Horace the scrapbook. "You 'ear Mervyn dead?" he asked.

"Yes, me 'ear," said Horace.

"Well, cha, we all dead one day an' when me see you fall me thought you were dead too. You know dat team finished, don't you, dat dem never play again?"

Horace began to look through the pages of the scrapbook. While lying in a hospital bed he had tried to reconcile himself to the thought that the team he had built had reached the end of the road. It had been a long and arduous journey and he had hoped the final destination would have been a more glorious one. And yet, he couldn't bring himself to answer Frank's question. "So Mervyn garn," he said, "it won't seem de same widout 'im."

"Nutten stays the same, man," said Frank. "There ain't no 'stop' or 'rewind' button fe life, jus 'play' an' none-a we know how long de tape 'as to run. It's de same wid Sabina Park Rangers, dem reached de *h*end of dem tape, man. Look, Horace, you an' dem took tings forward fe black players, maybe not as far as you wanted, but dem mek steps in de right direction. But it-a time now fe someone else to tek more steps from where you stop. Man, it-a long walk an' me an' you nah 'ave de time to see dat journey finished."

Horace took a while to flick through the scrapbook and pore over the cuttings. He reread the headline '*Sabina reaches final with wonder goal*' and could not help but savour that sweet moment of victory just one more time. "A long way from finished," he said softly. And with that he closed the book.

Also by Sylvester Young

What Goes Around

This much-acclaimed novel is a chilling insight into the minds of 'home-grown' terrorists. In the seedy, violent city where they live, former friends go their separate ways and become involved with two terrorist organizations. For Tyrone Swaby it is a matter of choice when he joins the 'Brothers of Islam' but for Robbie Williams it is his friendship with his old sparring partner Danny Maguire that gets him embroiled with an IRA operation taking place right on his doorstep.

'. . . a story that grips you from the first page . . .'
UNTOLD Magazine

' . . . Young's is a deftly assured debut which provides British crime writing with a vibrant new voice.'
The Times

'. . . A powerful and explosive novel . . .'
The Weekly Gleaner

'. . . *What Goes Around* is, to coin a cliche, a real page turner. The mystery and intrigue just keeps on coming as the suspense builds to an explosive ending.'
The Big Issues

Coming Soon

Sleeping Dogs Lie

The thrilling sequel to Sylvester Young's novel *What Goes Around*. Fugitives for several years, Robbie and Danny are living in Georgia, USA. But their past is about to catch up with them as they find themselves mere pawns in the sinister game of a secret service agent named Mitch, who is waging his own personal 'war against terror'.

For more information on upcoming titles and events please visit
www.raldonbooks.com